OFF TRACK

NASHVILLE FURY: BOOK 2

CHELLE SLOAN

Cover Design: Jessica Lynn Designs

Editing: Elaine York, Allusion Publishing

Line editing: Marla Selkow Esposito, Proofing with Style

Proofreading: Michele Ficht

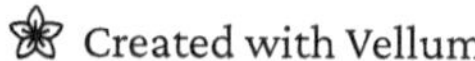 Created with Vellum

DEDICATION

To Kelly...
Book friends are the best friends. Thank you for going on this
journey with me.
Here's Davis for you. I hope I did his story justice.

PROLOGUE

BETHANY

"ARE you sure this dress looks okay?"

I had asked Sadie this question when I tried the dress on at the boutique connected to the salon I work at. I asked her again when I was checking out.

And now, as I ask my stepsister the same question while we wait for our Lyft to pick us up, I'm pretty sure she is regretting the fact she agreed to set me up on a double date.

"For the hundredth time, yes, it looks fine. You look great. Sexy. Davis won't be able to take his eyes off you. Now the car is here, let's go."

Bless my stepsister's heart for saying that, even though I bet if I held a gun to her head, she couldn't tell me the color of the dress.

It's cream. Modest on top, but so short I'll need to watch how I sit.

In other words: It's perfect.

I've been eyeing this dress for months, and I finally had an excuse to buy it. Tonight's double date with Davis could be my last first date. So, obviously, it deserves a special dress.

Don't think like that, Bethany. You always think those kinds of thoughts before a date and it always ends up in disaster. Don't set yourself up for failure. He could be like every other guy out there and be a complete jerk. Quit putting pressure on this.

I let out a heavy sigh I don't think Sadie hears as we ride to a downtown Nashville bar for our double date. I hate thinking like this. I know it's not healthy to put expectations on a date, especially with a man you've never met. Yet, this is where my mind goes every time I go on a first date—that this one will finally be *the one.*

I love love. I want to love and to be loved in return. I want the kind of love that is written about in songs, the kind of love you don't think is real. I want the happily ever after. I want the husband and the house and the three kids running around with the golden retriever chasing them at our home in the suburbs.

Every date I go on, I hope it's with Mr. Forever. I build up every guy in my head because I'm so tired of waiting for my forever to begin. Yet the only guys I can find these days are the ones who say they want the forever at first but are just saying what they know you want to hear. In reality, they only want one night. Which, of course, I don't find out about until the next morning. You know, after the one-night stand.

And I fall for it.

Every.

Single.

Time.

Because you are so desperate to find your happily ever after you ignore the glaring red flags.

I shake away the voice inside my head as the car turns onto the street where we are meeting her boyfriend, Hunter, and Davis, my date and a fellow coach with Hunter of the Nashville Fury, the city's professional football team.

I don't know a thing about football, but from the picture she showed me of my hopefully, last first date, I'd be willing to learn. I know there is something about a tight end, and I liked the sound of that.

I'm also a fan of the pants the players wear.

"So, tell me more about Davis," I say as I take the compact from my purse to make sure my makeup is still in place. "You barely told me a thing about him."

When Sadie and Hunter first started dating, I asked if Hunter had any single brothers or friends. Sadie thought I was joking. You would think since we've been stepsisters for more than ten years, she'd know by now I never play around when it comes to trying to find my future husband.

It's like she doesn't even know me sometimes.

Then again, Sadie and I are complete opposites. Today's impromptu shopping trip for this dress reminded me of that. When we went prom dress shopping in high school, I wanted to try on everything at the store while she looked like she was ready to make a run for it.

Today, I was in my glory, wanting to make sure I had the perfect dress for tonight. Sadie, on the other hand, barely paid attention to me and was glued to her phone, likely working on a story. As a reporter for the local newspaper covering the Fury, Sadie is always on her phone. I could have come out of the dressing room wearing a burlap sack and she would have told me I looked good. Her usefulness past connecting me with Hunter's friend is the extent of her involvement, so it seems.

"He's nice."

"Nice?" I ask, looking over at Sadie who is still typing furiously on her phone. "That's all you got? I mean, nice is good. Nice is a requirement. But I'd like a little more intel than that! What if he has a weird feet thing?"

Sadie must pick up on my desperate tone as she puts her phone away. "First off, I'd like to remind you this setup is solely because you refused to leave Hunter alone, constantly asking him if he had any single friends. Considering Davis is pretty much the only guy Hunter hangs out with, this is who you get. Secondly, how would I know if he has a weird feet thing? It's not something I'd ask him during an interview."

"Does Hunter know? Text him really quick. I can't go on a date with a guy who wants to suck on my toes."

"Why on Earth would Hunter and I ever talk about if Davis has a weird feet thing?"

"I don't know," I say in frustration, sliding down a little farther in the back seat. "I just want this to go well. What if we hit it off and one day we get married and we live next door to each other? Our kids can play together and we can take back-to-school photos every year! How amazing would that be?"

Sadie shakes her head, letting out a small laugh as she places her hand on top of mine. "While yes, that would be great to one day have, remember what we talked about. Please don't go into this date with your hopes super high that Davis is the one. In all honesty, I don't know much about him except his football background and that he and Hunter have become pretty tight in the past few months. Hell, I don't even know his first name except that he goes by the initial *R*. But what I do know is he strikes me as a guy who doesn't take much seriously. The players call him the fun uncle of the coaching staff. So while I want you to have fun, don't get your hopes up too high, okay? Let's just go and have fun and see where the night takes us."

"You're right. Thanks for talking me off the ledge."

I let Sadie's words settle as our car approaches the bar. This is just a fun night with friends getting drinks. Meeting someone new.

No pressure.

No expectations.

No planning our wedding an hour into the night.

The car slows down, and I see two men standing in front of the bar, casually leaning against the fenced-in patio. I can tell one is Hunter. But it's the guy next to him I can't take my eyes off of.

Davis. The picture Sadie showed me did him no justice.

The first thing I notice is his arms. His biceps are barely contained in his light blue button-down shirt, which is a beautiful contrast to his tanned, olive skin. He has chestnut brown hair that is just long enough to imagine slipping my fingers through. If I had to guess, his beard is supposed to look like a five o'clock shadow but is styled like that on purpose.

This man, by far, is the sexiest man I've ever met in person.

I'm now really glad I bought this new dress.

Our ride comes to a stop, and I take a deep breath before getting out of the car, closing my eyes to give myself one more mental pep talk.

This is just a date.

Don't go into this thinking he could be Mr. Forever.

Even though you know you'd make beautiful babies.

Just enjoy the night.

Be in the moment.

After all, there'll be time to plan the wedding starting tomorrow.

I feel the air hit my legs before I open my eyes. When I do, I see Davis standing next to the car, extending his hand for me to take.

And they say chivalry is dead.

"Thank you," I say, accepting his hand, though my words don't come out as confident as I would like. Half of that is to do with how sexy this man is. The other half is because the second my hand touched his, shivers raced through my body, despite it being an unseasonably warm November night in Nashville.

"I would like to say it's because I'm a gentleman," he says, not hiding that he is openly checking me out. And I'm guessing he's a leg man for as much time as he spends not looking me in the eye.

"You're not a gentleman?" I ask as we walk to the bar, his hand now resting on the small of my back.

He lets out a low chuckle as I carefully sit on a barstool. He leans in close, and I can feel his breath on my neck, his hand still on my back. "The things I'm thinking about right now are the opposite of a gentleman."

Another shiver goes down my spine. Between the feel of his hand and the words coming from his mouth, my body is quickly overheating. Thankfully, I get a reprieve as he releases his touch, pulling up a seat next to mine. I look around for Hunter and Sadie as Davis flags down a bartender and see they found a table outside.

I guess we're on our own.

"What is the opposite of a gentleman?" I ask.

Davis doesn't answer as the bartender takes that opportunity to take our order. Vodka soda for me. Beer for him. As he's trying to convince the bartender to put the drinks on Hunter's tab, I take the opportunity to give him a better look.

His dress shirt is rolled at the sleeves in the way that makes most women, including me, go ga-ga over. His eyes are a fascinating shade of blue that almost looks gray. Then there is his cologne. It's a combination of a woodsy and manly scent that makes me glad I have to cross my legs in this dress.

"The opposite of a gentleman," he says, suddenly pulling me away from my unladylike thoughts. "is a man who just meets a woman and can't stop looking at her legs, or wondering what they would feel like wrapped around him. The opposite of a gentleman is knowing we are here with our friends, but not being able to wait for the time we can leave. The opposite of a gentleman is wondering how I could know you from just a photo and a few words of conversation, but I already know I'm about to kick my friend's ass for not introducing us sooner."

I reach for my drink that was just put down in front of me, needing the liquid to cool me down.

What man talks like that? Definitely none I have ever been with. In my quest to find Mr. Right, I have dated douchebags and fuck boys. They tried to talk like Davis just did, but failed epically. Just sending a text saying, "U up?" isn't the way to lure a woman to bed. Then there were the responsible guys. The ones with 401ks, savings accounts, and square footage with their name on the deed. They *definitely* never talked like that.

But Davis? Davis knows what he wants. And apparently, right now, he wants me. Sadie might have said he doesn't take things too seriously, but I'm guessing that doesn't mean inside the bedroom. Unless he's a big talker. But judging by the way he's looking at me right now—with nothing but fire in his eyes —I would bet all the money I have in my bank account that this man can not only talk the talk, but can also walk the walk.

This guy isn't Mr. Forever. This guy has Mr. One Night written all over him. My dreams of this being my last first date are once again crushed.

"Cat got your tongue, princess?"

I ignore the pet name, not having any clue where he came up with it, and take another healthy sip of my drink as I gather courage for what I'm about to say.

Because I've never said it before.

One night.

Maybe one night wouldn't be so bad? At least this time I know what I'm getting into. There wouldn't be any surprise when I wake up tomorrow morning and he's already gone, quicker than the afterglow of what I expect would be a phenomenal orgasm—or three.

And let's be real, it has been a *really* long time since anyone has been anywhere near my bed. And definitely not a guy as attractive as Davis. Or with a man who can make my toes curl just with his words.

Yes! This is perfect.

I can't get hurt if I know what I'm getting myself into. This time, I'm in control. Right?

Well, at least going into it. If the way he's looking at me right now says anything, I have a feeling he's going to be in control for most of the night.

And I don't hate that. Not one bit.

"Not at all," I say as I lean a little closer to him. "I was just thinking I like the fact you're not a gentleman. Being a gentleman doesn't sound nearly as fun."

He lets out a small laugh. "I'm all about fun."

"I like the sound of that."

One night.

No one gets hurt knowing the expectations. What could be the harm in that?

CHAPTER 1
BETHANY

THREE MONTHS LATER

THE AUDACITY.

The absolute and sheer audacity of Hunter McAvoy asking me what he just did sitting in the position he is in. Apparently, no one told professional football's golden boy you don't ask that kind of question to the woman cutting your hair.

"Did you really just ask me what I think you just asked me? Because I know you are smarter than that."

"What?" he says, feigning innocence as our eyes connect in the mirror at my station. "All I asked was if you could come to Memphis and take pictures when I propose to Sadie this weekend. That's it. I don't know what you're getting so worked up about."

"You know that was not all you said," I say, pointing my scissors at him for extra emphasis.

"But that's the only part you need to focus on. Forget I said the other thing."

If it were only that easy.

What my likely—because he may not make it out of this haircut alive—future brother-in-law would like me to erase from my memory is that not only did he ask me to come to Memphis to take photos when he proposes to my stepsister, but he also invited his best friend to come as well to get the video.

And therein lies the problem.

His best friend is Davis.

The man I can't say no to.

Believe me, I've tried.

So many times.

I've never succeeded.

I'm so incredibly weak.

"You know I can't do that," I say, going back to cutting Hunter's hair. "You said it and now it's in my brain."

"Maybe if he's in your head so much, then you two, you know, should become more than two people who pretend they aren't sleeping together?"

Yup. This man is about to get a chunk of hair removed from the back of his head.

I give Hunter my meanest glare in the mirror as I go back to cutting his hair. The right way. I may want to "accidentally" cut an outline of a penis into the back of his head, but I'm way too nice.

Because he's about to ask my stepsister to marry him. If he had a horrible haircut for the biggest night of his life, I'd never forgive myself.

"We aren't sleeping together," I say as matter-of-factly as I can muster. "I don't know where you got that idea from."

Hunter looks at me through the mirror, trying to decide if he's going to call me out on my crap or not. Apparently, he chooses the former.

"So, you're telling me you two didn't leave my house after the championship game to go back to one of your places to hook up? And you two haven't been secretly hooking up for months, even though both Sadie and I know it's going on, yet neither of you will admit it to us?"

I turn my focus to his hair. If I make eye contact, he'll know I'm about to lie through my teeth. Again.

"Nope. I have no idea what you are talking about. Can you look down so I can clean up the back of your neck?"

I'm going to hell. Liars go to hell, right? They do. And I've booked myself a one-way ticket to meet Lucifer himself. Is it wrong I'm hoping Davis is seated beside me?

Because everything Hunter just said is precisely right. What was meant to be one night with Davis has turned into a months-long, not-so-secret hookup fest we can't seem to stop.

We aren't dating.

We have sex.

Correction: we have amazing sex.

That's it.

The first night we hooked up, Davis confirmed what I thought the moment I laid eyes on him—he doesn't do long term. He doesn't do commitment. What he does do is me... over and over and over again.

Just like he did that first night...

We stumble into his apartment, shoes and clothes already coming off, and we aren't even two steps inside.

How we didn't get kicked out of the Lyft back to his place is a mystery.

My fingers are frantically trying to undo the buttons of his shirt while his hands are cupping my ass, his mouth sucking on a spot on my neck that I didn't know could give me such pleasure. Just as I get the last button open, he stops.

"You don't have to stop," I say, pushing the shirt over his shoulders.

"I need to be upfront with you before this goes any further."

The tone of his voice makes me pause. "Unless you're about to tell me you have a wife and this is your sex apartment, we don't need to talk anymore."

I try to let my fingers go down to undo his belt when he stops me.

"No wife," he says, tilting my chin up so I'm looking at him. "There will never be a wife. This is only tonight. Do you understand that?"

It takes all I have not to laugh. I knew I had this guy pegged.

"I had no intentions of it being anything more than that."

I want to go back to undoing his pants, but he refuses to let my hands go.

"You don't strike me as a hookup girl."

I let out a defeated sigh. "I'm not. I want the husband and the kids and the whole nine yards. But not tonight. Tonight is just about that... tonight. No strings."

He quirks his eyebrow at me. "You sure, princess?"

"Yes," I say, dropping to my knees. "Now, where were we?"

It was just supposed to be one night. Yet here we are, three months later.

I knew he'd be good. What I wasn't prepared for was the man to be a sex god and to make me wonder if any of the previous men I had been with have any idea what they were doing.

He's attentive.

He's primal.

He makes me speak in tongues.

He has the most beautiful dick in the history of dicks.

Yes, dicks can be pretty. He proved that to me.

His is glorious. Long and thick and... it's just perfect.

And it makes me weak when it comes to him. That and the dirty words he whispers when he's making me see stars.

Which he has done. Many times. In many ways. In many places.

I'm addicted to him. And his dick.

It's bad. I'm bad. So, so bad.

God, let him be sitting next to me on that one-way trip to hell.

"Bethany?"

Hunter's words snap me from my Davis-induced daze. "Yeah?"

"You know because you reacted like I asked you to help me bury a body is very telling that you two are more than you let on. But if you insist on not admitting it out loud, Sadie and I will continue pretending we don't know what's going on."

I let his words hang in the air because I have nothing to say. He's right. When he asked me to come to Memphis and tried to slip in that Davis would be there, I reacted like a guilty person. Like someone who had something to hide.

Because I do.

I'm not this girl. I'm not the girl who has a month's-long relationship based solely on sex. We've never gone on a date besides the first night we met. We don't share meals. We don't talk about our feelings.

We have sex. It's what we do. What we do very well.

Well, it's what we did.

A week after the setup date that resulted in three mind-blowing orgasms, I was out with a few of my coworkers when I ran into him at a bar not far from our salon in the West End of Nashville. Before I knew it, we were calling a car and going back to my place.

Then there was New Year's Eve when we celebrated by him drinking champagne off of my chest.

And when we left Hunter's place at halftime of the championship game. And that was after we had round one in Hunter's garage. We were both winners that night.

And last Thursday.

And a bunch more times in between.

It's wrong on so many levels. But I give him credit, he never lied to me that this was anything more than two adults enjoying each other's company. I agreed to those terms because Davis might be fun, but he's not the guy to bring home to meet your family. And for the time being, I'm okay with that.

Until last Thursday.

God, I hate last Thursday.

What changed? I did what I promised myself I wouldn't do that first night—I envisioned our future. A future with Davis.

And I loved what I saw.

I don't even know where the thoughts came from. One minute I'm watching his spectacular, naked ass walk out of his bedroom to get us some water, then the next, I was seeing our future in vivid detail.

I pictured myself walking toward him on our wedding day.

I pictured him walking out of that bedroom to get me a snack in the middle of the night because the pregnancy cravings kicked in.

I pictured us with Sadie and Hunter, watching our kids play in the backyard of our neighboring houses.

When he came back and asked me if I was all right, I couldn't leave fast enough. This wasn't supposed to happen. I wasn't supposed to catch feelings. I don't even know how it happened. It's not like we have in-depth conversations about anything. Those thoughts weren't supposed to creep up.

Yet there they were. As clear as if they were happening in real time.

The next morning I texted him we were done. No more. How can I find what I'm looking for if I'm hooking up with him on a regular basis without the promise of a future? He said he understood and wished me luck.

I ignored the part where his well-wishes stung more than I anticipated.

But I want more, and I know Davis isn't the guy who that

can happen with. He has told me he doesn't do relationships. Plus, we are total and complete opposites. I'm born and raised in Nashville with no intentions of leaving. He's a coach for a professional football team, and his life could be uprooted at any moment. He's the guy who doesn't take life seriously and goes with the flow. I'm the girl who can't operate without her day planner and schedule book.

Hell, he won't even tell me his first name. I only know it starts with the letter *R* because of Sadie.

That's not what I want from the man I'm going to spend the rest of my life with. I mean, only knowing part of his name doesn't make for a solid marriage foundation.

I have been Davis-free now for six days. And just when I thought I was kicking the habit, here comes Hunter McAvoy strolling into my styling chair, asking me to spend an evening with the man I'm trying to quit cold turkey.

As I said, the *audacity*.

"So, can I count on you? To be there Saturday?" I look at Hunter, who is giving me his best puppy dog face. "I want this night to be perfect for Sadie. She deserves perfect. I want us to be able to remember it for years to come. And that only happens with photos and video. That is where you and Davis come in. Can you do it for me? For Sadie?"

I let out a sigh of defeat. Hunter knows I'll do anything for the woman who is not only my stepsister, but my best friend.

Even if that includes spending one more night in the presence of the man who is all sorts of wrong for me.

"Fine. But you owe me. Big-time."

CHAPTER 2
DAVIS

THE THINGS we do for friends.

That is one of the many thoughts going through my head as I sit at a hotel bar in Memphis, sipping on a glass of chilled, top-shelf tequila, waiting on the princess to arrive so we can play the part of paparazzi for Hunter and Sadie tonight.

Usually, I'm a beer guy. But I knew tonight called for something stronger.

Tonight, I have to be around Bethany and not touch her. I have to respect her wishes. I have to know and be okay with the night not ending with her in my bed.

As much as I'd like her to be.

"Yup, tonight calls for the hard stuff."

I must say that a little too loud because the bartender turns to see if I need a refill. I shake him off and take another sip of the cold liquor.

When Hunter asked me to come video the proposal and also happened to mention he was asking Bethany to participate, too, I played it cool. I believe I went so far as to pretend I didn't hear what he said, despite the moment he mentioned her name, my pants started to get tight.

That's the effect she has on me. Just the sound of her name gets me going.

No one knows that, of course. Not Hunter, who is not only my coworker and technically my boss but has also become my best friend. I have a feeling he suspects Bethany and I are more than acquaintances who were set up on one date, but he's never called me out on it.

If he only knew what we did in his garage at halftime of the championship game...

Or that she drives me crazy in ways I don't like to admit...

But he doesn't know that, either. Neither do my sisters. Definitely not my mother. My personal life is just that. Personal.

I glance down at my phone to see that it's seven forty-five. We are supposed to be at our spots on Beale Street at eight fifteen. I told Bethany to meet me down here now, and it's surprising she's not here, ready to go. I mean, never have I had such a punctual friend with benefits.

> Davis: You almost ready?

> Princess: I'll be down in five minutes.

> Davis: Is the princess actually going to be late for once?

> Princess: Just for calling me that I'm making you wait another five.

> Davis: You know you love it when I call you that.

> Princess: See you in fifteen.

I smile as I set my phone down and signal for the bartender to close my tab. I know she hates it when I call her that, which is why I continue to do it.

I love getting her fired up. Early in our... whatever you want to call it, I discovered when Bethany was riled up, it translated to off-the-charts sex. And nothing got her more worked up than when I called her princess. I don't know why, but it did.

So I kept doing it.

Yes, I know she hates the name. And I know she has called off our arrangement. That doesn't change the fact that pushing her buttons is one of my favorite things to do.

That and making her toes curl.

There is something about Bethany that is addicting. It's definitely not her constant need to look perfect for every occasion. I still don't understand why a woman needs to have perfect hair and makeup for a booty call when I'm going to mess up both.

It for sure isn't her deep-seated want to get married and have a family. That's good for some people, but I'm not one of them.

Yet since that first night, there has been something that has drawn me to her. Something about her I've never been able to say no to. Something that kept me coming back for more.

It's how she became the only woman I've slept with on more than one occasion.

Not that she, or anyone else, knows that.

I'm not a relationship guy. I'm the guy you have fun with. I'm the guy who doesn't take life seriously and is the life of the party. I'm not the guy you bring home to your parents. I'm the one your parents tell you to stay away from.

The dumb jock. The class clown. You name it, I've been called it my entire life.

At least that's who everyone thinks I am. I know I'm much more than that, I just don't correct them when they make the assumption. It's how I've flown under the radar and taken care of the business I have needed to.

I have everything I need and everything I can handle. Personally and professionally. I don't have room in my life for anything else.

"That is why it was best she left when she did."

Apparently, the combination of tequila and thinking about Bethany makes me talk to myself. In public. It shouldn't surprise me. The woman keeps finding ways to mess with my head.

Take our last night together. When I left my bed with her lying naked and sated, nothing seemed off or different. It was like any other night we chose to spend in each other's company. It wasn't until I got back to my bedroom, holding two bottles of water, that it hit me.

Looking at her lying in my bed hit me in the heart like it had never done before. I thought she was gorgeous from the first time I laid eyes on her, but at that moment, she was truly a vision. Her makeup and hair were a mess and all I could think about was what she would look like in the mornings. We had never spent a full night together, so I didn't know what she looked like in the morning light, before she had a chance to do her hair and makeup. I rarely got to see her like that, and frankly, I loved it more than when she was all done up.

And in that moment, I wanted to. I wanted to see her without the makeup. I wanted her to wake up in my arms before we went down to the kitchen to make breakfast; her wearing nothing but my shirt as we made our coffee. I wanted us to get so distracted by each other we forgot we had started making pancakes. I envisioned lazy days on the couch and date nights with Hunter and Sadie.

In that moment, I envisioned our future. And that scared the ever-loving shit out of me.

Those were the pictures in my head when the flash of Bethany sprinting out of my bedroom knocked the thoughts away. I was too stunned to stop her, though I know it was best I didn't. It's also why I didn't fight her the next day when she called our arrangement off.

She wants the whole shebang. She wants the husband and the house and the kids. How can she find that when she and I have become very good friends with benefits who don't have conversations past the ones where we are whispering filthy things into each other's ears?

It was a good move on her part to call things off. Though the thought of her with another man pains me in ways I'm not ready to admit; I know I'm not the guy for her. She wants forever. I'm not in a position to give that to her. Now or in the immediate future.

That's what I need to remember tonight.

My phone buzzes and I pick it up, thinking it's Bethany needing another five minutes. Instead, I'm greeted by a message from my sister who likes to sometimes think she's my mother.

> Abby: Please tell me you are not sitting at home alone on a Saturday night. Or worse, at the bar you always go to. Never mind. Maybe I'd rather you be at home than at that meat market.

I laugh, because when I tell her what I'm doing, she will never believe me.

> Davis: Actually, I am sitting in a hotel bar in Memphis waiting to go take video of my friends getting engaged.

> Abby: I don't know if you're being serious or not. Pics or it's not happening.

I laugh and do something I rarely do, snap a selfie and send it to her, making sure I get the sign that clearly says I'm in Memphis in the background. She'll get a kick out of that.

"You're wondering where I am, and you're sitting here drinking and taking selfies?"

Bethany's voice startles me, and I quickly put away my phone. My reaction gets a laugh out of her as she takes a seat next to me.

She's so close I could touch her, but I keep my hands to myself. The smell of her perfume gets me just like it does every time. It's something floral and sweet and screams Bethany.

And it's just now fading from my pillows.

"I had to do something while I was waiting for you," I say, taking another drink of my tequila in an attempt to recover. "I'm not used to you making me wait."

The look she shoots me lets me know she has picked up on my double meaning. The Bethany of old? She would have come back with a witty, and just as suggestive, comment.

I'm going to miss that Bethany. Hell, I already miss that Bethany.

But this Bethany? She just lets the comment hang in the air. When I take another look, her sapphire eyes look almost pained. Like she doesn't know what to do or say, and it's like every second in my presence is making her uncomfortable.

Out of habit, I let my hand graze down the side of her arm, wanting to put her at ease. I don't even mean to do it. But when she's this close to me, looking like this, I can't not touch her. She shivers under my touch before stepping back.

Shit, I didn't mean to scare her off.

"I'm sorry," I say, truly meaning the words. "I know what you said and I need to respect that."

"No apologies needed," she says, quickly standing from the barstool. "Old habits die hard. We should go, shouldn't we? We don't want to be late."

"Have you ever been late before? Or am I getting to witness a moment in history?" I say jokingly, hoping I can put a smile on her face.

"Ha ha. You are such the comedian," she says, a hint of a smile showing as we turn to walk out of the bar. "Just because I love being punctual doesn't mean I don't slip up from time to time."

"I doubt that, princess."

She turns and shoots me a look. "Do not call me that."

"You love it when I call you that."

She gives me a huff as she turns to exit the hotel. Having her in front of me gives me the chance to look at her uninterrupted. She's wearing a sweater dress that hits mid-thigh and heeled boots that come up past her knees. The sweater hugs her in all the right places and hangs off of one shoulder. It leaves plenty of room for my lips to find skin. Especially with her blond hair over the opposite shoulder. Hair that I'd love to wrap my fist around as those killer legs are wrapped around my waist.

Stop it. It's done. No more.

I know we can't get together. She was adamant in what she said, and I'd be an asshole to not respect her decision. I have two sisters. If I knew any guy they were seeing didn't respect their wishes, I'd beat their asses without question.

But looking at her now? Remembering the way her body felt in my arms? Or how she felt when she came undone on top of me that last night?

Fuck, I think I need another drink.

"Are you coming?"

Oh princess, those are three words that could get you in a lot of trouble—especially with tequila flowing through my veins.

I know I'm a bastard for what I'm about to do. Maybe the

tequila wasn't in fact my best decision because those words have now sparked something inside of me.

I might not be able to have one more night with her, but that doesn't mean I can't drive her wild.

I smile as I take a few steps toward her, putting my hand on the small of her back to bring her into me. Just like always, whenever we touch, an invisible spark passes through us. I thought it was a fluke the first time it happened, but every time it's the same feeling. God, I miss that feeling.

And it's another fact I choose not to overthink. So instead, I taunt her with the possibilities and the what ifs.

"Oh, princess," I whisper into her ear. "That will have to wait until later."

I press a small kiss on her neck right below her ear, and I can feel the shiver through her body.

"I told you we were done Davis... never again," she says quietly, though she isn't trying to remove herself from my hold.

"Never say never." I place one more kiss on her neck before letting go. "Now, let's go take some pictures."

"WHERE ARE THEY?"

I ask the question even though I know Davis doesn't know the answer. I check my phone for the hundredth time, reviewing the directions I now know by heart. We are right where we are supposed to be—outside a jazz club on Beale Street at 8:15 p.m. Yet, there is no sign of Hunter or Sadie.

"I'm sure they just got held up at the restaurant. Keep your panties on, princess. Or don't."

I shoot Davis a glare, even though he doesn't catch it because he's staring at his phone.

"Can you quit watching sports highlights for five seconds and concentrate," I say, tugging his arm so he can help me look for Hunter and Sadie over the crowd of people who have gathered at our meeting spot.

"I'm not watching sports," he says, reluctantly following me.

"Oh really? What could possibly be more important right now than making sure we don't miss Hunter's proposal?"

"I was checking to see how the stock I bought this week is performing."

"Funny," I say, not even giving him the time of day with

that response. "Put your phone away and keep on the lookout for them."

I have no idea what Davis was really doing, but he doesn't argue with me. He slides his phone into his pocket as we pace around the area Hunter told us to be at.

"Can you believe they are about to get engaged?" I say, doing my best to not make the silence between us awkward. We've never been together this much with our clothes on. "And at the spot where it all started for them. Is there anything more romantic?"

"I mean, he could have done it the first place they had sex. Or while they were having sex, but I guess then he wouldn't want us for an audience."

"Of course, you would say that."

"What? I'm sure that moment and location holds a special meaning for them."

I hate that I immediately think if that were the case for Davis and me, he would be proposing to me in his living room. Because that first night we couldn't even make it to the bedroom.

"It's not just the spot," I say, trying to divert myself from the thought of a naked Davis. "It's the whole city. Recreating the night. It's romantic."

Davis doesn't reply. We just keep looking for Hunter and Sadie, our phones at the ready so we can start capturing the moment as soon as we see them. I'm in charge of the photos. Davis is in charge of the video. I assume it's because Hunter knows I will be meticulous in making sure I get every angle. Davis just has to point in the right direction. Surely he can't screw that up.

"Is this what you would want?"

Davis's question catches me off guard. "Is this what I want for what? My engagement?"

"Yeah," he says with a shrug. "I mean, you're the one always talking about the marriage thing. I imagine you have had dreams of how your proposal would be."

I give him a look out of the corner of my eye, trying to assess the seriousness of his question. Is he messing with me or is he truly interested?

"You really want to know?"

"Yeah," he says, though he doesn't make eye contact. "Tell me all about it. What will it be like when your future husband proposes to you?"

"Well, first, I would want it to be a surprise. I would hate to know if it was coming."

"You said first. How long is this list?"

I give Davis a playful shove. "If you keep interrupting me, I won't give you the abbreviated version."

"Fine," he says, dragging it out like he's a toddler. "Keep going, princess."

"*Second* of all," I say a bit more exaggerated, skating over the fact he used that pet name. "I would want him to put a lot of thought into it. And I'm not just talking about a hundred candles and a trail of rose petals. I have always wanted my engagement to be special between the two of us. While I don't know the what or the how, I do know I want it to be something I tell our children and grandchildren about because it was so amazing. I want it to be completely unique, because it will only be meaningful to us. Something we will remember every day for the rest of our lives."

I brace myself for some sort of snarky remark from Davis. Maybe something about the candles burning down the house during my hypothetical engagement, or that I wouldn't let my future husband propose because my nails weren't done.

That remark doesn't come, though. Instead, he stops and turns to face me. And when he does, I see something in his blue eyes I wasn't expecting. It's not the normal look of lust like I'm used to. The look where everyone in the vicinity of us knows he has seen me naked.

I don't know what this look is. And the only word to describe it is... more.

More of what, I don't know.

"What?" I ask, needing to know what he is thinking.

"Nothing," he says, though the look in his eyes hasn't changed. If anything, it is getting more intense. Like he's trying to see through my soul.

Or kiss me.

Both are very bad ideas.

"Then why are you looking at me like that?"

"Like what?"

He takes a few steps closer to me and my breath hitches. He doesn't take his eyes off of me as he slowly places a loose strand of hair behind my ear. A tremble goes down my spine, just like always. I figured that reaction would eventually go away. It never did. If anything, knowing we aren't sex buddies any longer only amplifies the feeling. It's part of why I had to walk away. I knew it would only get stronger as time went on.

"Like you... miss me."

Before he can respond, I'm pushed into Davis with a force I didn't see coming. My hands immediately grip onto his chest as his arms protectively go around me.

"Watch it, asshole!" he yells to the seemingly drunk guy who just ran into me. The man yells back something inaudible to Davis as he haphazardly stumbles away.

"Are you okay?" Davis asks, rubbing his hands up and down my arms.

I nod, but I don't try to push away. I know I should, but I can't make myself, which makes it all the more disappointing when Davis quickly takes a step back.

"What?" The word slips out of my mouth, even though I should be glad he broke the contact. Being in Davis's arms like that leads to things I don't want to happen anymore. Things that can't happen anymore.

"I see Hunter and Sadie," Davis says, pointing over my shoulder. "It's time."

I turn to look in the direction he's pointing, and there they are, a seemingly confused Sadie being tugged down Beale Street by Hunter, who looks slightly frantic and very nervous.

It's go time.

I hurry and bring my phone to life, firing up the camera app to take pictures. But before I can start making my way toward them, not wanting to miss a second, Davis grabs my hand, pulling me back into him.

"You were right."

I tilt my head, slightly confused by his words. "About what?"

He gives my hand a squeeze before leaning in, his cheek brushing against mine.

"I do miss you."

"YOU'RE TELLING ME, that you, Mr. Hunter McAvoy, the man who went viral for a fake press conference where he professed his love... that all day you were an ass to the lovely Sadie. Then you spilled water on her, and this was all before walking up and down Beale Street for the equivalent of two miles before proposing? Sadie, sweetheart, maybe this guy isn't the one for you? You know I'm still available. It's not too late to change your mind."

Everyone laughs at my recap of the events leading up to Hunter's proposal as Sadie reaches for her now fiancé's hand, giving it a kiss before he puts it around her shoulders. Usually, I'd give them shit about being all over each other, but not tonight. Tonight is for celebration.

My best friend is getting married to the love of his life. And I couldn't be more excited for the two of them.

"He was. He did. And yes, I did," Sadie says, looking at Hunter with nothing but love in her eyes. "Thanks for the offer, Davis, but I'll have to pass."

The conversation flows as the four of us make ourselves comfortable around a table at the hotel restaurant. As a thank you to Bethany and me, Hunter reserved both of us rooms at the same place he and Sadie were staying. He also felt the need to emphasize that Bethany and I would be staying in separate rooms.

After we took some pretty epic footage of Sadie saying yes, we made our way back to the hotel. I figured they would want to spend the night alone—I know I would if I had just proposed. Hypothetically speaking, of course. But Hunter insisted the four of us celebrate together.

"Why would you pass on me?" I ask, taking a sip of tequila. Yup, I went back to the hard stuff. Still probably not a good idea. "I'm quite the catch."

Bethany and Sadie both let out simultaneous laughs as soon as the words leave my mouth.

"What?" I gasp, putting my hand over my heart like I'm offended. "Tell me one thing that makes me not husband-material."

"Oh, where do I begin?" Bethany chimes in.

I shoot a look to Bethany, who is giving me a devilish smile, like she's ready to expose all of my secrets.

"Name one thing, princess."

She sets down her empty champagne glass and sits up straight, like she's about to give a presentation to the class. "For starters, you won't even allow yourself to have a girl-friend, let alone get married. Kind of hard to get married without dating first."

"Nope. Doesn't count," I say, grabbing the bottle out of the ice bucket to give her glass a refill. "That's by choice. Doesn't mean I don't have the goods to be one if I wanted. Try again."

"Fine," Bethany continues, this time giving it a little more thought. "Oh! Your name. Kind of hard to get a woman to agree to marry you when you won't even tell your closest friends that vital piece of information."

"Strike two, my dear. That is also by choice. When the right woman comes along, she will be worthy of knowing my deepest secrets."

"What about me?" Hunter asks. "I'm your best friend. And your boss. I can't believe you haven't told me. Though, you know I could figure it out if I wanted to. I could just go look it up."

"Good luck," Sadie says, a sound of defeat to her tone. "I work for one of the biggest media companies in the country. We have access to records not many do, and I *still* can't figure it out. Who did you pay off to keep it a secret? And more importantly, why is it a secret?"

I hold up my glass, giving Sadie a cheers for her failed reporting efforts. "Don't you wish you knew. Maybe one day I'll give you the scoop. But only after you tell me if Hunter hadn't snagged you up, you would have gone out with me."

"Whatever you need to tell yourself to sleep at night. Randy."

The look I give Sadie is of utter confusion, while Bethany can't seem to hold in her laugh. "Randy? Who the fuck is Randy?"

Sadie shrugs while taking a sip of her glass of champagne, snuggling farther into Hunter's side. "If you're not going to tell us, then I'm going to assume it's something awful or something you despise. I know in the media guide your name is listed as R. Davis. Therefore, I'm going to keep guessing random names that start with *R* until I get it right. Or until I drive you crazy."

"Ooh, I want to play!" Bethany says excitedly, nearly bouncing on her seat.

"How much have you had to drink?" I ask her.

"Don't try and change the subject," she says, pointing her finger into my chest. God, I wish I could take it and bite it.

"Fine," I say, pretending to be exasperated, though I think their game is kind of funny. "If either of you guess it within the next year, Sadie can write an exclusive story on me centering around my name. If I win, I get lunch every day for a month."

I reach my hand across to Sadie. "Deal."

"Wait! What do I get, Romeo?" Bethany asks, a slight flirtation in her voice.

"Romeo, yeah, that's cute. So, what does the princess get?" I repeat, tapping my fingers to my lips, pretending I'm thinking of something really good.

What I want to say is I'll give her as many orgasms as she wants. That I will set up shop between her legs for as long as she will let me. That I will forever ruin her for that future husband she's so desperate to find.

Instead, I say the next best thing. I push her buttons in a way I know only I can.

"Why, the princess will get a tiara. Only the best, of course."

This earns me a playful slap across the chest, which I gladly take—anything to get her hands on me.

"You're going down, Davis," she says, leaning a little closer into me, not taking her hand off my chest. She's so close to me that all I can smell is her perfume. It drives me fucking crazy. Between that and the three glasses of tequila I've had tonight, my head is spinning.

Only thing is, I just don't know if I'm drunk off of the alcohol or her.

Probably both.

After a few more minutes and one more shot of tequila for celebration, Hunter and Sadie tell us good night, leaving just the two of us at our table. I order us each another drink, though we probably don't need it. But I'm not ready for my night with her to be over yet. And by the look she keeps giving me—filled with want and need—neither is she.

I'm going to blame that look on what comes out of my mouth next. That and the tequila.

"Want to make another bet?"

She gives me a flirtatious look, and if I had to guess, she knows where my brain is going.

"What do you have in mind?"

"You need to answer a question first."

She cocks her head to the side. "And what is that?"

"How drunk are you?"

She finishes off her glass of champagne, sets it down on the table, and inches even closer to me. Fuck, does she realize what she's doing? Any closer and she'd be straddling me. Not that I care, but she has to know she's playing with fire right now. Sitting beside her all night, I'm like a literal tinderbox waiting for a spark.

She's definitely the spark.

And by the look in her eyes, she absolutely knows what she is doing.

The little minx.

"Drunk enough to not care about what I said last week. Sober enough to remember this tomorrow."

Fuck. This woman is going to be the death of me.

"Then the bet is that I can have you naked in less than an hour."

I whisper the words in her ear, and as soon as they leave my mouth, I feel her shiver against me.

Good to know I have the same effect on her that she has on me. Not that I doubted it though. Together we've always been combustible.

"What happens if you win?"

I put my arm around her back, bringing her flush to me so I

can whisper my next words. "Then I'm going to make you come with just my tongue."

"And what happens if I win?"

I lean back in, placing a small kiss just under her ear. Right at the spot I know drives her wild.

"Then you get my tongue and my cock."

CHAPTER 5
BETHANY

THIS IS SUCH A BAD IDEA.

This is a very, very, very bad idea.

The worst idea ever.

I know that. My brain knows that. My heart knows that.

But my body? The body that is currently melting into Davis because he is doing something wicked with his tongue that is making me tingle in places I didn't know could tingle.

My body thinks this is the best idea ever.

One more night. What could be the problem?

You could fall for him... even more than you already have.

Drunk me is going to ignore that little voice. Because all I want right now is the man who is kissing my neck.

"I almost forgot how good you taste."

Davis's words bring me back to the present as we step out of the elevator and stumble down the hall to my room. I reach into my purse, fumbling around, trying to find the keycard. It would probably be easier if Davis wasn't sucking on my earlobe, but I love it too much to tell him to stop.

"Hurry up, princess," he says slowly into the ear he just finished nibbling on. "Or don't you want my tongue between your legs? You don't have to delay to win the bet. I'm going to eat that pussy, win or lose."

My legs nearly give out as I continue to dig through my purse for the keycard. If he only knew how badly I wanted him there. That every night since I told him we were done that I've dreamed about his mouth and the dirty, yet delicious, things he can do with it.

"Oh, thank God," I say as I finally locate the keycard and quickly insert it to unlock the room. Before I can take a step inside, Davis picks me up and swings me through the doorway, slamming the door shut behind him, pressing me against the hard surface. I don't even have a second to get my bearings before his lips find my skin again, this time concentrating on the exposed skin on my shoulder.

"God, I love your tongue." I know love probably isn't the best word to use with a man who is nothing more than a hookup. But it's true. His mouth can do things I never imagined. Can make me feel things that no other man has.

The first night we were together, I remember being surprised by how much he seemed to enjoy foreplay. I figured he would be one of those lick it once, flick it twice, three pumps and done kind of guys.

But not this man. This man loves using his mouth more than anything. His tongue should be deemed a wonder of the world.

And I have missed it every day.

"If you love that, then I think you'll love this even more."

He lowers me from his hold against the door. I start to make my way to the bed, but he kneels down in front of me.

"Not so fast. Let's see if you still taste the same."

Before I know it, my leg is over his shoulder, and I hear the sound of my lace thong ripping as Davis's tongue finds my center. My back is against the door again and I don't know how I'm going to keep my balance standing on one foot in heeled boots. All I know is that I'll do everything in my power to stay upright as long as he continues that thing he is doing with his mouth.

"Holy shit…"

The best part of Davis giving oral is that it's never the same twice. This man doesn't just have one move. He has every move.

Tonight? He has decided to devour me.

I'm not going to object.

He isn't just using his tongue; his entire mouth is in on the action. It's as if I am his last meal and he doesn't want to miss a single taste.

As many times as he has done this to me, he's never done it while I'm standing above him. The view from up here is… erotic. Powerful. Like even though he is the one pleasuring me, I'm the one in total control.

I might think I have the power, but as I glance down at Davis, I realize I am nothing but putty in his hands. Hands that are reaching around and grabbing my ass, bringing my core as close to his face as possible.

"Davis. Ah!" I moan as he sucks on my clit. The sensation drives me wild, and I start to move my hips, all but riding his face. All of this… it's too much. There are so many sensations and I'm not going to be able to last for long.

"Almost," I pant. "I'm almost there."

Yet he doesn't stop. If anything, he speeds back up. That's it. I'm done for.

"Davis!" I scream his name as I explode on his face. The man has made me orgasm many times from oral sex, but never this hard. Never this intense.

I don't have a chance to catch my breath before he scoops me up, takes five steps, and we both go crashing onto the bed.

The next few minutes are a flurry of limbs, torn clothing, and desperation. Each of us grabbing on to each other for dear life. Our mouths colliding in passionate kisses that could make me come again from the intensity of it all. Our clothes being ripped off—figuratively and literally—as we fall into the sheets.

"I need inside you," he says right before taking my breast into his mouth, sucking on it like his life depends on it.

"Condom..." I don't know how my drunken brain remembers to say that, but I have a feeling if I didn't, we wouldn't have used one. We've never been irresponsible before. But we've also never been so much in the moment.

Right now, we're in a bubble. It's just us. No thoughts of the future. No thoughts of how different we are. No thoughts of we ended this thing not that long ago, yet here we are.

It's just us.

Davis releases my nipple with one last pop as he quickly jumps off the bed, somehow immediately finding his pants. He quickly grabs a condom from his wallet and sheaths himself before he's back on the bed, kneeling between my legs.

"What is it you want tonight?"

He might be asking me, but I have been in this situation before to know that no matter what I say, I'm going to get what he wants to give me.

And somehow, it's always what my body craves.

"You."

He strokes himself once before positioning himself on top of me.

"Then that's what you are going to get."

With one thrust, he pushes himself inside me, his perfect length and girth filling me completely. I expected after what he did to me against the door, and the subsequent tearing of our clothes on the way to the bed, that this would be hard. Rough.

That he'd have me on all fours and be taking what he wants from behind.

That's not what he is doing at all. Right now, he's slowly moving in and out of me, making sure that I feel every inch of his cock as he thrusts. Our hips are circling in perfect unison, meeting each other at every right moment.

He sits back up, bringing my legs so they are fully wrapped around his waist. "I can't hold on, Bethany. Come with me."

"Yes." It's all I'm able to say as he begins pumping faster. I grip on to his biceps as he hits the spot that only he can find. Before I know it, I feel another orgasm rising in me, readying to let go at any minute.

"Now, Bethany. Come with me now."

And I do. With one more push, Davis and I come together, long and hard and perfect. It's the kind of orgasm I used to only read about when I snuck a read of my mom's romance novels. I have had friends who said that they had experiences like this, but now I don't believe them. There is no way to describe what just happened between us. And if I tried, people would think I'm a straight-up liar.

Davis collapses on me, and while I welcome his weight, this act takes me by surprise. Yes, he has collapsed on me before, but normally after a few breaths, he's up and disposing of the condom.

Now? Now it's almost like he's... cuddling me?

No, it can't be.

I then really question if I'm dreaming as he presses a kiss to my cheek before rolling out of bed to dispose of the condom.

Okay. Now we're back on track.

This is the part of our arrangement I know by the book. He gets rid of the condom, cleans up, gets dressed, plants another kiss on my cheek before saying some witty banter, and shows himself out.

Except, this time, that's not what happens. Instead, I feel the bed move. Though I know it's him, I almost want to turn and look.

But I don't. I just let the moment happen.

Davis in my bed. Wrapping me in his arms as we fall asleep together for the first time.

This might be a bigger mistake than the sex.

Holy crap on a cracker. Who is this man?

THE MORNING LIGHT creeping in from behind the curtain startles me awake. When I'm at my apartment, I'm never woken by the light. Blackout curtains are the best invention since smartphones, instant replay, and mobile banking.

That's not the only thing telling me that I'm not in my own bed, though.

I feel the mattress move as Bethany rolls to her side so she's now facing me, and by the looks of it, she's still asleep. Good. I'm going to need a few minutes to process the events of last night.

Hunter's engagement.

Tequila. Champagne.

Bets.

Going down on her against the door.

Sex so good I don't even know how to describe it.

Two drunk and sated people falling asleep together in a blissful bubble.

It doesn't shock me that Bethany is the first woman I've ever woken up next to—and that it doesn't surprise or scare me. Tack this up to another first that she doesn't realize she is for me. It's not that I don't want a relationship. I just know I can't put any more on my plate.

Sometimes I wish I were in a different situation. But wishing doesn't get you anywhere. I have my priorities. I have my duties for my family. I have a job that could change at any moment if the team I'm coaching doesn't perform well. Plus, during the season, I'm on the road for most of the year, and that doesn't count the travel scouting and off-season duties. None of that is good for a relationship.

So, unfortunately, there is no room for any woman. But if I were to make room for anyone, it would be this woman right here.

I roll to my side so I can unabashedly look at her while she sleeps. This is what I thought of that night. This right here.

Her blond hair is a mess over the pillow. Her mouth is slightly open, and every few minutes, a soft snore comes out. I think there is a little drool on the pillow, which makes me silently laugh. She would die if she knew I noticed that. The covers are tightly wrapped around her, but I know underneath lies a naked body that I would worship every day if I could.

In other words? She's perfect. And if I'm being honest, this is the most beautiful I have ever seen her.

And this will be the first, and last, time I'll ever see her like this.

For real this time. No more slips. No more drunk nights.

I could fall for this woman. So easily. And that can't happen.

The scary thing is, I don't even know much about her. We don't exactly "talk" when we are together. But from the little bit I do know? She's the type of woman I would go for.

She loves her family. She is a loyal friend to Sadie. The times I've made her laugh, I never wanted to stop hearing the sound.

And when we touch? I know it can't be a fluke that after months together, I'm still feeling the same spark.

That is why this has to be over. There's no room for her, or any woman, in my life.

"Mmm."

Bethany's low mumble alerts me she's awake. I start making my way out of bed, not wanting her to know that I've been staring at her for the past ten minutes like some sort of creep.

"You don't have to get up just because I'm awake now," she says, her voice groggy and still heavy with sleep.

"It's probably for the best," I answer, standing up as I look for my discarded clothes that are all over her hotel room. I locate my boxer briefs and quickly slip them on.

"You know, if we wanted to do things that were for the best, we wouldn't be here right now."

Her words cut me, even though I know they are true. When I turn back to look at her, she's sitting up, the sheets pulled up over her chest. I don't know if it's to hide her body from me or it's serving as a proverbial shield from the conversation we both know we're about to have.

Maybe both.

"Yet here we are," I say, throwing on the rest of my clothes before sitting next to her on the bed.

We both take each other in for a minute, a heavy silence filling the air. I look at her face, and it's swimming with a bundle of emotions.

Sadness. Resignation. Acceptance.

"Why can't we stay away from each other?"

I don't acknowledge her question, because I don't have an answer. And the only possible answer I have is one I can't and won't think about.

"I don't know, but this can't happen again."

She looks down away from me and nods, and I'm pretty sure I see a tear falling from her eye.

"Because you don't want anything long term," she says, sadness thick in her voice.

I let out a sigh. "And you want something that will last forever."

Our eyes find each other again, and I can see the pool of tears welling in her eyes.

"Hey there," I say, gently taking my thumb and wiping away a stray tear. "There's nothing to cry over. Certainly not over me."

She nods, quickly trying to wipe away the few other tears that have leaked out. "I don't know why I am. It's not like we were ever a thing. We aren't breaking up or anything."

Bethany might have said the words, but we both know that we essentially are. I damn well know she's the closest thing to a girlfriend I've ever had.

"I wish I could give you what you want," I say, lacing our fingers together, hoping she can feel the weight of my words.

"And I wish I could be enough to make you change your mind."

If she only knew. If she only knew that she is likely the only woman who could make me change my mind.

But I can't. I have my career. And my responsibilities. There isn't enough of me to go around. It wouldn't be fair to her.

So, to give her the opportunity at what she wants—what a girl like her deserves—I have to do the last thing I want to do. I have to walk away.

For good this time.

With our linked hands, I bring her a little closer to me and I'm relieved when she doesn't fight me away. I need to kiss her one more time.

When our lips meet, I can tell this time is different. I don't know if I've ever kissed anyone like this. With meaning. With emotion. Like I'm trying to convey words through the act.

I hope she can feel my goodbye, because I can feel hers.

It takes all the power I have to break the kiss. I don't move right away, instead letting our foreheads rest against each other before I place one more kiss on her cheek before I get off the bed.

This is it.

Last night was our swan song. This morning is our goodbye.

"I'll see you around," I say, grabbing my phone and wallet.

"Yeah. I'll see you around."

I don't turn back to look at her. If I do, I'll crumble.

Instead, I walk out of the hotel room with the knowledge that I just gave up the only woman who could have made me want to change.

CHAPTER 7
BETHANY

MAYBE IT'S because I'm southern, or maybe it's because I'm a blonde cosmetologist, but I've always had an affinity for the movie *Steel Magnolias.* Something about that movie just draws me in.

As an adult, I have truly come to appreciate the strong leading ladies, the story that will rip your heart out and show how people can be vulnerable yet strong at the same time.

Then there's the quote. The one line I feel so deep in my soul that I know I'll remember for the rest of my life... heck, maybe that's the whole reason why I went into cosmetology as my chosen profession. But the movie quote has resonated with me since the first time I saw it on the big screen.

I don't trust anybody who does their own hair. Dolly Parton is a true queen, and we should all bow down to her greatness. Of course, that could just be the southern girl in me talking too.

Ever since then, I have wanted to be a cosmetologist. When I was eight, all of my dolls had different hairstyles. When I was thirteen, I asked for wigs for my birthday to practice different cuts and styles. In high school, my friends came to me before prom to do their hair and makeup.

I must say, we had the best-looking senior prom dates this side of the Mississippi.

I first wanted to become a cosmetologist to make women, and men, feel their best. I remember whenever my mom came home from the hairdresser, she had a certain glow about her. She always looked different, and not because a few inches of hair were gone. She was confident. She had an extra sway to her step.

I wanted to make people feel like that. So, when my friends were agonizing over college finals and internships, I was graduating at the top of my class from cosmetology school, about ready to start at one of the most successful salons in Nashville.

Over the years, I've learned being a hairstylist is more than giving people a good cut and color. It's about giving people time to themselves. It's about giving people an ear if they need it. It's about helping people feel beautiful inside and out.

And I am darn good at my job.

"Can you believe it?"

Considering I have no idea what Ruthie, my eighty-six-year-old client, just asked me, I'll amend that last thought to say, "except today." Today I am failing miserably. Not at the hair part. I have done Ruthie's hair every week for five years now. I could do her hair in my sleep.

But the other part of my job? The chatting and the talking and the being interested in my clients' conversations? I am completely out of it. I've had five other clients in my chair today, and I don't think I said ten words total to them, much less could tell you about anything that they talked about.

"I really can't, Ruthie." Not looking at her, so hopefully, she can't tell I'm fibbing straight through my teeth. "But stranger things have happened."

"You think there is something stranger than a twenty-something hottie asking me to be his sugar mama? I mean, I am a catch, but even I know I can't snag a twenty-year-old anymore. Maybe a few years ago, but these days I'm focusing more on the sixty-and-over crowd."

"Wait. What did you say?"

"Oh my dear," Ruthie says, shaking her head in laughter as she looks at my confused face. "You were so out of it, I just started talking about random things to see if I could get your attention. You missed the one where I said Elvis was living in my basement, and that I think next time I'm here we should shave all my hair off."

"Oh wow," I say, trying to laugh off that I've likely been spacing out the entire time I've been styling her hair. "I'm sorry. I'm just a bit out of it today."

"That's not just any kind of out of it. That look on your face is because of a man."

I raise my eyebrow, wondering if I'm really that transparent. "And how would you know that? Weren't you the one saying last week men weren't good for anything anymore?"

She gives me a shrug. "Just because they are good for nothin' doesn't mean we don't want them. I don't want to want Lester at the senior center, but the man does something to my lady bits that I didn't think worked anymore. Even if he cheats at cards. Moral of the story, we might not want men, but that doesn't mean we don't need them in some ways. Now, talk to me, dear. Lord knows, I've told you enough of my problems over the years. What has my favorite hair girl looking lost?"

I let out a large sigh and a small smile as I look at Ruthie's reflection in the mirror. Not only is she my oldest client, but she's also my favorite. And that isn't because she makes the world's best chocolate chip cookies, or because she gives me a bottle of moonshine each year at Christmas (that I'm pretty sure she distills herself). She's a spitfire. She tells it like it is.

She keeps me on my toes. She's the definition of age is only a number.

And right now, she is the only person I want to talk to.

"You're right," I begin. "It is a guy."

"I knew it. I'm going to guess he's got you in knots. And not the good kind."

I give a small shrug, not sure how I want to say this. "We had an... agreement."

"Y'all were naked bed buddies."

"Is that what you used to call it?" I say, trying to hold in my laugh.

"We didn't call it anything because it wasn't polite to talk about back then. But we aren't talking about me. Why did you two call it quits?"

"We want different things," I say matter-of-factly. "And neither of us are willing to budge. So we called it quits. I just didn't realize it would be this hard."

That is the truth. It's been nearly two weeks since Memphis. I was a wreck driving back to Nashville after that night, which was expected. But I didn't expect it to last this long.

It's ridiculous that I am feeling this way. We were never anything serious. We were friends with benefits. Plain and simple.

Friends who had one last unforgettable night that is making me wish for things I can't have with him. And it wasn't just the sex. Hanging out with Sadie and Hunter made me wish that we were a normal couple on a double date. It was easy. Effortless. And it made me want more.

"Giving up someone you care about is never easy," Ruthie says as I give her one last spray. "That's why you need to get back on the horse."

I wasn't expecting her to say that. "I need to what?"

"Sweetie, I'm the one who wears the hearing aids. Not you. You heard what I said, my dear. Get back out there. Find yourself a new man. The only way to get over someone is to get under someone new, isn't that what the younger crowd says these days?"

"What?" Did she just say what I think she just said? "I don't think that's how it works, Ruthie."

"Actually, my dear, I think that's exactly how it works."

"I'm not just going to go out there and sleep with the first man I meet to get over someone I shouldn't even be hung up on. I'll be fine. By next week I'll be good as new."

I can't believe I'm having this conversation with an eighty-six-year-old woman.

"You might be. But maybe you need a little help. Now I'm not saying you have to sleep with Gavin right away. I'm just saying he might help you get over the man who is haunting your thoughts."

Now she is really confusing me. "Gavin? Who is Gavin?"

"The man I'm going to set you up with."

I'm pretty sure at this point, my eyes are bugging out of my head. "You are what? Huh? Who? I am so confused."

I take the gown off of Ruthie and she slowly stands from my chair. "Gavin is the grandson of a very nice man I've met at the senior center. He's new to Nashville. Just got transferred for his job at a bank, if I remember correctly. So, he needs to meet new people his own age. And he's going to be your date this Friday."

"Oh, is he now?"

Ruthie nods before grabbing her cane so we can walk to the front of the salon. "Bethany, my dear, I love you like you were my own grandchild. And the look I saw on your face today was of someone who is in pain. And I don't want to see that. I only ever want to see your beautiful smile. Now, I'm not saying that you need to sleep with Gavin, or even marry him, but I'm saying that you need to do something to take that frown off your face. And Gavin is the way to go about doing just that very thing."

She's right. Because since Davis and I have been sleeping together, I quit dating. I didn't mean to; it just kind of happened.

And maybe someone like Gavin is who I need, even if I only know his name and his job. If he works at a bank, that means he has a stable job. I know the guys I've dated in the past who have jobs like his haven't been the most exciting, but maybe a little on the boring side is what I need now.

Yes. I need stable. Guys in the banking industry who are looking out for their future—both personally and financially. Not football coaches who refuse to think past the next game.

Maybe Gavin won't be so bad?

"Fine," I say, walking to the computer to ring her up. "I'll go out with Gavin."

"That's right, you will," Ruthie says as I help her put on her jacket. "And make sure you wear something nice. Something that shows off the girls. Even at my age, the guys like the girls to be on display."

"Goodbye, Ruthie," I say, waving and laughing as she leaves the salon.

Maybe this won't be so bad? If anything, it rips the Band-Aid off and gets me back into the dating world. And maybe it will help me get over a man I should never have had to get over in the first place.

I LOVE THE DRAFT. It's my favorite part about coaching professional football.

Don't get me wrong, I love helping players develop. A win on Sunday is a feeling you can't replicate. Calling a play that leads to a big score? It's a pure adrenaline rush.

But the draft? The draft is months of planning, strategizing, and scouting, concluding with a three-day chess match against thirty-one other teams to see who can put the best moves together.

It's like the stock market of professional sports.

And I fucking love it.

Except not right now. Right now, I'm ready to pull my hair out.

"What happens if Phoenix takes a running back at number eight? Then Orlando takes a defensive back at fourteen, and Sacramento takes a linebacker at twenty. Who let me remind you, is the guy we love. And where does that leave us? We need defense this draft."

This is about the tenth hypothetical question Hunter has asked me in the past half hour. And the only reason he is asking me is because I'm the only coach left at the Fury facility. The defensive coordinator and the other position coaches said goodbye a long time ago. They got the hell out of Dodge as soon as they could.

I told them to save themselves. I'd throw myself on the sword for them because I could see the spiral Hunter was about to go down. He gets this way around draft time. He tries to predict every team's every move. It's an impossible task.

And it stresses everyone the fuck out.

"Up shit creek without a paddle."

This gets his attention. "Huh? What did you say?"

"You heard me," I say, kicking my legs up on the table in our conference room that has turned into draft central. "We're up shit creek. Obviously, you have it all figured out, and it's not going to go well for us because of hypothetical picks that are likely to not happen, so we should just pack up and go home. Don't even bother drafting. Maybe I can cash in some of my stocks and take a vacation to Aruba. I hear it's nice there in April."

The look he's giving me screams he doesn't appreciate my sarcasm. I, however, think I'm hilarious.

"We have to plan for everything. We can't just draft by the seat of our pants."

I let out an exasperated sigh and pick up a football that was left on the conference table. "And like I've said for the hundredth time, there is no way we can plan what is going to happen before our pick is on the board. There are twenty-one other teams picking before us. Killing yourself to try and see the future is not healthy. All we can do is put together our board of best players and go from there. So sit the fuck down and take a breath."

Hunter lets out a defeated sigh before slinking into a chair, beating his head with the football I just tossed him.

"We can't fuck this up."

"I know," I answer honestly. "And we aren't going to. But you seriously need to get your panties out of a bunch and relax. You're stressing everyone out."

I believe in my words, but I get where Hunter is coming from. This draft is easier said than done. A big reason we made the playoffs this past season was because we had the number-one pick last year and drafted our franchise quarterback, Bryce Donald. We knew Bryce was our guy from the moment we set eyes on him. He was the total package. Great athlete, hell of an arm, and he's the All-American boy that moms across the country want their daughters to bring home. He was a home run pick. From there, we just had to decide who our best players were and let the cards fall where they may.

We knocked the draft out of the park. It was a feeling like no other. It was the first draft I was a part of where I was in the room where the decisions were happening. I still get a rush thinking about that day.

It reminded me that I've come a long way since my lowly days as a glorified towel boy in Denver. That was my first professional coaching job, if you could call it that. After a few seasons there, I somehow was able to get hired with the Fury as a low-level offensive assistant. I didn't care though. I was moving up.

Now, three years later, I've gone from no-name assistant who was partying with the players, to wide receivers coach, to offensive coordinator. I'm Hunter's right-hand man to run his innovative offense.

So I get his stress. We need to nail this draft, even though we are picking at number twenty-two. We are a team on the rise and after last year's playoff season we don't want to lose momentum.

"How many players are we scouting this week?" I ask, trying to get his mind off of the actual draft.

"I forget the total number, but every coach is somewhere," Hunter says, looking at our scouting lineup. "You are going to be heading to Michigan and Ohio Friday."

"Sounds good to me. Both have a killer craft brew selection."

Hunter all but rolls his eyes at my response. "Between flights of beer, can you remember to scout players? I'm going to head down to Alabama for Pro Day. Always good for me to make an appearance at the alma mater."

"You just need your ego stroked since Sadie is out of town."

Hunter launches the football back at me, which I catch with ease. "Says the man who isn't getting anything stroked right now."

"Maybe I am. You don't know what I do when I leave here."

"I know you aren't sleeping with my future sister-in-law anymore. I also know that you're a dumbass for not even trying with her."

The look I shoot Hunter is meant to kill. I'm not an idiot to think he didn't have an idea what was going on with Bethany and me, but this is the first time he has brought it up to me.

"You don't know shit, McAvoy."

I throw the ball back to Hunter a little harder than I should as I stand from my seat and head to one of the many whiteboards around the conference room. I grab an eraser and find an insignificant portion to erase. Anything so I don't have to look Hunter in the eye right now.

If he knows we aren't... whatever we were, then why did he bring it up? Dick move, in my opinion.

Since I left her hotel in Memphis two weeks ago, I've been doing everything I can to keep busy and keep my mind off of her. I've put in twelve-hour days at the Fury facility. I'm at the gym twice a day. I'm in constant motion to keep my mind from going to that dark place where all I do is think about Bethany.

Because if I don't stop, I don't have time to play the what-if game. If there is one thing I'm good at doing, it's what-ifing a situation to death. I know I made the right decision, but that doesn't mean it doesn't suck any less.

I made my bed. Now it's time to lie in it.

"You know you can talk to me," Hunter says, his tone now not as harsh. "You helped me when shit almost blew up with Sadie. The least I can do is return the favor. However you need it."

I know he means well, but talking to people about my personal life isn't my favorite thing to do. Nor is asking for help.

When you ask people for help, they take it as an invitation to know everything about your life. The easiest way to get around that? Don't ask for help. Never show weakness. Paste a smile on your face and deflect with a joke. It works every time.

I found out at an early age that if you're joking around and always happy on the outside, no one asks how you are doing. How could you *not* be happy? You're the life of the party! You might be struggling more than you ever have in your life, but if you're laughing and joking, no one is the wiser to what's going on behind the scenes.

No one will know that your piece-of-shit father up and left one day and never came back, leaving you, your mom, and two younger sisters to fend for themselves.

No one will know that you had to become the man of the house at thirteen.

No one will know that those responsibilities still follow you to this very day.

"No favor to return," I say, though I still don't make eye contact.

"She's going on a date this weekend."

His words catch me off guard. I freeze at the board, not knowing what to do next.

She's going on a date? Already?

No, this is what I wanted. What she wanted. This is what I knew was going to happen when we called things off. She wants to settle down. Start a family. It just can't be with me.

But I just didn't think it would happen so soon.

"Good for her," I say, not looking back at Hunter. "I hope she has a good time."

"You're a fucking liar, Davis."

I let out an irritated breath. "How am I a liar?" I ask, finally turning to look at him. "She's a good girl. She deserves to be happy. If dating some random dude makes her happy, then great. I'm happy for her."

Hunter just shakes his head at me, notably frustrated at my reaction. "Fine, if that's how you want to play it, I'm not going to press you. But answer me one thing. Not as your boss, but as your friend. Why? Why won't you give her a chance?"

Fuck. I liked Hunter much better when he was spewing out random draft scenarios.

I really don't want to answer his question. That answer could open a Pandora's box of information that I have worked my ass off to keep stored away under lock and key.

If I was going to tell anyone, though, it would be Hunter. I didn't have a lot of close friends growing up; I kept everyone at arm's length to make sure that no one knew what me and my family were going through. Hunter isn't a shithead teenager who would run his mouth, though. He knows what it's like to want to keep family things a secret.

Yet, I can't bring myself to tell him the full truth.

"I have a lot on my plate. Family stuff," I begin, though I

know I'm still being pretty vague. "My mom and my sisters come first. Always. There's no room in my life for anyone else."

Hunter nods, though I can tell he knows there is more that I'm leaving out.

"Does Bethany know this?"

I shake my head. "No. And I'd appreciate it if she didn't. I have my reasons. That's all anyone needs to know."

Hunter stands and walks over to me at the whiteboard. "You know she'd understand."

"I don't want to have to make her understand."

"I get it," Hunter says as he gives me a hard pat on the shoulder. "But I don't get it at the same time. Thanks for telling me. I promise that I won't tell Bethany, or Sadie."

"Thanks. I appreciate it."

"Actually, no, that's not it," he says, slightly frustrated. "I get that you have your reasons, and in your head, you've made sense of them. But the right girl? The one who is made for you and only you? She would understand that you have other people in your world besides her. She wouldn't make you pick. She'd be your teammate. Your partner. Your best friend. She'd be right there beside you, supporting everything that is important to you. And that feeling? The feeling of having someone like that in your life? It's better than any win on a Sunday will ever make you feel."

I let Hunter's words roll around in my head as we pack up our things and make our way to our cars in the parking lot of the Fury facility.

I get what he's saying. In theory. I know he's found his person in Sadie, but from what I can tell from other relationships I have seen, they are unicorns.

Do I wish things were different? Yes. I also know that dreams are for fools. The real world doesn't allow for dreams. Just responsibilities. Heavy responsibilities.

As for Bethany? She deserves more than just to be someone else I'm responsible for. She deserves a man who can put her number one at all times.

"Hey, Hunter," I say as I open my car door.

"Yeah?"

"Just make sure he's not a douchebag."

Hunter nods. "I'll kick his ass if he is."

CHAPTER 9
BETHANY

I AM CONFIDENT.

I am beautiful.

I am not going to go into this date thinking I just met my future husband.

I have said these words to myself at least ten times in the fifteen minutes I've been sitting in my car outside of the Mexican restaurant where Gavin and I agreed to meet. I've been trying to psych myself up to go inside the restaurant, but I can't seem to move from the car.

I don't know why I'm so nervous. It's not like this is my first, first date. Heck, it's not even my first setup or blind date.

Liar, you know why you're nervous. It's because this is your first date since you met Davis.

Ugh, sometimes the voice inside my head is a real twat waffle.

I didn't mean to go on a dating hiatus when I met Davis. It just kind of... happened. I know we weren't a couple. We didn't go out to eat or get drinks or even see each other in the light of day. Yet somehow, it feels wrong for me to be dating other men. I've obviously taken the friends with benefits scenario with Davis to the next level.

I should have known then that I was in deeper than I should have been.

But that's no more. Tonight starts a new chapter. A Davis-free one.

"Just have fun. Don't put pressure on yourself or Gavin. Just have a nice dinner and see what happens."

Maybe since I'm saying those words out loud and not just in my head, I'll listen to them a little better.

I check the time, five minutes until seven.

Check the hair and lipstick.

Deep breath.

Here goes nothing.

Gavin and I exchanged a few texts before tonight—compliments of Ruthie and his grandfather playing matchmaker—and we figured out this place was a good central location for the both of us. Plus, Mexican is always a safe first date spot, in my opinion. There are drinks, chips and queso, and it's a laid-back atmosphere.

And if you don't like tacos, then we don't have a future together, and it's best I learn that early.

From the little I talked with him, he seems like a nice enough guy. He was polite. He didn't ask for a picture of my boobs before he learned my last name, and when I asked him for a picture so I would know what he looked like tonight, he didn't send me one of him holding a fish or his junk. He's already better than almost every guy I've met on the dating app I just rejoined this week.

"Bethany?"

I turn to my right to see the man who looks just like the picture Gavin sent me standing in the lobby, looking adorably nervous.

"Hi. Gavin?"

"Hi," he says, letting out a relieved breath. "I was so

worried I wasn't going to recognize you and say hi to the wrong person."

"Well, put those worries aside. Here I am. It's nice to meet you."

I reach out my hand to shake his as he simultaneously takes a step toward me, arms open for a hug. What comes next is the most awkward thirty seconds in my entire dating history of fumbling hands and repeated apologies.

"I'm so sorry," he says nervously, taking a step back and rubbing his hands down the front of his pants.

I touch his shoulder, trying to ease his discomfort. I ignore that I don't feel one bit of a spark when my hand makes contact with his. "No worries. I never know if people are huggers, so I always err on the side of caution. Come on, let's go grab a table."

We follow the hostess back to our booth as we both get settled in before saying another word.

The silence lets me take him in a little more. He has light brown hair that I would bet my cosmetology license on gets more blond in the summer months. He has kind eyes hidden behind a set of stylish glasses. His shy smile is highlighted by the slight dimple in his right cheek.

He's very attractive. Some might even say that he's hot in a Clark Kent before he becomes Superman kind of way.

Unfortunately, since he doesn't look like a tanned, brown hair, blue-eyed football coach, I am feeling absolutely nothing.

Don't. Don't compare him to Davis. Davis isn't an option. Get him out of your head.

"So, since I'm new in town, what's good?"

"Do you want an appetizer?"

We laugh at our second awkward moment of the night. Luckily, the waitress saves us from ourselves to take our drink order while also placing two glasses of water down in front of us.

"Do you do this often?" he asks.

"You mean talk at the same time as my date and shake their hand when they try to hug me? Can't say I do."

His shoulders visibly relax as my attempt at humor does the job. "At least you'll be able to say this date is memorable."

I hold my water glass in the air. "To a memorable first date."

He returns my gesture, and just like that, the blundering part of our date seems to be over.

We get served our drinks, place our food orders, and begin what I like to call standard interview date questions. We are both twenty-nine, yet neither of us is dreading our next birthdays. He's originally from North Carolina, went to college at N.C. State and recently moved to Nashville when his bank transferred him here. He used to spend each summer here with his grandparents, and when the opportunity presented itself to move here, he jumped at the chance. He likes cats over dogs, though doesn't want either, isn't a big sports fan, and has no opinion on whether pineapple belongs on pizza.

When it's my turn for the inquisition, I tell him how I was born and raised here, and how these days, not being a Nashville transplant is a badge of honor. I tell him the CliffsNotes version of my family history—that it was just my mom and me until she met Sadie's dad, Mike.

Guys don't get the full version of my sad childhood until at least date five. No first date wants to hear that sob story, especially the part that I've never met my father.

"I want to apologize again for earlier."

I give him a questioning look. "What for?"

He lets out a breath like he's trying to give himself courage. "I was so nervous for tonight. It's been a long time since I went out on a first date. And then my grandfather showed me your picture and you are gorgeous and... yeah. Needless to say, I might have psyched myself up a little too much for tonight."

This guy really is too sweet.

I reach out and touch his hand, hoping to calm his nerves. I again ignore that there is zero zing when our skin makes contact. I hate that I look for that now. The spark never even crossed my mind until... him.

"There is nothing to be sorry for," I say, trying to reassure him. "I haven't been on a first date in a while either. So, I'm a bit out of practice myself. Normally, I'm better judging whether someone is a handshaker or a hugger."

He laughs, though there isn't much humor in it. "I doubt you're as out of practice as me."

"How about this, since we seem to be great at doing things at the same time, on the count of three we'll say how long it has been since we've been on a first date."

"Promise to not make fun of me?"

I shake my head. "Cross my heart. This is a judgment-free zone. Ready? One... two... three."

"Four months."

"Four years."

I don't mean for it to happen, but I choke on my water. "I'm sorry. I didn't mean to respond like that. Wow, four years?"

He laughs, handing me a napkin. "I'd probably react like that too. But that's the answer. I was in a long-term relationship before I moved here."

"Is that why you moved?"

He shakes his head and immediately reaches for the second round of drinks the waitress just delivered. "No, but I'm not going to lie and say that the opportunity didn't come at the right time."

"Can I ask what happened?"

"We wanted different things," he said, a somberness now to his voice. "I guess we should have figured that out earlier. I wanted marriage and kids and a family. She wasn't opposed to the marriage part, but she didn't want children. I thought after a while she might change her mind, but she didn't. We realized, way too late, that it was best if we went our separate ways."

His words hit me straight in the gut. Is this what Davis was trying to save me from? He knew upfront that he would never change. Was it better to cut ties early like he did? Or was it better to be Gavin? To have four years of love with someone before you decided to move on with your lives?

Honestly? Both sound pretty crappy to me.

"Why do I have a feeling that you understand everything I just said?"

I shake my head as I smile. "Am I that transparent?"

"Nah, I just recognize that look."

I take a drink of my margarita. "Why can't two people who have deep feelings for each other want the same things? Finding love shouldn't be this hard."

This earns me a laugh. "If I knew the answer to that, we wouldn't be here tonight."

We both let the comment settle and take each other in.

This man is going to make some woman very happy someday. He's nice and sweet and good-looking. He has a good job, he's family oriented, and wants the exact same things I want in life. On paper, he checks every single box.

That is, except one. He's not the man that I can't get out of my head and the one I want in my bed.

"Gavin."

"Bethany."

Again, all we can do is laugh.

"We are really good at that," he says.

"That we are."

"Though I think that might be the only thing we're good at."

Thank the heavens he said it first.

I reach for both of his hands and give them a squeeze. "It's not fair to you that my mind is still with someone else."

"And though I know I need to at some point, I'm not ready yet to get back out there."

We let our words hang in the air, though the silence isn't uncomfortable. In fact, it feels right. All in all, it's a very pleasant date. We finish our meals with great conversation because the elephant in the room has been let free. If I felt one ounce of attraction to this man, I know I'd already have our wedding planned out.

Instead, I'm going to go home and dream of the man and the life I can't have. I know I'm going to need to get over him and the idea of us, eventually. But that's not going to be tonight.

Or likely tomorrow.

Maybe someday.

"Bethany?" Gavin says as we approach my car. "I know this is going to sound weird, but I want to say thank you."

This I wasn't expecting. "For what?"

He brings my hand to his lips and gives it the gentlest kiss. "For making me realize that I can do this. Maybe not now, but eventually."

It's like this man can read my mind.

"Then I should say thank you as well."

He quirks an eyebrow at me. "For what? Talking over you three times?"

"No," I say, giving him a kiss on the cheek. "For showing me that I'm not ready either."

CHAPTER 10
DAVIS

I'M TIRED.

I'm hungry.

I'm horny.

Put those all together and I am one grumpy-ass moth-erfucker.

I've been scouting for the past four days, making my tour through colleges in Michigan and Ohio. At the last minute, Hunter requested I swing over to Indiana to watch a few kids, and that was all before my flight was delayed twice due to a late-winter snowstorm.

I might be originally from Pennsylvania, but I have become quite acclimated to the mild winter Nashville offers. I have no love lost for Midwestern snowstorms.

Normally, after a trip like this, I'd go home, shower the day away, hop into the sports bar not far from my apartment and grab food and a drink. If the stars aligned in my favor, I'd meet a willing woman to help me scratch the itch that's been festering since Bethany and I ended our arrangement.

Unfortunately, that's not in the cards for me tonight. Instead of having a relaxing night, I'm heading into the Fury offices to have a debrief meeting with Hunter.

I told him it could wait until tomorrow. He then went on a twenty-minute rant about draft strategizing and having to get this draft perfect, and the hidden gem of the draft could have been in the players I watched this week, but I might forget if we wait until Monday morning.

I know when to pick my battles. This wasn't one of them.

Just as I'm trying to think of ten different ways I can get Hunter back for making me come in on a Sunday night, including what I'm going to make him buy me for dinner, my phone rings. And since it's eight p.m. on Sunday, there is no question as to who it is.

"Hello, favorite sister."

"How do I know you don't say that to Sara too?"

"Have you no faith in me? I'm a man of my word."

I'm pretty sure she snorts before answering. "Whatever you need to tell yourself to sleep at night."

"I sleep just fine, thank you very much."

"I take that as code for I'm still not sharing my bed with anyone for more than a few hours at a time so no one is stealing the covers?"

Leave it to my sister to get to the real reason for tonight's weekly check-in. Some weeks she calls to give me an update on our youngest sister. Sometimes she calls to talk about Mom. Most weeks, she gives me hell about not settling down yet.

"Is this going to be the topic of tonight's phone call? To try and meddle in my life?"

"What are little sisters for?"

"I thought once we became adults you'd quit annoying me."

This earns me another laugh. "Again, what are sisters for?"

We might give each other shit, but besides Hunter, Abby is my best friend in the entire world. I know that might sound weird to some, but if you grew up how we did, it would make sense.

Abby and I are Irish twins, though that's the only thing Irish that flows through our veins. I was born in January, and by December, my mom was taking care of two kids under the age of one. Considering we both share our mother's dark hair and features, people just assumed we were twins for most of grade school. We got tired of correcting people and just rolled with it.

Being basically the same age helped later in life when our dad took off. We went from being seemingly normal preteens to adults overnight.

When my parents were together, we weren't rolling in the cash, but we weren't starving either. Mom worked in the school cafeteria, and Mitch—I try not to think of him as Dad even though I look nearly identical to him—had a steady job with a construction company. I never had a pair of new Jordans or the latest gaming system, but I knew even at a young age we were better off than most.

Then one day, everything changed.

Mitch left without warning. It was a Saturday, and he said that they were getting overtime on a job. We didn't think anything of it.

That was until it was dark out and there was no word from him. We didn't have enough money for a cell phone back then, so all we could do was wait.

Sometimes I think my mom is still waiting. She used to sit outside in our backyard on an old tire swing for hours, just staring off into the distance. She said she was doing it to clear her mind, but I think she was waiting to see if he'd come home.

He never did. We never saw him again.

Next thing we knew, our lives were turned upside down. Mom picked up a second job waitressing. Abby became a second mother to our younger sister, Sara, who was a toddler when he took off.

As for me? I hated seeing my mother working herself to the bone. So along with school and football, I picked up every odd job I could. Every penny was either saved or spent on necessities.

Abby and my mom hated me working. They both wanted me to concentrate on school and football. They promised me that helping around the house was enough. But I couldn't sit back and watch them suffer. I had to do what I had to do. That was the man-of-the-house mentality that was almost ingrained in me—not by my father, of course.

So, from the age of thirteen until the time I graduated, I never went to a party. I never had girlfriends or went to the prom. It was school, football, and work. That's all that mattered because at the end of the day, I needed to help my family.

And to this day, I'm still living that lifestyle. Now just for different reasons. But still for my family.

Anything for my mom and sisters. They come first. Always.

"Did you really call just to nag me about my personal life, or was there a real reason?"

"I'd be lying if I said it wasn't partly for that. I hate that you are alone, Davis. You know you don't—"

"Stop right there," I warn, knowing where my sister is going with this conversation. It's a speech she likes to give at least twice a month. "Why else did you call, Abby?"

I hear the defeat in her sigh before she goes on. "I stopped and saw Mom the other day."

"How was she?"

"It was a good day. She remembered my name."

I hate that this is now what's considered a good day for my mom. But that's the reality with early-onset Alzheimer's.

"That's good."

"I was also told to tell you to expect a call soon from the billing department at the facility. Something about terms in her insurance changing."

As if this night couldn't get any worse. "Can't wait for that one."

"As if getting older and sick wasn't hard enough."

"Don't worry about it, Abbs. I'll take care of it."

I hear her take a deep breath. It's the kind of breath these days she reserves for scolding my two nieces or me. "You know you don't have to carry the load anymore. We aren't kids, Davis. I'm a grown woman. And despite what you think, so is Sara. We are in this together."

"I said I'll handle it, Abby." My voice growing frustrated, but I don't know how many times I can have this conversation with my sister. "You have a family of your own, and that's where your energy should be. I want Sara to worry about college, not this. I said I'll handle it and I will."

Silence weighs heavy on the line, even though we've gone round-and-round on this ever since my mother was diagnosed. The early signs started becoming apparent when I was in college, though I have always wondered if they were there earlier and I just didn't realize it. Abby stayed at home and went to community college because she felt guilty about leaving Sara, who was still in elementary school at the time. That turned out to be a blessing in disguise because when we realized something was wrong with Mom, things happened at warp speed.

From what started as forgetting a few things turned into her going missing, which led to the early-onset Alzheimer's diagnosis. We were able to find a facility for Mom within an hour of Abby, and she has been the point person physically since I can't be there. That and basically raising Sara.

As for me? I'm the one footing the bill. I don't mind. Take my money. Take it all. As long as my mother is getting the care she needs and my sisters are provided for. That's all that matters, and if I have to give up aspects of my life for that to happen, then so be it.

"I hate what all of this has done to you," Abby says, her voice now softer.

"What do you mean?" I ask as I turn into the Fury facility.

"Since the moment Dad left, you put your life on hold. Then Mom got sick and you went into overdrive about helping us. I know we had to back then. But now? Davis, this shouldn't be how it is. Sara and I shouldn't get to live our lives while you suffer."

"I don't suffer, Abby," I say, exiting my car and making my way inside the building. "I've made my choices. Mom is safe and cared for. You and Sara are happy. I don't regret a thing."

"One of these days, big brother, you will. And when that day comes, you're going to realize that a promise you made to yourself when you were thirteen wasn't worth it."

I let the comment go and say goodbye to my sister as I head down the hallway to our coaching offices. Every Sunday call is like that with her. She makes sure I'm alive, updates me on Mom, and makes some sort of comment about my personal life. If I didn't love her so much, I'd quit answering.

She acts like I'm suffering because I've chosen to prioritize my family's needs over my own. When Mitch left, I became the man of the house. It's a responsibility I have never taken lightly. A man doesn't turn his back on his family. A man doesn't let his family suffer when he has the means to make sure they don't.

The day he left, I vowed to myself that my mother and sisters would never want for or have to worry about anything. Not for food, for clothes, for anything.

It's a vow I still hold true to this day.

It's why I won't get into a relationship. If I did, I don't know if I could balance it all. How can I be there for someone else, as well as my mom and sisters? How could I provide for two families? How would I prioritize?

I never wanted to know that answer, which is why I've kept women at arm's length my entire life.

Except her...

As if my mind is playing tricks on me, I hear her laughter coming from one of the offices as I walk down the hallway.

No. It can't be. What is she doing here?

I take a few more steps toward the voices and realize my mind isn't messing with me. Sadie and Bethany are sitting in Hunter's office. The door is open so I'm able to hear what they are saying without them realizing I'm here.

"So how did it go?" Sadie asks. "You can't tell me about a first date, then give me no follow-up details."

Bethany doesn't answer for a minute. Then she does something I rarely hear her do.

She giggles.

"He was like no one I've been out with before," Bethany answers, a happiness to her tone that simultaneously makes me happy for her and want to punch a wall.

I forgot Bethany had a date this weekend. I was able to block that out of my mind while I was freezing my ass off scouting players we might draft.

"In a good way?"

"In the best way. Sadie, it was the best first date I had been on in a while."

"Tell me everything. Consider this payback for all the times you made me gush about Hunter."

"Well, he was nice, and sweet. Once we got past the first-date jitters, he was easy to talk to."

"And…" Sadie probes.

"And yes, he was very good-looking."

"You're holding out on me. What else?"

"He was just about perfect. He wants the same things I want. He wants a family and to settle down. He has family in Nashville and wouldn't mind staying here. I honestly didn't think a guy like him existed."

I don't hear whatever else Bethany says because every ounce of blood in my body starts boiling.

I knew she had a date, but I figured it would be with some tool. From the little bit of her dating history I know, that seems to be her luck. Selfishly, I hoped it didn't change.

From the sounds of it, that's not the case.

You knew this could happen. You didn't try to prevent it. You made your bed. Now lie in it.

"You're here."

I nearly jump out of my skin at Hunter's words. "Dude, give a guy a warning."

"Not my fault you were eavesdropping."

"I wasn't eavesdropping."

The look Hunter flashes me lets me know clear as day he doesn't buy it. "Whatever. And before you ask, Sadie and I were on our way to dinner when Bethany called her. Since we had to make a pit stop here to meet you, she told her to come here and catch up."

"I didn't ask."

"You didn't have to. Come on, let's get this over with so we can get out of here."

Hunter signals for me to follow him down to our draft conference room. In doing so, we have to walk past his office. I know I shouldn't, but I take a peek as I walk past.

Bad idea.

I almost forgot how beautiful she is. Especially now,

talking and laughing with Sadie. She looks happy. Lighter. Like she doesn't have a care in the world.

And that's all I want for her is to be happy. Even if it's with some douche canoe who is "sweet."

Fuck a bunch of sweet.

As if she could hear my internal dialogue, she takes that moment to look up. The second our glances connect, I see the light leave her eyes.

I put that look there. Because I was a selfish bastard who couldn't stay away from her, I put that look in her eyes.

No more. If the douche canoe makes her happy, then I need to stay as far away as possible.

Because I can't give her what she wants. And apparently, he can.

"You coming?" Hunter asks, standing at the doorway to the conference room.

And I do the only thing I can. I walk away from her without saying a word.

CHAPTER 11
BETHANY

"HELLO? WHERE Y'ALL HIDING?"

Normally, when I show up at my mom and stepdad's house for Monday night dinner, I'm greeted with the sights of my mother flying around the kitchen and Mike reminding her she's only cooking for five of us, not an entire army.

Today? Today I've walked into an empty house, though I see both my mom and Mike's cars in the garage. The oven isn't on; nothing is in the crockpot; there aren't any signs that my mom plans on cooking tonight.

"AHHHHH!!! MIKE!!!!!"

No.

No.

No. No. No.

Did I just hear what I think I just heard?

No. It can't be.

"YES!!!!"

Oh my God.

It is.

My mom is having sex.

And she's a screamer.

When you grow up with a single mom who never brought

men home, this wasn't something that happened. I don't have the childhood memory of accidentally walking in on my parents and them giving me a flimsy excuse about why they were naked in bed that I only buy because I'm a kid. Even when she and Mike started dating, I don't believe they even spent the night together when I was home until they were married and we all moved in together. Then again, he was my English teacher, so I'm going to assume that also had something to do with it.

And now, hearing what I'm hearing, I'm glad that I don't have to sit in his class every day knowing these are the sounds that the two of them make together.

I will never be without the knowledge that when my mother orgasms, she screams for all the neighborhood to hear.

I don't know how long I stand in the entryway. It has to be more than a few minutes because before I know it, my mom is coming downstairs, fixing her hair like she just freshened up in the powder room, not getting a mid-afternoon quickie from my stepdad.

"Bethany! Oh dear! When did you…?"

Her question trails off because at this moment, I'm guessing she can read the horror on my face.

"Long enough," I say as I look away, trying not to make eye contact with her.

"Well, you're an adult. I'm sure you can appreciate the act of two—"

"Mom, please," I say as I follow her into the kitchen. "I beg of you. I never want to talk about this again."

"Oh, come on, Bethany," she says, pulling chicken out of the refrigerator. "We used to talk about this stuff all the time."

It's true. To an extent. My mother and I have always been extremely close. I never knew my father. They were engaged when she got pregnant with me but decided to postpone the wedding until after I was born. She says every day that was a blessing in disguise because after two months of fatherhood, he couldn't handle it and split. Signed away his parental rights, never to be heard from again.

Apparently, fatherhood is easier to dispose of than a used condom.

Since it was just me and her, we became this weird combination of mother-daughter and best friends. She never pulled punches with me. I had the birds and the bees talk long before my friends did. I wasn't embarrassed when I first got my period. I even ran home and told her all the details about my first kiss.

There has never been a part of my life when I didn't think I could talk to her.

That is, until now. Hearing your mom cry out her husband's name during an orgasm is crossing the line.

A big one. One that can never be uncrossed.

"Please, Mom, let's forget about it," I say, trying to busy myself by starting to make the salad.

"You know sex is a natural thing," she says, and I swear on my best flat iron that if she goes into the lecture she gave me when I was in sixth grade, I'm going to lose it.

"Yes, Mom. I do. Now please—"

"And it's natural as you get older your sex drive..."

Oh God, she's really never going to stop.

"Mom!"

"And you know you arrived a half hour early."

Just as I'm about to protest again, my stomach makes a sound that I've never heard it make before. Not even on my twenty-first birthday after ten lemon drop shots and a trip to Taco Bell. Who knew that my mom talking about sex could make me physically sick?

"Bethany?"

I hear my mom, but I don't answer as I sprint to the bathroom that is just off the kitchen.

There is no such thing as vomiting gracefully. And for the next ten minutes, I try to figure out what in the heck I ate to make this my current reality.

After I left the Fury facility last night, I was craving hot chicken, which I rarely do, and picked some up on the way home.

Maybe it was the potato salad? Yes. That had to be it.

"Bethany? Are you all right?"

Sadie's voice travels through the door, but I don't answer right away. First, I make sure I'm confident that whatever just happened is over before I stand and start rinsing my mouth out.

Gosh, that was a weird turn of events. And hopefully, a one-time thing.

"Give me a second."

Convinced I look like I didn't spend the past ten minutes unloading my guts, I open the door to see Sadie standing in front of me, a concerned look on her face.

"Are you okay?"

I laugh it off the best I can. "Yeah. I don't know what happened. I have it narrowed down to bad potato salad or hearing our parents having sex."

This makes Sadie's eyes go wide.

"Did you just say...?"

I give her a devilish smile. Because if I have to know this, so does she.

"Oh yes. And fun fact. My mom's a screamer."

———

The rest of the night is Monday dinner business as usual. My stomach stopped revolting, my mom quit trying to talk to me about sex, Sadie retreated to the study to conduct a phone interview, and Hunter and Mike had their now-weekly debates over the best college football players of all time.

Just a normal Monday night at the Benson-Hall household.

"You sure you're okay?"

Ever since my episode earlier, my mom has asked me this question every five minutes or so. I thought me loading the dishwasher would give me a reprieve. Not so much.

"For the hundredth time, I'm fine, Mom. I think I just had some bad food last night. Please stop worrying."

"You're my baby, I'll never stop worrying."

She wraps her arms around my waist as I lean back into her embrace. I know everyone says that their mom is the best, but I'm pretty sure mine would win every time.

"That's our job as parents. We will worry until the day we die," Mike says, entering the kitchen with Hunter and Sadie right behind him. "Even though you two are adults, and soon starting families of your own, you're still our little girls."

I know the second part of that comment was directed toward Sadie, but I'm not going to lie that it doesn't sting a bit that it's *only* directed to her.

I never really thought about having the stereotypical family growing up. I had my mom. We were happy. That was all I needed.

Then she met Mike.

I remember when she first told me about him. I remember thinking to myself that this was the happiest she ever looked. She couldn't stop smiling. She would just stare out the window in a daydream, and I never wanted to disturb her.

That was when I decided that I wanted to find a love like theirs. And I didn't want to wait until I was in my forties.

I want it now.

Maybe because I'm so desperate to find it is why I haven't. I know there's a saying about you find love when you're least expecting it, but I think that's a bunch of bull crap.

Although, my mom didn't expect to meet Mike during a PTA meeting.

And Sadie didn't expect to meet Hunter when she did. Heck, they never really should have ever even gotten together. A coach and a reporter dating is super taboo in their world.

Yet here they are. Happy and engaged.

And here I am. Puking alone because of bad potato salad.

"Bethany, are you okay?"

Just when I think my mom is asking me if I'm about to get sick again, I realize it's because I've started crying.

"Yeah," I quickly say, wiping away the stray tear. "I should get going. I have early clients tomorrow."

Considering how this night has gone for me, my mom doesn't press about me leaving early. I quickly tell everyone good night and make my way back into the Nashville city limits toward my apartment.

Normally, when I'm in my car, I find my Top 40 country station and blare the radio. Tonight, I choose to drive back to my apartment in silence, only my thoughts keeping me company.

I've always been happy for Sadie and Hunter. I don't know why tonight, all of a sudden, I feel a pang of jealousy toward them. There's nothing to be jealous of. They found their love story. Mine is coming soon.

Hopefully. Maybe.

Crap... there go the tears again.

What is with me tonight? As much as I want to blame it on

hearing things no child ever wants to hear, I know that's not it. One minute, I'm my normal happy self. One minute, I'm crying over nothing. One minute, I'm throwing up.

This isn't like me.

Maybe it's my time of the month? Yes, that has to be it. Good ol' Aunt Flo is on her way to town and it's throwing me all off.

At least, that's what I'm going to blame it on. Because being the depressed single girl who realized today her mom has a better sex life than she does is not an option.

CHAPTER 12

BETHANY

"DON'T HATE ME."

I'm not even three steps inside Hunter and Sadie's condo when my stepsister says that statement and drags me into the half bathroom just off the entryway.

"Why am I hating you? Did you forget the wine? Sadie, I said I'd order the pizza. You had one job for girls' night, and that was to get the finest bottle of ten-dollar wine Target has to offer."

"No, I didn't forget the wine," she says in a loud whisper. "But I want you to know that when I invited you over tonight, I really thought it was just going to be the two of us."

That makes my eyes go wide. "What are you talking about?"

She looks toward the door, even though it's closed, before looking back to me. A look of guilt is written all over her face. "Between the time I told you to come over and now, Hunter might have moved the draft strategy session to here."

"Sadie..."

"And he might not be alone."

When Sadie asked me to come over tonight because Hunter

was working, I jumped at the chance. For some reason, I was feeling extra emotional and really didn't want to be alone. What better way to fight the depression, pre-period blues than with pizza, cheap wine, and a binge-watch of the new historical romance series on Netflix?

Guess I'll never find out.

"It's fine," I lie.

Sadie raises her eyebrow at me. "Really? You aren't mad that Davis, whose name is not Ricardo, is here, and you had no prior warning?"

I mean, I am mad. Not mad, just... mentally unprepared. But I can't tell her that. Sadie knows the bare minimum of what went on with Davis and me. She definitely doesn't know what happened in Memphis. She doesn't know that the real reason my date with Gavin is going to be a one-and-done is that the entire night I spent comparing the two men.

I should have told her about us when we first started. It would have made everything so much easier. I don't even know why I didn't. Maybe because I felt ashamed? I'm not one to have a month's-long hookup. But what's done is done. I've made my bed, and now I have to awkwardly lie in it.

"I'm not mad. They can do their thing and we will do ours," I say, trying to play it off. Though I take the time in the bathroom to make sure that the little makeup I wore today still looks good.

"Are you ever going to tell me what happened with you two? I thought maybe after Memphis things would change. You seemed to be getting along so well at the bar."

I make eye contact with Sadie through her mirror, a sad look gracing her face. It matches the look on mine.

"Everything is how it is meant to be," I say, my tone resigned. "Now, where is this wine, and you better have bought more than one bottle."

She lets out a sigh. "As long as you are happy, that's all that matters. I love you, sis."

Sadie gives me a side hug before we exit the bathroom. I let her leave before I give myself one last glance-over, fighting back the unexpected wave of tears that almost hit me from Sadie's words.

Deep breath. Check.

Makeup? Good.

Hair? Messy, but in a cute and styled way.

Heart? Locked up. Tight.

I take one last resolving breath and leave the bathroom. I kind of hoped that I'd at least get past the kitchen before I saw him, but of course, that's not my luck.

Standing at the counter, in all his muscled, sexy glory, is Davis.

And he's wearing gray sweatpants.

Dear Lord Jesus and Queen Dolly, give me the strength to resist.

His back is turned to me, which gives me two choices right now. I can quickly walk past him and not say a word, hoping he gets the idea and doesn't talk to me. I do need a wineglass, but I'll just drink from the bottle if it affords me the chance of avoiding him.

Or I could suck it up, say hello, and attack the elephant in the room head-on. Be an adult. Let him know that I'm the bigger person here and that his presence means nothing to me.

"Why don't you take a picture? It might last longer."

Or Option 3: Get caught staring at him when I didn't even know he knew I was there.

"I have no idea what you mean," I say, even though I totally was just staring at his butt. "I'm just about to get myself a wineglass."

He turns to look at me, a devious grin on his face. "Wineglass, huh?"

"Yes, a wineglass," I say with more confidence than I'm feeling as I walk toward the cupboard.

I might have given myself the option of talking to him and being an adult, but I didn't take into account what it would feel like to be in his orbit again. Every step I take closer to him, the more my body reacts to his mere presence.

"I didn't expect to see you here tonight," he says, now leaning against the counter, his arms crossed in a way that should be casual yet is ridiculously sexy when he does it. God, that smirk on his ridiculously handsome face is more potent than I remember.

"I can say the same for you," I say as nonchalant as possible. "I didn't picture you as one who worked past five o'clock."

Yes! Fight off his vibe with sarcasm and snark. Good plan!

He quickly puts his hand over his heart. "You wound me, princess. What makes you think that I'm a clock watcher?"

"Excuse me for thinking that the fun uncle of the Fury works overtime," I say, now standing directly in front of him. "I didn't think those two things went together."

We might be playing a game of verbal cat and mouse right now, but I can't deny the pull I feel toward this man.

And I hate that I do. He is the worst possible man to feel like this toward. Is it ever going to not happen when we are near each other?

Even though I know what I'm feeling is all kinds of wrong, it doesn't mean I don't want to pull him into Hunter's garage and have a repeat of the championship game night where he made me see stars against Hunter's truck.

"Fun uncle, huh?" he says, taking a step toward me. "I've heard that I've been called that. I also get dumb jock a lot. But I don't know if I agree with that one."

I quirk my eyebrow at him, doing my best to ignore the

overwhelming effect his cologne is having on my body right now. "Then how would you describe your work habits? I mean, you are the man who once told me that if it isn't fun, it isn't worth doing."

Just as I'm about to pat myself on the back for how I'm handling this interaction, Davis leans a little closer.

Oh God... No! Stay strong! He's just a man!

But I don't know if I have enough strength to fight back all of the feelings my body is processing right now. His lips are inches away from my ear and his breath on my neck right now has a direct path to my core.

I feel myself getting weaker by the second.

"I'm a much bigger proponent of the phrase 'work hard, play harder.' You remember that, right? You remember how hard I like to play, don't you?"

Dear seven-pound, eight-ounce baby Jesus, give me the strength right now because I don't think I can resist.

Before I can answer, Davis continues. "But the question is, does your new boyfriend play like I did? Does he play hard, Bethany?"

The noise inside my head right now sounds like a ten-car crash on Interstate 40 during rush hour.

"What did you just say?"

I'm genuinely confused. Who is he talking about? Gavin? How does he even know? Did Hunter tell him something?

Then it hits me.

Sadie... Sunday night... the Fury facility... making eye contact with him before he walked away without even an acknowledgment.

That must be it. He must have overheard me talking to Sadie about my date with Gavin. Though by how he is talking, he must not have heard the part where I told Sadie that there was no chemistry and we are going to just be friends.

Davis takes a step back, a satisfied look on his face. "You heard me. I was just asking if your new boyfriend likes to play hard, too? Or is he one of those guys who plays it safe? You didn't strike me as a girl who would be attracted to that kind of guy, but what do I know? I'm just the dumb jock who doesn't know the meaning of the word serious."

"Don't put words in my mouth," I say, my blood now simmering. "And who I do or don't see is none of your business."

"It's not," he says, trying to play nonchalant. "I just think it's funny that you go from me to what I'm now guessing is some nice guy who is all about giving you your two-point-five kids. But hey, whatever floats your boat."

Is this man serious right now? The sheer audacity of him!

I don't even justify his outburst with a response. I don't correct him about Gavin. I can't. I don't trust my words right now. Instead, I shove my way past him, open up the cupboard and get a wineglass. A big one. I'm going to need the whole bottle after this interaction.

"Nothing to say, princess?"

I take a breath, trying to even my tone as much as possible despite Davis being ridiculously infuriating right now.

"Who I am seeing is none of your business."

A shit-eating grin forms on his stupid handsome face. "Ah, then that's all the answer I need. I hope that Mr. Nice Guy gives you everything you want."

"You!" I scream, slamming my wineglass on the counter. It might have shattered, maybe just cracked. I'm not sure. "You have no right to ask about who I am or am not seeing. What Gavin and I do or don't do is not your concern."

"Ah-ha!" he says, a smug look on his face. "So you are seeing someone. Gavin's his name, huh? That didn't take long."

"This is all because of you! How dare you try and throw

stones at the type of man he is. You've never met him. Remember, you did this. You're the one who didn't want more. You're the one who couldn't bear to have his perfect little fun life be complicated by such hassles like a girlfriend or responsibilities. Or God forbid, a family and a future."

"Don't you talk to me about family or responsibilities," he answers, his voice now going down an octave. "You have no idea what is on my plate."

I am livid right now. "How can I? How can you? You won't even tell me your name! You won't tell anyone. I don't know if you're an only child or you have eight siblings. I know nothing about you. And that's your doing. I wanted more. You didn't. That was that. So before you come around here giving me hell for moving on with my life, remember each and every reason that I'm doing it."

My breathing is heavy, and I can't believe all of that just came out of my mouth. This isn't me. I'm not the one to yell at anyone. I hate confrontation. I used to try and break up fights at recess because they made me sad.

Then I look over Davis's shoulder and see Hunter and Sadie standing outside the kitchen, looking at us in shock. Davis turns when he sees my eyes fixed on them, his shoulders dropping when he realizes that we just had a full-fledged screaming match in their kitchen.

"I'm sorry," I say, running to grab my purse, embarrassment and a million other emotions raging through my body. "I need to go."

"No," Davis says, gently putting his hand on my shoulder. "You stay. Hunter, I'll see you tomorrow."

All I can do is watch him as he grabs his keys and makes his way to the door. What happens next is something I never expected.

"You're right," he says, though he doesn't turn around. "This is all my fault."

And then he walks out.

Why does it feel like this time him walking away means forever?

CHAPTER 13
DAVIS

I TURN the treadmill up to eleven, hoping that the punishing pace will do the damage I'm seeking. My normal run is somewhere around a nine, so hopefully, this does the trick.

It won't. Nothing will. Nothing will make up for how I treated Bethany tonight.

Could I be any more of an asshole?

The moment I left Hunter and Sadie's place, I wanted to turn around and apologize. I know I should have. Maybe it was my pride that didn't allow me to do it.

More like my shame.

When I drove away, I considered heading to the bar, and finding some faceless and nameless woman to get lost in for the night. But the more I thought about it, the more I couldn't stomach that thought.

Instead, I drove home and found myself in the gym of my apartment complex. When I was in high school and was mad at the world for the hand my family and I were dealt, I'd take my frustrations out on weights or a heavy bag.

And when that wasn't enough, I went on a run. A long, punishing run.

But tonight, even that isn't working. That's how much I fucked everything up.

Where did I think I had the right to question who she was seeing? Or to act the way I did? If I knew a man was treating Abby or Sara like that, I'd pummel him to within an inch of his life.

Bethany was right. Every word she said. I'm the reason nothing is happening between us. I'm the one who refuses to budge. Granted, my reasons are valid, but still, it's because of me. How can I be upset that she is seeing someone new?

I can't be. Yet I am. And I'm not sure how to process all of that.

"I don't regret a thing."

"One of these days, big brother, you will. And when that day comes, you're going to realize that a promise you made to yourself when you were thirteen wasn't worth it."

Abby's words from a few weeks ago come to the forefront of my memory. Is this what tonight was? Regret? No. While I might regret how I treated Bethany, I don't regret why we aren't together. I made a choice back then, and that was to put Mom, Abby, and Sara first. Always. Just because my balls had barely dropped at the time doesn't mean anything. I meant what I said, and I'm going to stick with it until my dying day. I won't be like my father and dismiss the family responsibilities that I have. Real men don't do that.

As long as they are taken care of, I will regret nothing.

Except living with the knowledge that I put the look of anger and sadness on Bethany's face tonight.

That sobering thought sends a jolt through me and I jump to the sides of the treadmill, letting the belt keep running as that image goes through my head.

What kind of man talks to a woman like that? I pride myself on being a man for my family, but what kind of man am

I to make a woman feel bad about herself? To chastise her about her dating life?

Fuck, I really am an asshole.

I don't think this was the type of regret my sister was talking about. Neither is what I'm about to do.

"Hello? Davis?" Abby says when she answers, confused as to why I'm calling. "Is everything all right? What happened? What did you do?"

I sit in a nearby chair, thankful that no one is in the gym right now. "What makes you think I did something?"

"Because you are calling me, unprompted, on a Wednesday night at nearly midnight. Spill it. What did you do?"

I run my hand over my face, wondering where to even start. "There's this girl."

I've never begun a sentence like that to my sister. Therefore, I didn't expect the high-pitched noise that came from the other end of the phone that I'm pretty sure only dogs can hear.

"Abby, settle down. It's not like that."

The line immediately goes quiet. "What do you mean, *it's not like that*? Oh God, did you fuck it up already? You are such a fucking man sometimes."

I let out a sigh I'm sure she can hear. "It wasn't supposed to be serious between us. But..."

"But then it got serious?"

I let out a sigh. How do I explain this? "Yes. No. I don't know. She wants more than I can give her. She wants what you have. The husband and the kids and the happily ever after. I can't give that to her, so I told her to move on. And she did."

"You did what?" Abby yells, and I'm pretty sure the only people who have ever heard her voice reach this volume are her children and husband. "Why on God's green Earth would you tell her to do that?"

"You know why."

"Are you meaning to tell me," she begins, then has to take a deep breath before continuing. I haven't been yelled at like this since I was ten. "That you met a woman you liked enough to actually keep around for more than a night. And I'm going to assume she felt the same way about you. And because you decided when you were thirteen that you were going to provide for us that you turned her away? Wow, big brother, you are a special kind of dumbass."

"You know I had to," I say, trying to defend myself.

"You did not. We are all adults, with our own families now, not children. Don't use us as an excuse to run from commitment."

This gives me pause. Is that what I'm doing?

No. She's wrong.

"Abby."

"Ri—"

"Don't. Do not use my full name."

"If a situation called for it, it would be this one."

"I didn't call you for a lecture."

"Then why did you? Why did you call me to tell me about a girl I'm never going to meet because you're an idiot who pushed her away because of a decision you felt you had to make when we were kids?"

I don't answer right away because I honestly don't have any idea how to. She's right. I made that declaration when I felt our backs were against the wall. We were struggling, and I hated seeing my family suffer. Mitch leaving put us in an impossible situation that no family should ever have to endure.

I never thought about the future when I decided to put the family on my shoulders. I never thought there might be a day when I'd want more. And now, to have more in my own personal life, I'll have to let down the family I'd die for.

That is not an option.

"I called because... I don't know. She and I, we have mutual friends. We saw each other tonight. It didn't go well. I said some stupid shit and... I don't know, Abby. I feel horrible."

"Do you feel horrible because of what you said or because you're in this situation to begin with?"

I take a moment to think about that. The real answer is both, but I wouldn't have to be sorry if we never started sleeping together.

But then I would have never known her. And I hate that most of all.

"Do you think I can do it all?" I ask, ignoring Abby's question.

"Brother, there has never been a time in your life that I didn't think you could do anything you put your mind to. You got good grades while working thirty hours a week, while also playing football well enough to earn a scholarship. You have put this family on your back—carrying a heavy burden that no one person should have to carry—while also moving up the professional coaching ladder. Don't sell yourself short. If you think she's the one, do not let us hold you back. You know that's not what Mom would want."

Abby's last words are a straight knife to the gut. "Low blow, Abby."

"I know when to play the ace. And now is the time. If you want to see where this goes with this girl, then go for it. Quit using us as a shield. You have to live your own life. If anyone deserves happiness, Davis, it's you."

Is she right? Can I do it all? I never thought I could. The mere thought of it made me panic. But not as much as just the mere thought of Bethany being with another man.

"I don't know if I can fix this, Abbs," I say, knowing how badly I fucked up tonight.

"Well, you better try. I want to meet the woman who made you finally get your head out of your ass and tell her thank you."

CHAPTER 14
BETHANY

BEING BORN and raised in Tennessee, I pride myself on being a southern woman.

I always say please and thank you. I refer to my elders as sir and ma'am. I love anything with my initials monogrammed on it. I still say my prayers every night, and I believe that white shoes have no place on your feet after Labor Day.

I might be a lady, but that doesn't mean I don't cuss a little.

Not often. Only in certain situations.

Like when someone tells me they only have Pepsi products. Because Diet Coke is *not* the same as Diet Pepsi.

Or when a certain football coach is making me forget how to string together sentences.

Or when I'm two weeks late on my period.

That last one requires all the swear words. And it's all I've been saying all morning.

How in the fuck did I not realize I had missed my period?

I didn't even realize I was late until this morning when I looked inside my medicine cabinet and saw the box of tampons. The box that hadn't been opened this month. That unopened box caused a slew of cuss words to be formed in my head.

Then I did the math. I should have started two weeks ago. I've never been regular, but I've never been *this* late. I'm not on the pill, but I am always careful. Always. No condom, no entry.

We were careful, right?

The thought sends me into a whole new level of panic. Because if this is true, then it means...

Davis... what will he think?

Oh God. Davis. The last time we spoke at Hunter and Sadie's was... well, it wasn't pretty. The things we said to each other, neither of us can ever take back.

Besides that, the man fears commitment like I fear snakes. As in, don't put it within fifty miles of me unless you want me to full-on freak-out. If what is happening now is what I think is happening right now, he is going to flip the entire fuck out. There's no use in sugarcoating that reality.

Breathe, Bethany... deep breaths.

Maybe this is nothing. Yeah. Maybe this is just my body being weird and I'm panicking for no reason. We were safe. Every time. Yeah. No reason to freak-out.

Except I have been an emotional basket case recently. And there were those few times that I felt pretty nauseous. And the time I threw up at Monday night dinner for no apparent reason.

And now that I think about it, my boobs are super tender.

Shit. Shit. Shit.

Fuckity-fuck-fuck.

The next few hours are a blur. I vaguely remember canceling my appointments for the day. I know I had to be a walking zombie when I left my apartment because I did so without putting on makeup or doing my hair. That never happens. After all, southern cosmetologists never allow that to happen. Somehow, I managed to drive myself to a drugstore, where I proceeded to buy ten different pregnancy tests.

Now I'm standing on my mother's doorstep, frozen in place, holding a bag full of sticks I'm supposed to pee on that will tell me if my life is about to change forever.

How did I get here? I mean, I know that I drove myself, even though I don't remember much of it. But theoretically speaking? How did I get here?

We were careful. I think back to that night in Memphis, which is where this had to have happened. We used a condom. We always did.

Except they aren't always reliable. I don't know what's wrong with me, but for some reason, right now, I'm reminded of the scene in *Friends* when Ross and Joey find out that condoms aren't one hundred percent effective.

And I just start laughing.

Hysterically.

On my mother's porch.

It's official. I'm certifiably insane.

And this is how my mother finds me when she opens the door—no makeup, wearing clothes I don't think are clean, laughing my ass off as I hold a bag full of pregnancy tests.

"Bethany? What's the matter?"

I don't know why, but those three words snap me out of my hysteria. And I do what any woman in my situation would do.

I fall into my mother's arms and cry.

———

"Sweetheart? Can I come in?"

I stir when I hear my mom's voice. Why is Mom waking me up?

When I slowly open my eyes, I realize that I'm in my bed in my teenage bedroom and everything comes rushing back to me.

Missing my period.

Buying the tests.

Making my way here and proceeding to cry myself to sleep.

"How long was I out?" I ask, slowly sitting up in bed as my mom comes and sits next to me.

"A few hours."

She hands me a glass of water, and bless her heart, she doesn't start asking me questions. That's just her way. Helen Benson, formerly Hall, does not prod. She waits. She makes you feel calm. Next thing you know, you're telling her your entire life story.

"I'm guessing you know why I'm here?" I ask, wanting to know where to start.

"I have an idea, but why don't you tell me everything from the beginning."

I look up at the ceiling, wondering where the beginning even is.

When Davis and I first met?

When we refused to stay apart, even though we knew it was for the best?

The night Hunter and Sadie got engaged?

"I'm late."

"By the bag full of pregnancy tests, I gathered as much."

"The fath... his name is Davis."

"The one who coaches with Hunter?"

All I can do is nod. "I swear, we were careful."

She puts her hand on my ankle and gives me a reassuring squeeze. "I have no doubt you were."

I don't know what to say next, so I say the only thing I know to be true right now. "I'm scared, Mom."

And I am. I'm scared for the result. I'm scared of the unknown. I'm scared of what Davis will say. I'm scared of everything.

"I reckon you are, but let's not completely freak-out until you take a test... or ten," she says, grabbing the bag and holding it up for me. "You have a variety to choose from."

I laugh, her bad attempt at a joke just what I need. I rummage through the bag and grab one and make my way to the bathroom to find out my future.

"Here goes nothing," I say to no one as I lay the test next to the sink and sit on the toilet, setting my phone timer for three minutes.

The longest three minutes of my entire life.

Do I want children? Yes. One day. But I never thought it would be like this. It wasn't supposed to happen like this. I was supposed to meet the love of my life, date, get married, have some years that we got to spend together, then babies. It's always ended with babies in my scenario.

In that order.

At that moment, I think back to growing up with just my mom. I love my mother and I treasure the bond we have together. Growing up, I never thought about what my life would have been like if we had a traditional family. Then she met and married Mike.

What would it have been like to have a father? Someone to take me to the father-daughter dance and teach me sports? What would it have been like to have a sibling? Yes, I consider Sadie my sister, but we didn't grow up together. And we are the same age. What would it have been like to have a little sibling?

Once I knew what I missed out on, I vowed that I was going to do things differently than my mom. I was going to date and find a man I couldn't live without, and in turn, he couldn't live without me. We would get married and eventually start a family.

If this test shows what I think it's going to, that is likely never going to happen.

Davis doesn't want a family. Hell, he doesn't want a girlfriend. Am I going to be alone like my mom? My dad couldn't handle the responsibility and left before I knew him.

Will that be Davis? Will he want nothing to do with me or the baby before it even arrives? Will he think he wants a part of it, then realize he can't handle it?

I don't even let myself think about him accepting us and becoming a family. No sense in dreaming of an outcome that will never happen.

Beep. Beep. Beep.

The timer on my cell phone goes off, and though I stop it, I don't move. I don't reach for the test. I just sit there, allowing myself a little more time before knowing whether or not my life changes forever.

You can do this.

You're a strong woman.

No matter what this says, you'll do what you need to do.

One... two... three.

I stand up and turn toward the counter. With one last breath, I look down at the test, and staring right back at me are two distinct pink lines.

"Bethany?"

My mom's voice comes through the closed door, but I don't answer.

I'm pregnant.

"Bethany, are you okay?"

The tears start slowly coming down my cheeks as I turn and open the door. As soon as I make eye contact with her, she can read it on my face.

And for the second time today, I fall into my mother's arms and cry.

CHAPTER 15
DAVIS

TO SAY the Fury front offices are a dumpster fire right now would be the understatement of the year.

The draft begins tomorrow. Hunter has gone through so many scenarios and driven himself to the brink of insanity. He was doing no one any good, so the other coaches and I kicked him out. I'm guessing he made it home by the last texts Sadie sent me.

Sadie: You're an asshole.

Davis: I mean, I am. But why this time?

Sadie: Because you sent my fiancé home the night before his first draft as head coach, and instead of driving you crazy, he's driving me crazy.

Davis: This is what you signed up for when he put a ring on it.

Sadie: You're a fucking asshole, Randall.

Davis: Still wrong. Keep trying. You still have 11 months.

I laugh as I prop my feet on the desk and take a look around my office.

My office.

Who would have thought a mid-level college football player from bumble fuck Pennsylvania would one day be the offensive coordinator on a team that every football pundit is saying is the future of football?

Surely not me. And probably not any teacher or coach I had back in school. The only one who saw me for my potential was my mom.

Football was the only thing I did growing up that was for me. I had to keep a part-time job to help out around the house when Mitch left, which my mom reluctantly agreed to. However, she gave me one condition when she signed my work permit, I had to still play football.

I didn't know at the time why. In middle school, I was good but not great. It's not like a lot of middle school football teams are making big plays with their wide receivers. If you ask my coaches from back then, they'd probably remember me more for my wisecracks in the huddle than my playing ability.

Then came high school.

My body developed, I gained some speed, and I was playing with a quarterback who could throw the ball. Next thing you know, I'm getting scholarship offers. I knew that was going to be the only way college was going to be an option for me, so I went to Pitt. It wasn't the highest ranked school that offered me a scholarship, but it was close to Mom, Abby, and Sara if they needed me.

I learned a lot in college.

I learned it was easy to transition from the class clown in high school to the life of the party.

I learned that I was never going to have a career as a professional wide receiver in the league. I was good, but not great. Plus, players are always one injury away from having their careers eliminated. My focus was on how best to provide for my family after college. It didn't take me long to realize that you could have a longer career coaching than playing. And if I wanted to provide for Mom, Abby, and Sara for the long run, that was my better move.

I also learned I was really good at finance—a skill that has served me well over the years. Turns out having a side hustle as a stock trader earns you and your family a pretty penny. So, while being a graduate assistant on the Pitt football team, I also received my MBA. I figured it was a good Plan B in case coaching football didn't work out.

I know using the MBA would be more responsible, but it didn't sound nearly as fun as coaching. And trading stocks on the side means I can have my cake and eat it too.

And that's a lot of fun.

"Coach? You wanted to see me?"

I look to my doorway and see our quarterback, Bryce Donald, leaning against the frame. I almost forgot I asked him to come in tonight.

"Yeah, Bryce, have a seat."

At this time last year, Bryce was about to be our number-one pick in the draft. When we were scouting him, he had all of the makings of a franchise quarterback. At Clemson, he guided his team to a national championship. He is a good-looking kid who comes from a good family. He's well-spoken and has a cannon for an arm.

Last year, he was named Rookie of the Year. He's exactly who you want to build your team around.

And all of that is going to his head.

And I need to put a stop to it. Now.

"I'm guessing you know why I asked you to come in?" I ask, taking my feet off my desk.

"Not really," he answers, almost sounding bored with my question. "I kind of figured you needed a wingman for tonight."

The fact that I used to party with players is not serving me well right now. "I heard that you've been having some fun this offseason."

He laughs, a cocky tone to it. "So you *are* asking if you can tag along. Coach McAvoy too boring now that he's wifed up? I mean, I could always use another wingman. I hate to send home too many ladies disappointed."

Who is this kid? This isn't the guy we drafted last year. That guy was polite. Said please and thank you.

After the season ended, it was like a switch flipped. It started with an article from one of the blogs showing Bryce and a few other players partying on Broadway. It was the end of the season and we had a good run. We didn't think anything of it. It was twenty-somethings letting off a little steam.

The problem is, for Bryce, it didn't stop. His name has been popping up on blogs, both local and national, nearly every night showing him at a different bar. Usually with a different woman on his arm.

This kid could break every record in professional football if he does things the right way. But if this train continues? His career is going to be over before it starts, and he doesn't even realize it.

"Are you listening to yourself? You sound like any other fuck boy running around this town."

"Except I'm not. My face is on twenty billboards in the city limits alone. Those country music guys got nothing on me. So what if I'm blowing off some steam before the season begins? Is it now a crime to go out and have some fun? That's rich coming from you."

"It's not," I say, trying my best to keep my temper even.

"But it is going to be a problem if your antics carry through into camp. And you do have a behavior clause in your contract. I'm just trying to talk to you before things get out of hand."

I pause to try and get a read on him. All he looks is annoyed.

"You're my quarterback, Bryce," I continue, hoping I'm not talking to a wall right now. "This team depends on you. You do your teammates no good if you're drunk every night. You do us no good if you knock up some girl whose name you don't know and have your face plastered across the tabloids every day. Or if you wreck a car and get arrested for DUI. You're better than this."

The look he is giving me screams of privilege and the it-will-never-happen-to-me mindset.

"I thought you were the cool coach. What the fuck gives? Why you riding my ass?"

That's it. I'm about done with this kid.

"I'm riding your ass because someone has to. I'm not saying you have to live like a priest, but for God's sake, Bryce, you have to see that this behavior is only going in one direction."

"I can do whatever I want and spend my free time however I want. I'm a grown man."

"Then act like one!"

He stands up, fire now in his eyes. "You sound just like Cole. Neither of you know what it's like to be me."

Cole Campbell is his best friend and a lineman on the Fury. The two have played together since they strapped on their first shoulder pads. At least someone is trying to talk some sense into him.

"No, I don't," I say, trying to calm my voice. "All I know is that I see a talent like this league has never seen, and he is one bad move away from ruining it all."

He doesn't reply. Instead, he just stares at me like I'm wasting his precious time.

"Are we done?"

I let out a defeated breath. "With this conversation? Yes. And I'd rather not have more like this in the future."

He turns and storms out of the office, and if I'm not mistaken, I hear a wall being hit on his way down the hallway.

I had hoped to talk some sense into him. I've always had a good relationship with the players, and I was hoping I could get through to him before Hunter had to sit him down for a come to Jesus meeting.

Sometimes being the fun coach isn't always so fun.

CHAPTER 16
BETHANY

I HAVE NEVER BEEN a football fan.

Growing up, it was just the sport I cheered for in the fall on Friday nights. I knew that when we ran the ball to the end of the field, it was good, and when the other team did, it was bad.

When Sadie and Mike came into our lives, they lived and breathed it. Whenever they talked football at the dinner table, it sounded like a foreign language to me. My mom wanted to learn a little because she knew it would make Mike happy. Me? I was fine not knowing anything.

Therefore, it's safe to say that I have never in my twenty-nine years on this Earth sat at home and watched the draft. I had no idea what to expect. Sadie made it sound like it was as exciting as the Grammys.

Newsflash: It's not.

"Are we really just going to sit around all night and watch guys talk, then announce a name, some clapping, and then more talking?"

"Yes," she says, acting like I just asked the dumbest question in the world. "I told you to bring your wine because we were in it for the long haul tonight. We have another hour before the Fury pick."

I let out a groan as I slink back into her couch, bracing myself for what this night has in store for me. I told Sadie I would watch the draft with her because, well, she's a little out of sorts tonight. It's the first time in her career she hasn't worked on draft night because of her promotion to the investigative team at *US Daily*. She doesn't know what to do with herself. Add on that this is Hunter's first draft as head coach, and she is pacing around their condo like a southern mama at a beauty pageant before they name the ultimate grand supreme winner.

Or like me trying to figure out how to tell my baby daddy that he is a baby daddy.

Oh God, I have a baby daddy.

I always hated that phrase. It sounds so juvenile. But at the end of the day, that's who he is.

Who am I? I am a confirmed, seven-weeks pregnant, confused, scared, expectant mother who vomits every morning at eight thirty like clockwork and is currently craving apples.

Oh, and I'm the person who still isn't sure how to tell the man who wants nothing to do with her that he's about to become a father.

"What? They took Jarrett! You've got to be kidding me! This fucks everything up!"

Sadie's outburst nearly makes me jump off the couch that I have become quite comfortable in. "What are you yelling about?"

"That!" Sadie says, pointing to the TV like I'm supposed to know what *that* means.

"What? It says that Milwaukee took a linebacker."

"Exactly!" Sadie is back to pacing. Between watching her walk around and the nausea that likes to creep up sometimes at night, I'm about to be sprinting to the bathroom soon. "Milwaukee was supposed to take an offensive player. *Everyone* thought that. And that was the guy Hunter wanted. And their second choice was also already drafted. This screws everything up!"

Sadie turns on a dime and heads to the kitchen. "Did you bring wine? I'm out and I need more if this is how the night is going to go."

Oh shit.

"I forgot it."

This makes her stop in her tracks. She hasn't stopped moving since I got here. "You forgot wine? Who are you and what have you done with my sister?"

I shrug and try to look anywhere but at Sadie. "I had it on the counter and then just forgot."

She just shakes her head at me, though she must have bought it because a few minutes later, I hear her giving a "woo!" from the kitchen.

"I have vodka!" she yells, her voice much more excited than it was a few minutes ago. "Want me to make you a drink?"

I'm not an alcoholic by any means, but if it's me and Sadie and a girls' night—even if we are watching football stuff rather than our normal Netflix or reality shows—I always have a cocktail. She was so nervous tonight she hasn't noticed that I haven't been drinking.

"I'm good," I say as nonchalantly as possible.

"You're good?" she asks, making her way back to the living room. "Everything okay? Is watching the draft stressing you out where you don't drink? What gives?"

No, Sadie. Everything is not okay.

"Yeah, just had a headache today. Figured I should play it safe with water."

Sadie seems to buy my flimsy excuse and turns her attention back to the talking guys on TV.

No, I have not told Sadie yet. It's killing me not to. Especially now, when it's just the two of us.

Luckily, the day that I showed up at my mom's house crying with a bag full of tests, she was the only one home. I left before Mike got home from work, and I begged her not to tell him yet. Or rather, not to tell anyone.

I don't want anyone else to know before I have the chance to tell Davis.

It only feels right. I have no idea how he's going to take it. But I couldn't stand the thought that he would be the fifth person to know. If Sadie knew, that would mean Hunter would know. I didn't want to put him in an awkward situation.

So, for right now, only my mom and I know the secret. Even though I have to tell Davis soon. And that thought has scared the crap out of me.

I have tried to think of a million ways to do it. And like the universe is mocking me, I swear every video I see on Facebook right now is cutesy ways women are telling their husbands they are pregnant. Just today, it was a man going on a scavenger hunt leading to the positive pregnancy test. Of course, he was over-the-moon excited, scooped his wife into his arms, and kissed the heck out of her. You know, because she'd just made them one big happy family and all with that little gem of an announcement.

And here I am, just hoping that when I finally get the courage to do it, he doesn't tell me to get out of his life and slam the door in my face.

I need to do it soon. I'm driving myself mad with the "what will he do or not do" scenarios. I wanted to do it this weekend, but Sadie kept saying how the draft is super important and stressful, so I told myself I'd wait until it's over.

She informed me the draft ends Saturday night.

Sunday it is then.

"Woo-hoo! Great pick guys! Great fucking pick!"

I turn my head to the TV where I see the cameras first following a guy who is no more than twenty years old up to the stage.

"That's Dexter Smith," Sadie says, even though I didn't ask her. "He's the best wide receiver in the draft. They wanted defense, but you can't pass a player like him up. He is going to be a game changer for Hunter and Davis. They have to be ecstatic!"

I can't share in Sadie's excitement because the cameras have now shifted to the Fury draft room. I recognize it from when I was there a few weeks ago. The cameras are zooming in on Hunter and Davis giving each other that one-arm hug thing that guys always do. They break away and Davis is pumping his fist and clapping his hands.

I've never seen this side of him before. He looks so excited. Light. Happy.

And I'm going to be the one to ruin that for him. Literally crush that carefree vibe right out of him.

"Bethany! Why are you still sitting down? It's time to celebrate!"

But I can't. Instead, all I can do is run to the bathroom and cry. And pray that I don't puke.

WE FUCKING DID IT.

Somehow, someway, we came away with a better draft than we did last year.

In every scenario that Hunter dreamed up over the past few months, none of them had Dexter Smith dropping down to us. In the rest of the rounds we were smart, took players we personally scouted and drafted needs for our team.

The talking heads on sports radio are already calling us the favorite to win it all this year.

And this is why I love the draft.

"Thank God, it's over," Hunter says, falling unceremoniously into his desk chair. "I'm wiped out."

"Oh, come on," I poke, taking a seat on the couch in his office. "It's not like the last four days were busy or anything."

The draft is a three-day affair, and Sunday is the day we invite all non-drafted players to rookie camp. It's a four-day whirlwind when you are not only putting together your team puzzle but also watching what thirty-one other teams are doing as well.

Screw Christmas and New Year's, these are my favorite days of the year.

"What now?" I ask, genuinely curious as to what Hunter is going to want to tackle next.

"Right now, we are going to leave this building—that I feel like we've lived in since Thursday—knowing that we've earned a few days off. I don't know what you're going to do, but I'm going to go home to my fiancée and do many things that I'd rather not talk to you about."

"Yeah, yeah," I say as I stand up from the couch. "You go home to your woman. I'm going to go out with the boys. Celebrate our draft haul."

Hunter lifts an eyebrow. "Boys? Who the hell are your boys?"

I gesture down the hall to the other assistant's offices. "Gumont and Martinez. I think I still saw them around earlier. They can wingman me."

"I'm pretty sure they have already taken off," Hunter says as he gathers his things. "Because they also missed their wives or girlfriends since they've barely seen them in four days. Face it, Davis, you're the lone bachelor on this staff."

I am? When did that happen? And why is that realization not sitting well with me?

Being a bachelor has never bothered me in the past. I was happy for my friends who were coupled up or getting married. Hell, I'm your go-to guy when you want a bachelor party thrown. I'm the guy who will lead everyone to the dance floor at your wedding.

Now the thought of everyone in my circle going home to someone is hitting a little harder than I care to admit, even though it's my choice that I'm going home to an empty apartment.

"Whatever," I say, trying to play it off. "Tell Sadie I said hi. And that my name isn't Robert."

Hunter lets out a small laugh as he gets up to leave his office. "Will do. See you in a few days."

And then there was one.

"Fine," I say to no one, gathering the rest of my things and making my way to my truck. "I've been going to bars by myself for years. Who cares if I'm celebrating alone?"

That's at least what I tell myself as I pull out of the Fury facility and make my way to the sports bar by my apartment that has never let me down.

Though the more I think about it, the more I wish I was going home to someone.

And not just anyone.

Bethany. The blonde beauty who knocked me on my ass the first time I saw her.

After my talk with Abby, when she basically called me a dumbass for how I treated Bethany after our last encounter, I really sat down and thought about it. Could I do it? Could I be a boyfriend? A husband? Could I give a woman forever?

I had honestly never thought it before. I was the guy women came to for a good time. My family always came first, and that stretched me thin enough on top of my job responsibilities. It was easy if I kept women at arm's length. Better safe than sorry.

Then I thought of the morning I woke up next to Bethany in Memphis. How content and happy I felt. It was a damn good feeling. One I wouldn't mind having more of.

But then I fucking blew it.

For a second, I had convinced myself I could do it. That I could be there financially and emotionally for Mom, Abby, and Sara while still being able to be a good partner for Bethany. I grew up with a father who was barely there before he was completely gone. I don't want to be that man. I refuse to be that man.

Then I think about the other side of the coin. She's moved on. I'm assuming she's still dating the douche canoe. But even if she isn't, would she even give me a chance?

I know for damn sure I wouldn't after the things I said to her.

So I never called. I never texted.

And now, here I am. Alone after the biggest weekend of my coaching career and no one to share it with.

I pull into the parking lot of the sports bar, and as soon as I turn off the ignition, I hear a text ping from my cell phone.

> Princess: I know you had a busy weekend.
> But can you come over tonight? I need to talk
> to you. It's important.

I do a double take as I read the message again.

Bethany? Wants to talk? Important?

This has to be some sort of sign. Half of me is excited and the other half is confused as fuck, though.

Why does she need to talk? Is it because of our blowup at Hunter and Sadie's? I can't think of another reason why.

Then there is the excited part of me that can't help but think this is a sign of some sorts. I usually don't believe in that cosmic bullshit, but I can't deny that I've been thinking about her nonstop for the past twenty minutes—okay, weeks—and here she is. Asking me to come over.

To talk.

This is it. This is my opening. I can do this. If there's a woman worth taking the leap for, it's her.

And this is my chance to make that jump.

> Davis: Sure. I'll be over in twenty. Is everything
> okay?

> Princess: I hope so.

Now I'm even more confused.

CHAPTER 18
BETHANY

HE'S HERE.

Even though I had all weekend—and the better part of a few weeks—to figure out how to tell him, now that he is here and knocking on my door, I have no clue what I'm going to say.

How do you tell someone their life is about to change forever?

I know you said you didn't want a family…

So, remember how we used a condom? Funny story about that…

Surprise! You're going to be a daddy!

Honestly, when I texted him, I had no idea how I was going to tell him. I just knew if I didn't do it tonight, then I didn't know when I'd work up the courage again to do so.

Be strong.

Be brave.

No matter what, everything is going to be okay.

I take one last deep breath and open the door. My legs almost give out at the sight of him. He's dressed very casually in a Nashville Fury hoodie and joggers, his beard is a little longer than usual and his hair looks like he's been running his hands through it all day.

"Hey, princess."

Oh God. The tone in his voice is so gentle. Tender even. Likely because he has no idea why I've asked him over here, and the last time we saw each other it was a toss-up of whether we were going to fight or fuck.

"Hey. Come on in."

My words are lame, but I'm just happy I'm able to find some. Between the sight of him, the smell of his cologne that is slowly taking over my body, and the insane amount of hormones swimming through me right now, I'm a jumbled mess inside.

I take a seat on the couch and instinctively grab a pillow to put over my stomach. I know I'm not showing yet, but the defense mechanism makes me feel a little more protected. Davis takes a seat next to me, but somehow I feel like we are miles apart, not just one cushion.

"Thanks for coming over."

"Actually, you beat me to the punch."

I quirk an eyebrow. "I did?"

"Yeah," he says, turning slightly so we are now facing each other. "I've thought about messaging you a dozen times since the last time I saw you."

This is a surprise. "You have?"

"Yeah," he says, taking a deep breath before he goes on. "Bethany, I was an ass that night at Hunter's. I could spew twenty different reasons about why, but they are all bullshit. You did nothing wrong, and I acted like a jackass. I'm sorry."

Wow, I wasn't expecting this. I know his admission is delaying the reason he's here, but I can't say I hate his words.

Maybe this won't go so bad after all?

"Thank you. I appreciate the apology. But I need—"

"Wait, let me finish," he says, inching a little closer to me. "I know you're seeing someone else right now, and this is the absolute wrong time to say this, but I can't stop thinking about the possibility of an us."

Wait, what?

"I'm... You.... What? I'm confused."

He laughs quietly while reaching for my hand. "Bethany, when I found out you started seeing someone, it drove me insane. I know I told you to. I know I told you to move on because I couldn't give you what you wanted. That I'm not the guy you need. Hell, I still don't know if I am. But I do know that I'd never forgive myself if I didn't take this chance now."

Is he?

Did he just?

What in the name of Dolly Parton is happening right now?

Out of all the things I thought might happen tonight, this is the *last* thing I considered. And if this were three weeks ago, I'd be shouting from the rooftop. I'd be calling Sadie and screaming in her ear. I'd be kissing the ever-loving daylights out of him before he uttered his next words.

Now? Now, I don't know what to do because everything that I wasn't expecting to ever happen with us, he's now telling me is a possibility. Giving us the green light. My emotions are all over the freaking place right now.

So I do the only thing that I've become good at over the past few weeks.

I cry.

"Bethany?" Davis asks, concern laced in his voice, as he puts his arms around me. "Shh. What's wrong? What did I say?"

"Nothing," I'm able to say in between sobs. "You said everything I've dreamed of hearing."

My tears last for another few minutes, and in that time, he just holds me. I'd be lying if I didn't say I took a few extra seconds to relish what it feels like to be in his arms. To have his protectiveness surrounding me.

Because this might be the last time I'm ever here.

"Talk to me," he finally says, brushing a loose strand of hair off my face. "I can't handle tears. Tell me what I can do to make them go away."

Oh, if it were only that simple. There's not a thing he can do to make this baby growing inside of my stomach go away. And as happy as what he told me makes me, I'm still so unsure of how he will react when I break the news to him.

I sit up, wiping away the stray tears running down my cheek. "I just wasn't expecting that. You took me by surprise, that's all."

Not half as surprised as I'm about to make him.

"I know. And I'm sorry. You're dating someone and it took me so long to get my head out of my ass and—"

"No," I say, cutting him off. It's my turn to talk. "I'm not seeing anyone."

"But I thought?"

I shake my head, wishing that this was the biggest hurdle we were going to have to overcome tonight. "I went out on one date with someone. I'll admit, I let you think it was more because I was mad at you, but it was never anything serious. He was nice. We wanted the same things in life. But..."

"But what?"

I take a deep breath, ready to admit a truth I've been trying to deny. "He wasn't you."

Before I know it, Davis's lips are on mine, and I'd be a liar if I didn't say this was the single best feeling in the world right now.

We've kissed before. Usually in the heat of the moment as we are in the process of ripping each other's clothes off. Those kisses have been sloppy and desperate. A means to an end.

This kiss? This is different. This has warmth. Feeling. Emotion. Commitment.

Dare I say something deeper?

His hands are cupping my face, holding me with a tenderness I've never felt before. Our tongues are meeting in perfect harmony. I feel this kiss in every cell of my body. I wish I could just stay here for eternity, letting this man consume every part of me.

But I can't. I know I need to stop this. This can't go on without him knowing everything.

With every ounce of strength I possess, I gently push him away. My body goes cold the second our lips part, but I can't let this go on anymore.

"Davis…"

It's now or never.

"I don't know why you stopped that, but I'm going to need you to change your mind," he says, trying to scoop me onto his lap.

"Davis. Wait," I say, holding my hands up. "Before anything else happens, I need to tell you the reason I wanted you to come over tonight."

He lets out a defeated breath but doesn't retreat back to his end of the couch. Instead, he takes my hands in his, placing soft kisses on the tops of each of them.

Okay, so I haven't scared him away completely, that's a good sign.

"Then tell me. Because I almost forgot how much I have missed your lips and plan on doing a lot more of that tonight."

The smile on his face right now is boyish with a touch of mischief in it. I hate that with my next words, that smile is likely going to fall from his face. That with what I have to tell him, I'll either go from being a hero to a zero in a few minutes.

I'll go from that perfect familial unit to a single mom, like my own, as soon as the words leave my lips.

Damn... I can't do this.

Maybe I should wait.

Ease him into being in a couple before I drop this bombshell. Let him get used to an us before we become a family.

What's going to happen next, though?

"Hey, it's okay," he says gently, seeing the level of panic on my face. "Whatever you need to tell me, it's okay. It's you and me now. If you're willing to give me a chance, then we are in this together."

I can't stop myself from laughing. "You say that now."

He shakes his head. "I'm confused. And you're killing me, princess. Just tell me whatever it is."

I take a deep breath and resolve myself to say the two hardest words I've ever said in my life.

"I'm pregnant."

"YOU'RE WHAT?"

I couldn't have heard her right. No. No way she just said that.

Though the more I look at her, the more I know that she said just that.

And at this second, I feel the ground falling out from under me.

"I'm pregnant, Davis. It's... It's yours."

Instinctively, I stand up and start pacing around her living room. I know I heard her correctly. She has said it twice now, yet I still don't believe her.

I'm pregnant, Davis. It's yours.

"You're pregnant?"

"Yes."

"And you are telling me it's mine."

Fuck. I shouldn't have said that. And by the look she is giving me right now, she's thinking the exact same thing.

"Yes, like I said, it's yours. Contrary to what you might have thought about my dating life before, I don't sleep with every man I meet."

"I'm sorry," I say, knowing how it came out. "I'm just... This is a lot."

She nods. "I know. Trust me. It's been a lot for me. But it's true. We're going to have a baby."

We're going to have a baby.

I pick up the pace of my steps, my mind going in circles because right now, nothing makes sense.

How did I get here in the blink of an eye?

Just a few minutes ago, her lips were on mine and everything was right in the world. I was just a guy who was praying this amazing woman would give me a chance to date her properly. And I didn't even know what I was getting into then. But I knew I wanted to try. For her.

Now... now everything has changed.

"But we... we always used condoms," I say, still trying to wrap my mind around this. "Didn't we? I don't know how this happened? We were always safe."

"I know," she says, her voice weak and distant. "I guess they mean what they say that they aren't foolproof."

I mean, I knew that. But... that doesn't happen in real life. Does it?

"When?"

"Memphis. I'm seven weeks."

"That means you're due..."

"The doctor said she'd give me a firmer date next appointment, but it's looking like end of November."

I don't reply, because I have nothing more to add.

Instead, I just keep pacing.

It's the only thing keeping me upright at this moment.

My universe is slowly toppling over right before my eyes and I can't make it stop. I've only ever felt like this once in my life, and that was the day we realized Mitch was gone for good.

Then I knew my world was never going to be the same, but that was different.

This? This is so much more.

I'm going to be a father.

It's my job to make sure that Bethany has everything she needs. I'm the one who is going to be responsible for this child's well-being. I'm responsible for making sure it is clothed and fed and provided for.

I've assumed this role before with my own family, so it won't be a problem, right? Only this time, I also need to be a partner for Bethany. To make sure I never make her or this child ever want for anything and to always have her back.

It's my job to make sure I do everything Mitch didn't do for us growing up.

Which means there is only one thing left to do.

"Marry me."

My words shock her. At least, that's what I think by the look on her face. Her jaw is open, her eyes are big, and she is looking at me like I have three heads.

"What did you just say to me?"

Shit. I'm doing this all wrong. But this is uncharted territory for me. I really have no idea what I'm doing, just what will be expected of me, and I'm already screwing up.

So I get down on one knee and take her hand in mine.

"Marry me."

"Is that a question or a command? I'm kind of confused here."

"Does it need to be a question?" Now I'm the one confused. "We are having a baby. We should get married. You've always wanted a husband and a family. So, let's do it. Let's be a family."

She doesn't answer. Instead, she stands from the couch, throws her hands in the air, and storms into the kitchen.

So, is that a yes?

"Where are you going?"

The sound of cupboard doors being slammed shut is the only answer I get until Bethany comes charging out of the kitchen, carrying three bags of different-flavored potato chips.

"What are you doing?" I ask because I genuinely have no clue what is going on.

"Well, I wanted vodka. I thought if I got drunk, I could understand your level of crazy," she says, throwing the chips on her coffee table before sitting back down on the couch. "But I can't have vodka because of your super sperm breaking through the condom. So, then I thought that maybe eating my frustrations and emotions would serve two purposes since I'm hungry all the freaking time. But my cravings change every three seconds, and right now it's potato chips, but I didn't know what kind I wanted. So, I brought all the chips. Get it now?"

I don't think I've blinked since she started talking.

"I... I don't—"

"Exactly. What I'm doing is nuts to you. Well, guess what, bucko, what you just said? Marrying you because you think that's what is expected—and not because it's something that you wanted? That's equally insane."

I sit down next to her because I need to steer this conversation back around.

"I thought you wanted to get married? That was the whole reason we ended things before. And now that there's a baby in the mix, marriage is the obvious solution."

She lets out a deep breath, almost trying to calm herself as she tears into the bag of Funyuns and shoves a few in her mouth, taking a moment to chew and swallow before speaking. "I did. I do. I don't know. But I don't want a husband just because of the situation. I want to get married for love. Not out of pity. What you are asking of me right now is clearly out of pity and obligation."

"Pity? This isn't because of pity or obligation." I take her hand in mine, hoping I can get through to her. "Bethany. You? This child? You're my responsibility now. It's now my job—"

"Your what?"

"My responsibility."

"Oh! Your responsibility," she says as she shoots back up and starts walking in circles, now tearing into the bag of Flaming Hot Cheetos as I silently wonder if that's the best choice of food to eat while pregnant. I don't dare ask that, though. She's starting to scare me. "Well, that makes the proposal *all* that much better! Where do I sign up for that?"

"Yes," I say matter-of-factly, ignoring her sarcastic remarks. "You're my responsibility. You are carrying my child. You both are my responsibility now."

She turns to face me. The look on her face, I admit, scares me a little.

Bethany. Is. Pissed.

"Why are you mad? I thought this is what you wanted?"

And now she's crying.

Holy shit. I heard about pregnancy hormones; I knew they were a thing, but I've never seen them in action.

"Not like this," she says, trying, but failing to hold back her tears. "Not like this."

I walk to her and bring her next to me on the couch. "What do you want then? Tell me, because I can't take the tears. But please know, you tell me what you want, and I'll make it happen."

She takes a few breaths, letting the tears subside.

"Do I want you to be a part of this child's life? Absolutely. And if you want to be with me because you care about me and you meant the things you said earlier tonight? Great. Let's give us a try. And yes, someday I want the husband and the house and the family and the golden retriever. I didn't lie to you when I said that. But not like this. I don't want a proposal or a husband out of some sort of misplaced feeling of guilt and responsibility. I don't want you to regret me in ten or twenty years. I don't want you to see our baby and realize you can't do it, but you feel tied to me. I want a husband who wants me because he can't imagine spending the rest of his life without me. Not one who only proposed because he got some life-changing news and feels that it's the right thing to do. So, no, Davis, I won't marry you. Not now. But if you meant what you said earlier, I do want to give us a try. I want you in my life."

Fuck. She's right.

I did all of that. I asked her the most important question of her life because I was panicking.

"I'm so sorry," I say, bringing her on to my lap. "You're right. But yes, I did mean it. I do mean it. The baby changes nothing."

She snuggles in a little closer. "I like the sound of that."

"Which part?"

"The one where you say I'm right."

I tickle her sides, and the sound of her just-been-crying laughter is music to my ears.

For the next few minutes, we just sit with each other, letting the night's events replay. At least, I am. Bethany's breathing has slowed down and her eyelids are starting to flutter.

Holy fuck, I'm going to be a father.

Why does that not scare me more than it should? Yesterday, I didn't think I could even handle a girlfriend, let alone a family of my own. Yet somehow, while this news is the most shocking of my life, I'm not as rattled by the enormity of it as I would have thought.

I have a feeling I know why.

Because of the woman in my arms right now.

"We're going to have a baby," she whispers, her eyes still closed.

"Yeah, we are. From this point forward, it's you and me, princess. Team Davis."

She lets out a laugh. "You know what this means, right?"

"What's that?"

"I'm eventually going to have to know your first name."

CHAPTER 20
BETHANY

I'M STIRRED awake by the feel of Davis's arms wrapping around me, bringing me closer to his naked chest.

If this is what it's like waking up with him every morning, then sign me up.

I don't open my eyes yet for fear that the second I do this bubble will burst. That last night didn't happen. That if I open my eyes, he won't actually be here. Instead, I take in the feel of his warm body against mine, his muscular arms holding me tight as I replay the events of last night.

Will you give me a chance?

I'm pregnant.

One of those announcements would have been enough for one night. But the two put together? That's a lot for anyone, especially for a man who just weeks ago wanted nothing to do with a committed relationship, let alone a family.

How could he change his mind so fast? What happened that made him want to give us a try? And then throwing a child on top of it and he didn't run for the hills?

No. Not only did he not run, he threw out two words I never thought I'd say no to.

Marry me.

What was he thinking?

How did I have the sense to say no?

I mean, I've been denying my true feelings for this man for months. And here he is, saying that he wants to give us a chance and that he wants to be a family.

Yet, I know he wasn't saying it for the right reasons.

I believe you should get married for love, not out of responsibility or obligation. I meant what I said, I don't want him to regret anything. I don't want him to leave because he made a rash decision and he didn't know what he was getting into.

I don't want to feel like my mother did. I don't want our child growing up like I did, even though I had a wonderful childhood, never knowing my real father still bites.

"Good morning, princess."

Jesus, take the wheel; his morning grumbly voice is enough to make my panties melt off.

I don't respond, instead snuggling closer to him while cracking open an eye to see what time it is.

8:28 a.m.

Oh no.

No. No. No.

Please, let this be the one morning I'm not sick. Please, just let me stay here for a little longer. Don't burst the bubble with...

The sound my stomach makes screams that it does not care that I'm in bed with a sexy as hell man. And from the sound and feel of it, I have approximately ten seconds to get to the bathroom or else Davis is going to see something that might completely change his mind.

I furiously break away from his hold, throw the covers off of me, and sprint across the hall to my bathroom.

"Bethany? You okay? Princess? What's happening?"

I don't answer him. If I answer, I'm not going to make it.

Instead, I slam the door shut and lift up the toilet seat for what has become my new morning ritual.

Morning sickness, like my inner voice, is a real twat waffle.

No. Scratch that. Whoever named it morning sickness is the twat waffle.

Because it's not just morning sickness. At least for me, it isn't. I find myself kneeling before my toilet like clockwork at eight thirty each day. It also hits me somewhere around mid-afternoon. And any time I smell freshly cut grass. Which in the spring in Nashville is a lot. What in the name of all that's good and holy causes puking from that?

Like I said. Twat waffle.

I don't know how I don't hear Davis come into the bath-room. Yet I feel his presence without even looking up. My fore-head is resting on my forearms across the toilet as I feel his hands bring my hair away from my face. Next, I hear the water running before I feel a cold washcloth on the back of my neck.

Since I found out I was expecting, I mentally prepared myself that I could be doing this on my own. That I'd be okay being my own wingman during these next seven months and beyond. I mean, how many times did he tell me he was never going to have anything serious, let alone a family? I believe his words were, "I wish I could give you what you want." I figured, if anything, he'd send a few checks and be on his way.

But for at least for right now, he's here. And this cold wash-cloth means more to me than he could ever know.

"You're probably going to want to rethink sleeping arrangements," I say, slowly backing away from the toilet until my back makes contact with the bathtub.

"Not a chance," he says, taking the washcloth and wiping away the sweat on my forehead. "I told you last night, we're in this together. The question now is, what can I get you? Water? Food?"

The sincerity in his voice is enough to send me into an emotional spiral. And the look in his eyes? There is so much caring and warmth in them that I don't know how I keep back the tears.

"Nothing," I say, giving his hand a squeeze. "Just you being here is more than enough."

———

"What is all this?"

Davis looks up at me, a big smile across his face. "It's breakfast. Now, sit."

My oh my, he's bossy today.

I forgot how much I love bossy Davis.

It's likely the very reason we are in this situation. Except last time it was Bossy Davis in the bedroom, not Bossy Davis in the kitchen. But with this baby growing inside of me, I'm really, really liking Bossy Davis in the kitchen.

After my morning episode, Davis insisted that I take a bath, relax, and that he'd take care of breakfast.

Who was I to argue with that? I figured I'd be greeted with a bowl of cereal. Maybe a bagel from the coffee shop down the street.

I was not expecting a breakfast buffet.

"Here," he says, placing a glass of orange juice in front of me as I take a seat at my small dining room table. "Is orange juice okay?"

"Yeah, it's great," I say, still a little confused and shocked by the feast laid out before me. "Did you order everything DoorDash had to offer?"

"Pretty much," he says, putting a plate down in front of me filled with bacon, eggs, pancakes, and waffles. "I didn't know what you liked. Or how much you were eating now. So, I played it safe."

I know I'm pregnant when a man hitting a few buttons on a food app is cause enough to make me cry.

I'm able to hold back the tears and dig into the best breakfast I've had in a very long time. Eventually, Davis makes himself a plate and joins me at the table.

It strikes me at this point that this is the first time we've shared a meal together. Well, by ourselves, where Hunter and Sadie weren't with us.

"God, we've done this completely backward."

I meant to say that to myself, but apparently, I said it a little louder than I intended.

"Not completely," he says, taking a sip of coffee before continuing. "We did at least go on one date first."

I laugh. "You're right. Though, I wouldn't say we dated."

"No, we didn't, princess. No, we didn't."

We sit in silence for a few minutes, and at least for me, my brain is going in twenty directions right now.

But the biggest question is, what now?

I didn't think past telling him because I couldn't predict the outcome. That was the major roadblock, and until I knew how he felt about everything, I didn't want to think about anything past that. There wasn't any point until I knew where he stood.

Now it's here. And now I don't have a flipping clue what to do next.

"We need to figure some things out," he says as if he's reading my mind.

"We do. I feel like there is so much to do and no time to do it and it's overwhelming."

Davis puts his fork and coffee down and takes my hands into his. Before, every time we touched, I felt a spark go through us. Now? The spark is still there, though this time there is something more. Now the spark is followed by a sense of warmth that makes me feel like everything is going to be okay.

"I agree. I suggest that first we figure out our living arrangement."

I offer him a confused look. "Well, I have a place to live and so do you. I don't see why that is the top priority?"

"Bethany, look around," he says, scanning my small one-bedroom apartment. "There is not enough room here for a baby. My apartment is bigger, but I'm too close to downtown. That's not a place we want to raise a baby."

He's not wrong. My apartment is very small. I didn't have to think of anyone else when I leased it. I can barely fit my clothes in here, let alone things for a baby. His place is nice, but he's right. I don't want to be listening to crowds when I'm trying to get the baby down for a nap.

"Okay, I see where you're coming from, but there is one important thing you're missing."

"And what is that?"

"I said I wasn't marrying you."

He picks up on my teasing tone as the look on his face goes from serious to mischievous in a heartbeat. How does this man have so many sides to him? He's serious and practical. He's also playful and boyish.

I don't know which one I love more.

I'm also going to ignore that my brain went to the word love rather than like.

"That's right, you did say that," he says, now a glint in his eye that screams he's up to something.

"What is going through that head of yours?" I say, taking another bite of bacon because we might be having a huge, life-altering conversation, but it's still bacon. And I'm still pregnant.

"You might have said no last night, but I do intend on marrying you one day. And it's going to be the proposal of your dreams."

"Oh, do you now?" I'm trying to play it off, but inside? Inside, I'm screaming like a teenage girl. Does he remember what I told him in Memphis? About what I wanted my proposal to be? Something special for just the two of us? I wonder what he would do?

I shake my head from those thoughts. That is a long time from now. Right now? I'm just going to focus on that he is here and he wants to give us a shot.

For now, that's more than I could have ever hoped for.

He brings my hand to his lips before continuing. "I thought about my life without you in it. Or you spending the rest of your life with the douche canoe—"

"His name was Gavin."

"Whatever. He's irrelevant," Davis says, scooting my chair closer to his. "What I'm saying is, that if I'm going to marry you one day, then one big thing needs to happen first."

"And what is that?"

He stands up, takes my plate, and places a kiss on my forehead. "I need to take you on a proper first date."

CHAPTER 21
DAVIS

I MUST SAY, for knowing that I'm going to be a dad for less than twenty-four hours, I'm pretty much already killing it.

After I left Bethany's today—she kicked me out after her second wave of nausea hit because she wanted to nap before our date—I decided to do what I do best.

And that is to come up with a plan.

Not many know this side of me. My former teammates saw the guy who would play pranks on the freshmen. My players see the fun coach who makes jokes in between drills. My fellow coaches expect me to make the inappropriate comment during staff meetings.

That might be part of my personality, but the other part is on the complete opposite end of that spectrum.

I plan until the very last detail is in place.

It started when Mitch left. There were budgets to create in order to make sure we had enough for food and anything extra we needed that month. There were calendars to keep so Mom, Abby, Sara, and I knew when any of us had anything going on. The refrigerator in our house always had notes and reminders on it written in Mom's handwriting. Was this the first sign of Mom's eventual diagnosis? I always wonder that.

No matter what the reason they were there, it's how we survived. And it's how I've been surviving ever since.

The second I get home, I pull out my laptop and start googling everything from "how much does it cost to have a baby" to "best daycares in Nashville."

Both of those answers have price tags that slightly terrify me.

I order four parenting books off of Amazon, quickly skim a blog about what Bethany is feeling right now and tips to help with morning sickness, and even look at pictures of what a seven-week-old fetus looks like.

Just as I'm closing my laptop, and before I get lost in the rabbit hole that is birthing videos—those look positively terrifying, by the way—my phone vibrates on the table with an incoming call.

"Hello, favorite sister. To what do I owe this pleasure?"

"Because, dipshit, you didn't answer your phone last night, and you didn't call me back," Abby says, her voice scarily creeping up to her mom tone. "God forbid me wanting to check in on my brother to make sure everything is okay."

I laugh as I make my way into my bedroom to start getting ready for tonight. "Everything is fine, Abbs. Actually, more than fine."

"Why do you sound so cheerful, and what have you done with my brother?"

If there is one person on this Earth who knows that my class clown persona is more of a diversion than anything, it's Abby. And she's not afraid to remind me of it.

"I'm no more cheerful than normal," I say, entering my closet to look for something to wear.

"The only thing that makes a man sound like this is that he's getting sex, about to have sex, or is having sex right now. Which, when it comes to you, I'd rather not know about."

I laugh. "No sex for me. Sorry to disappoint you."

"Then what has you sounding like you just won the lottery?"

I could drag this out a little more, but I'm expecting a solid half hour freak-out from her, and I don't want to be late picking Bethany up.

"Remember the girl?"

"The one who I told you to get your head out of your ass about? Vaguely."

I'm glad my sister can't see me roll my eyes. "Yeah. Her. Well... I have some news."

"Are you about to tell me you're in a relationship? Holy hell, I never thought I'd see the day! Oh my gosh, you're actually not going to die alone! Wait. Let me record this so I can play it for Sara. And Mom. They will never believe me."

The next few minutes are filled with Abby shouting exclamations, asking questions so fast I'm not sure what she said, and ramblings about how I better bring her home soon for the rest of the family to meet.

"Are you done yet?" I ask, loving that I still have one more big bomb to drop on her tonight.

"I... I think I am," she says, catching her breath. "What can you tell me about her? What's her name? Is this serious? Or are you getting my hopes up only to break up with her in a week?"

"Well," I say, finding a black button-down and dark jeans. "It's serious enough that you're going to be an aunt."

My news has its desired effect on Abby. Complete and blissful silence. Never once in my entire thirty years of existence have I ever been able to shock my sister silent.

I'm going to need to write this down somewhere in a journal or some shit to revisit time and time again.

"Abby? You okay?"

"Did you just say... You're going to? I'm going to be?"

I chuckle, setting the phone down and putting it on speaker so I can put on the shirt. "Yes, Abby. You heard me correctly. And before you ask, no, it wasn't planned. Yes, it's a surprise. But Bethany is pregnant. She told me last night."

If I thought my sister was screaming gibberish earlier, then I don't know how to explain what happens next. All I know is that by the time she starts speaking coherently again, I've finished getting dressed, brushed my teeth, and styled my hair.

"I have so many questions I don't even know where to begin," she says, wrapping up her incoherent conversation with herself.

"Well, the answer to one of those questions is no, you can't post all over social media about this. Not yet. I haven't asked her when she wants to tell everyone, so please wait until I give you the okay?"

"Fine," she says, though I know her grumble is only half serious.

"Are we done here? I'm taking Bethany on a proper date tonight and you're holding me up."

"Look at you. My big brother is finally leaving Neverland."

"You're such a comedian."

"I'm quite serious. You have gone from eternal bachelor to ready to buy a minivan in the blink of an eye. Then again, you are the one who doesn't back away from a challenge. Nope, my older brother meets the bull head on."

She's not wrong. When Mitch left, I didn't flinch. We came up with a plan and it was full steam ahead. That plan never included me having a family of my own. My sisters have always hated that I made that choice. Abby and Sara have been on me for years to try and settle down. They said just because I insisted on helping the family on the financial end years ago, that didn't mean I had to put my life on hold now. I'm sure if

Mom was mentally capable of knowing what was going on each day, she'd have my ass as well.

Turns out, all I needed was the right woman to give me the push I needed.

"Any other questions, sister?"

"Yes. When do I get to meet her?"

I smile because there is nothing more that I want right now than to introduce Bethany to my family. Next month being May will be tough with rookie camp. But by June, we will have some downtime before training camp opens. Sara will be out of school and living with Abby for the summer. And Mom... it's been a while. Even if she doesn't know who I am.

It's time to go back to Pennsylvania.

"How does June sound?"

CHAPTER 22
BETHANY

"I AM SO SORRY."

I reach for Davis's hand and give it a squeeze. "For the twentieth time, you don't need to apologize. You didn't know."

"But I should know. I should have known all of this!"

If this is truly going to be my last first date, it's going to be memorable for sure.

And not in a good way.

Things started off great. Davis picked me up, and I was able to keep my hormones in check from the sight of him in a black button-down with the sleeves rolled up and dark-washed jeans. He wore the cologne that makes me go weak. I deserve a medal for not pulling him into my house and skipping dinner altogether.

From there, it went downhill fast.

We drove into downtown Nashville and as soon as he parked the car, I knew where he planned on taking me.

A sushi bar.

Being pregnant, I can't eat raw fish.

If that was the only oopsie moment of the night, we still could have chalked this up to a win. However, that might have been the highlight.

In an attempt to make it up to me, he tried to surprise me again, and drove a few streets over to an Italian restaurant.

If this were a normal date, I would have been all for it. I love lasagna. Except right now, the smell of garlic and I are not friends. At all. As soon as we pulled up to the restaurant, the scent overtook my senses, and I had to make a mad dash from his truck.

Throwing up in a Nashville parking lot at seven on a Monday night, completely sober, is not one of the highlights of my life.

His last attempt at trying to surprise me came in the form of Indian food. The only problem is that I'm allergic to peanuts and peanut oil. With so many dishes using those ingredients, I play it safe and don't eat there.

"How could you have known?" I ask, trying my best to soothe him as he drives back to his apartment.

"I should have known about the sushi," he says, his voice still edged with frustration.

"Okay, maybe. But the garlic thing just started this week. And the Indian? It's not like our restaurant preferences ever came up in conversation."

He pulls the truck into a spot, puts it in park, and lets out a defeated breath. "I know. I just hate that I don't know any of these things. I'm your... I should know."

I lean over the center console and bring his lips to mine. Not a deep kiss, but one I hope tells him that he's doing nothing wrong.

"How about this," I say, placing one more kiss on the corner of his lips. "We go upstairs. Order our weight in hot chicken because that is the only thing I am craving right now, and we get to know each other in all the ways we skipped over before."

He smiles and leans over, taking my face in his hands for one more kiss. When he releases me, the smile on his face is one that makes the rest of this disastrous date worth it.

"Let's do it, princess."

———

"What do you mean, you've never seen *Die Hard*!"

The look on Davis's face right now is a combination of horrified and hilarious. Well, he's horrified. I find it hilarious how horrified he is.

"So? What's the big deal?"

"What's the big deal? What is the big deal!" he shouts as he paces around his living room. I think he's pacing harder now than when I told him I was pregnant. "How are we supposed to raise our child with the knowledge that *Die Hard* is, in fact, a Christmas movie if you've never seen it in the first place!"

I want to laugh. It is so cute how serious he is about this. But if I laugh, I'm afraid I'll open up another can of worms about the merits of *Die Hard* as a Christmas movie, and I'm not ready for that.

Plus, the man has never seen *Steel Magnolias,* so I think we're even. How can he lecture me about the greatness of *Die Hard* when he doesn't know the amazingness of a cast featuring Dolly Parton, Julia Roberts, Shirley MacLaine, and Sally Field?

The answer: he can't.

The beginning part of our date might have been disastrous, but the last few hours have been amazing. After our food arrived, we began learning all of the things about each other that we should have already known for two people who have seen each other naked as many times as we have. Take, for example, I had no idea he was from Pennsylvania. He was equally surprised to discover that I have never traveled west of the Mississippi.

Things we agree on: Pineapple doesn't belong on pizza; dogs over cats; and neither of us see what the big deal is about *Star Wars.*

Things we don't agree on: I think Christmas is the best holiday while he is Team Thanksgiving; I'm a morning person, while he is a night owl, which will be great when it comes time for late-night feedings; and of course, the atrocity that I've never seen *Die Hard.*

"Come, sit down," I say, patting the spot next to me on the couch. "You're making me dizzy."

He makes his way over, and not only does he sit down next to me, but he also brings my feet across his lap, rubbing small circles into my arches.

Oh, I could get used to that.

"What else do you want to know?" he asks, continuing to work my arches. If he keeps doing that, the only thing I'm going to want to know is how quickly he can get me naked.

"Tell me something no one else knows about you."

The circles on my feet stop almost instantly and the temperature in the room drops a few degrees. I didn't realize that question was so loaded. But now I'm wondering what his answer will be... or if he'll even respond.

"Remember when we were in Memphis and you were giving me shit for being on my phone and I told you I was checking a stock?"

I laugh. "Yes. I remember thinking that was a pretty well thought-out fib. You could have just said you were checking Instagram. Or sending another selfie."

He laughs. "Well, it was the truth."

"It was?" I say, the curiosity heavy in my voice. Though by the look on his face, he is one hundred percent serious. "You… are you a stock trader?"

"Kind of," he says, readjusting my feet on his lap. "When I was in college, we weren't allowed to have jobs. NCAA rules and because of our scholarship, but I helped support my mom and sisters, and needed to figure out a way to still be able to do that. I had taken a few business and finance classes and started reading up on the stock market. Apparently, I'm good at it. I made smart buys, sold when the time was right, and I made a pretty penny from my investments. Ever since then I've been buying and selling on the market to help support my mom and sisters, without having to dip into my coaching salary."

When I asked this question, I expected the answer to be something like, "I have a sixth toe" or "I can tap dance." No way did I expect all of that.

"Can I ask why you had to support your family while you were in college?"

He takes a deep breath before answering. "It's two-fold. My dad took off when I was thirteen. One day he was there, the next day he was gone. We never saw him again. On that day, I made a promise to my mom and sisters that I would help in any way I could. So I picked up part-time jobs while I was in school and continued playing football. I hated seeing my family suffer because my asshole father left us in the dust."

I reach for his hand, wanting to offer some comfort. "What's the second part?"

He slowly rubs his thumb over the top of my knuckles. "When I was in college, my mom was diagnosed with early onset Alzheimer's. It… we didn't see it coming. She needed medical help that neither my sisters nor I could provide. We found a facility for her, but it isn't cheap, and insurance only covers a fraction of what she needs. I take care of the rest."

Wow. Out of all the answers he could have given, this wasn't what I expected to hear.

Though, now I feel like I have a few more pieces to the puzzle that is Davis. I can't imagine what it's like feeling like the provider of a family, especially when you live hundreds of miles away from them. And he's been doing this since he was a teenager? Now his words about "I can't give you what you want" make more sense.

He was already trying to juggle life. He was trying not to add more to his already-overloaded plate.

Then here I come, baby on board. Adding more to his responsibilities.

"Is that why you pushed me away? Why you didn't want a relationship?" I ask, wanting confirmation.

He nods. "I've always felt like if I tried to settle down, I'd let down someone. Either them or my hypothetical girlfriend or wife. It wasn't fair, so I decided a long time ago to never have someone else in the equation, and then I didn't have to worry about letting someone down."

"Then I came along. With baggage."

He smiles, kissing my hand. "Then you came along. And with baggage I'm excited about."

I know he didn't ask me, but after his confession, I feel like I owe him one as well. One that's been weighing heavily on my mind since we decided to give this a shot.

"I didn't have a dad either," I say, my voice soft. "That is something else we have in common."

Concern covers his face in an instant. "Do you want to talk about him?"

I shake my head. "There's really nothing to talk about. He and my mom got pregnant with me when they were engaged.

They decided to not get married until after I was born. That was a blessing in disguise, because not long after I arrived, he realized he couldn't do it and took off. I've never met him."

Davis gathers me in his arms and places me on his lap, his lips softly kissing my cheek. "I'm so sorry."

"I'm not," I say, meeting his tender gaze. There's not a trace of the alpha man I know he can be. Or the jokester.

This... this is the true Davis.

And now I know, right here and now, that I could fall head over heels in love with this man. That if he were to leave me down the line, I don't know if I could recover.

"Davis?" I ask, my voice quiet.

"Yeah, princess?"

"Make me a promise."

I hope he can hear the sincerity in my voice right now. "Anything."

"If you can't do this. If you sit back and realize fatherhood isn't for you, please let me know. There will be no hard feelings. I think I turned out okay because I never had a dad, so I honestly didn't know what I was missing. I think it would have been worse if I had memories of him. So please... I know we are giving this a shot and we've made no promises, but promise me this. If you don't think you can handle it, leave now. I'll be all right. But I'd rather this child not know you at all than miss you every day of its life."

He doesn't answer. Instead, he takes my face in his hands and kisses me like I've never been kissed before—with so much passion that I can feel his answer without him saying a word.

This kiss is more than the one we shared in Memphis when we thought it was goodbye. This is more than the kiss the other night when we decided that we would give this a chance.

When our lips release and I look into his eyes, I can see everything he is thinking and what this kiss means.

This kiss screams of forever.

"I'm in this. I'm all in. You'll never have to worry about that. Our child will never not know me. I give you my word."

And then he kisses me again, and I know that we might have done things completely backward, but we are right where we are supposed to be.

OVER THE LAST week or so, Bethany and I have gotten on the same page about a lot of things.

We have agreed that we are going to find out the gender of the baby when the time comes.

We have agreed to at least start looking for a bigger place to live. Even if something happens where we don't work out, I want to make sure she has the room she will need for our child. Surprisingly, she didn't put up a fight on that one.

Probably because I convinced her of that while I was rubbing her feet and kissing her senseless.

We have also agreed that we don't want to announce this to the world until the twelve-week mark. Her mom knows. Abby knows. However, there are two important people who don't know. Yet.

Hunter and Sadie.

As in, they still don't know.

And it's more than time that they know—about everything.

"Do you think they are going to be mad?" Bethany asks as she straightens the pillows on my couch for the twentieth time.

"No. I don't think they are going to be mad," I say, bringing out the appetizer tray that Bethany insisted we make for them. I didn't tell her I know she only pushed for it because she's craving mozzarella sticks. "I think they are going to be excited for us. And relieved everything is in the open."

When we decided to come clean with them, I thought the best way to do it was to invite them over under the ruse of watching the hockey game—our fellow hometown Music City Rockers are in the playoffs. Little do they know Bethany will also be here and we will finally tell them everything.

I'm not worried a bit. Bethany has been freaking the fuck out all morning. Case in point? She's now reorganizing the appetizer tray.

"Hey," I say, taking her hand and pulling her into my chest. Her arms immediately go around my neck as I place a reassuring kiss on her forehead. "Relax, princess. Are they going to be surprised? Yes. Are they going to be happy for us? Also, yes. Imagine how good this is going to feel when we don't have to pretend in front of them anymore."

She nods, but I don't think my words reassure her as much as I'd like. "I just don't want them to think we are trying to steal their thunder."

"We aren't stealing their thunder. This little one will be here long before they walk down the aisle."

After two months of being engaged, and two months of listening to Hunter's mom nag them on a daily basis, they finally set a wedding date. They are getting married in June of next year.

Gotta love planning a wedding around the calendar year of professional football.

I realize then that not only did my words not cheer Bethany up, they actually make her start crying.

I should have known better. She cried at a dog food

commercial yesterday. And again at a drug commercial that promises to clear up warts.

These hormones are no joke.

"What's wrong?" I ask, wishing I could say something to help her. I have figured out how to soothe her when she's sick in the mornings. I've figured out how to help her wind down after a long day at the salon. But the crying? The crying I haven't figured out a remedy for yet.

"Our baby," she says between sobs. "Is going to be six months old when they get married. She'll almost be a year!"

While yes, she is correct, unfortunately, I don't have time to help her work through this one because as soon as the words leave her mouth, a knock on the door signals Sadie and Hunter are here.

"I'll get that," I say, wiping away some stray tears with my thumb. "Go to the bathroom and do what you need to do. Come out when you're ready. We got this."

She nods and gives me a small kiss before making her way down the hall.

Here goes nothing.

I barely have the door open when Sadie comes barging in. "Where is she?"

"Good luck, man," Hunter whispers, patting my shoulder as he enters my apartment.

"What are you talking about?" I try to play dumb, but it's no use. Sadie is currently looking in every corner of my living room and kitchen as if Bethany is hiding in plain sight.

There go the fluffed pillows.

She shoots me a look that very clearly says that she isn't buying my act. "Bethany. I saw her car outside. I'm tired of y'all sneaking around. At first, I was fine with y'all doing your thing on the down low. If anyone can appreciate a secret relationship, it's us. But come on, it has gone on long enough,

Rudolph. Just admit you two are sleeping together so we can quit pretending we don't know when we obviously do know!"

All I can do is laugh at Sadie's tirade, which only earns me an even meaner look.

Damn, she can be scary when she wants to.

"Oh, Sadie. You have it mixed up on so many levels," I say, really wanting to laugh at her outburst. "And my name is not Rudolph."

"I figured it wasn't, but I'm running out of *R* names. And don't try to distract me. Just tell me what I have wrong. We'd love to finally know the whole story."

"I don't know personally if I'd go so far as to say love," Hunter chimes in. "But I am interested."

Just as I'm trying to figure out a way to stall, Bethany returns from the bathroom. She doesn't even stop to say hi to Sadie and Hunter. She just immediately comes to me and slides her hand into mine.

"Where would you like for us to start?" Bethany asks, her voice much stronger than it was just a few minutes ago. "Because you're right, we need to come clean about a lot."

Sadie stares down at our joined hands, then back up to us, confusion now covering her face. "I don't know? I guess we'll start with why all of a sudden you asked us to come over today after months of us begging for you two to tell us what the hell was going on. And don't say that you really invited us over to watch hockey because that's a bunch of crap."

"You sure that's where you want to start?" Bethany asks.

"Yes, Bethany!" Sadie exclaims, becoming more frustrated. "Just spit it out. You're killing me here."

"You sure you don't want to sit down?" I ask, because I know the effect of the bomb about to be dropped. And I wish I had been sitting down.

Sadie lets out a groan. "For the love of all things holy, spit it out. I can't—"

"I'm pregnant."

"... keep waiting for you to tell me. Wait, what did you say?"

Sadie's eyes grow large as she realizes what Bethany said.

"What did you say?"

Bethany softly laughs as I decide I'll clean this one up. "How does the name Aunt Sadie sound?"

———

Bethany

"Oh my God. When? Where? How? I mean, I know how, but... how? I need every detail. Well, not every detail, but a lot of them."

Once we tell Hunter and Sadie the news of the day—followed by five minutes of shock and bewilderment—the two rush toward us in a flurry of hugs and congratulations.

I must say, it's a huge relief.

Things have settled down, and now it's time to face the firing squad. Though now I'm not as nervous for their line of questioning as before.

"Memphis," I say, loving that I'm finally able to talk about this in the open.

Hunter's jaw drops as he stares wide-eyed at Davis. "This is because of me! You are welcome, dude!"

Davis laughs. "Sure, McAvoy. Take all the credit for something you had a minimal part in."

"I'm serious," Hunter says, taking a jalapeño popper from the appetizer tray. "If I wouldn't have pushed so hard for you two to come to Memphis for the engagement, I doubt we would be here now. And if I wouldn't have invited you back to the hotel that night to celebrate with us, then I'm guessing you wouldn't have ended up in the same room together. Therefore, this is all because of me, and I will accept you giving your child Hunter as a middle name and yes, I will become his godfather."

We all laugh. And it feels so good to laugh about this. Today is really the first time since I found out I've felt good about this whole unexpected pregnancy. I'd been so worried about what Davis would think, then what Hunter and Sadie would think, that laughter hasn't been present much. Combine that with general worry about how everything is going to change, well, I really haven't sat back and enjoyed this change of life plans.

Until now. Right now? I feel like everything is going to be okay.

"What if it's a girl?" Sadie asks. "You do know that's a possibility."

Hunter waves her off. "Nope. My money is on a boy."

"Well, I'm going with a girl," Sadie says, setting down her glass of iced tea. "I have to keep things interesting. Plus, I love you, Bethany, but you raising a boy is slightly terrifying."

"Hey! I could raise a boy. He could play football and stuff."

"That's right, princess," Davis says, bringing me in for a quick kiss. "You can do whatever you set your mind to."

"This is just weird," Sadie says.

"What?" I ask, wishing that Hunter and Sadie weren't here so that kiss could go a little deeper.

"You and him kissing. In the open. Not hiding. I'm not used to it yet."

Davis and I look at each other and all we can do is smile. She's right. That's the first time we've kissed in front of people. Out in the open. Free to be... whatever we are. I feel the weight of months of hiding, questioning, and frustration lift off my shoulders.

"Well, get used to it, Benson. It's going to be happening a

lot more," Davis says, scooping me onto his lap. "Did we sneak around for months? Yes. Why did we hide it? I guess because it wasn't a real relationship, and we didn't want you two, or anyone else, judging us for the arrangement that at the time, we were both okay with. At that time, that reasoning seemed logical. Now we know it was a bunch of bullshit. All that matters now is that we're in this, and we're going to have a baby together."

I really need Hunter and Sadie to leave now. Between that speech and my hormones? I need this man naked and me on top of him.

Which would be the first time I've seen him naked since we decided to give us a real shot. Don't ask me why now, all of a sudden, he's taking things slow. It's driving me bonkers, and if he doesn't have sex with me soon, I'm going to combust.

"So, from the time we set you two up, until Memphis, you were sleeping together?" Hunter reiterates.

We both laugh. "For the most part. Yes."

Sadie slaps Hunter on the shoulder. "I told you they hooked up after the championship game!"

Davis and I both look at each other before busting up laughing again.

"What?" Hunter asks. "What is so damn funny?"

By the time we get our laughter under control, Sadie and Hunter are looking at us like we are from another planet.

"Let's just say," Davis begins. "Your truck is quite durable."

CHAPTER 24
BETHANY

"WHY IS everyone looking at me funny?"

I have to look up from my phone to see what the heck Davis is talking about. We are sitting in the waiting room of my ob-gyn for my ten-week appointment. I told him there was nothing super exciting that was going to happen today, but he was insistent on coming with me.

It's pretty adorable.

As I take a look around the waiting room, I can only guess as to why every woman here—and even a few men—are looking at Davis.

Frankly, he's the best-looking man in here. And he's covered in Fury gear from head to toe since he came straight from the facility to the appointment. Rookie camp starts soon, and apparently, that's a big deal to prepare for. Or so I've been told.

He's also built like a brick house and looks almost cartoon-like sitting in these small waiting room chairs.

"They probably think you're a player," I whisper, giving him a look up and down, signaling to his clothing. "Also, if you didn't know, you're pretty good-looking. I bet they are checking you out."

This earns me the smirk I love so much. "I did know, but it's always nice to hear it from the mother of my child, princess."

"Are you ever going to stop calling me that?" I ask. I used to loathe that name, but I must admit, it's growing on me. Though, I refuse to tell him that.

"Not a chance."

"Why do you even call me that?"

He leans in like he's going to kiss me on the cheek, but instead whispers in my ear. "That's my secret to keep."

I'm half-tempted to roll my eyes, but I'm stopped as a nurse calls us back.

"You ready?" I ask.

He stands up and holds his hand out for me. "I'm ready. Let's go meet our baby."

I don't know if he knew the double-meaning I packed into my question, but either way, I'm glad for his answer.

Every day I wake up wondering if this is going to be the day he realizes this isn't what he signed up for. He has given me no indication that he has one foot out the door, but my insecurities—packed with my own childhood ordeal—keep letting my mind travel down that road.

"Right in here," the nurse says. "Let's get all your vital signs checked out."

"Is she okay?" Davis asks, his voice concerned as the nurse takes my blood pressure.

The nurse smiles at him. "First time?"

Davis looks slightly embarrassed. "Yes, ma'am."

The nurse takes off the blood pressure cuff and enters it on my chart. "Everything is fine. We just need to do this each time she comes in. Everything is normal. Just wait here a few minutes, then the doctor will be in."

The nurse leaves and all I can do is laugh.

"What?" Davis asks. "I'm just making sure you're okay!"

"It's just my blood pressure. What are you going to do when they start strapping heart rate monitors to me?"

"Why would they do that?"

On cue, Dr. Janet Stewart walks into the exam room. "Because we like to make sure that the baby's and the mom's heart are working. You know, that's kind of my job."

"Hi, Dr. Stewart," I say, trying to hold back my laughter at her response to Davis. "Let me introduce you to the baby's father."

"Hi, ma'am. I'm Davis." He extends his hand, and if I'm not imagining things, I think he's shaking.

Is he nervous? The Davis I know is the definition of calm, cool, and collected. The man who is the center of attention and thrives when the spotlight is on him.

I knew there were going to be many layers of Davis. And every day since I told him about the pregnancy, I get to see a new one.

"None of this ma'am stuff. That is one thing I've never gotten used to living in the south. You can call me Dr. Stewart. Now, what million questions do you have for me, Mr. Davis?"

Bless Dr. Stewart's heart, because Davis came in today with no less than fifty questions, and she answered each and every one of them. I knew he's been reading parenting articles, but I had no idea how deep he had gotten. As in, he asked her if I was allowed to talk on my cell phone because of possible radiation transfer.

He also asked her about sex.

So many questions about sex.

If she was shocked, she didn't show it. Instead, she took the opportunity to ask him about the Fury's upcoming season. Apparently, she's a huge fan.

And she reassured him that sex is just fine.

"Now, if we're done with that, let's get to the good stuff," Dr. Stewart says, putting on a set of gloves. "Bethany, lie back and lift your shirt up. It's time to look at this baby."

I do as she instructs as Davis positions himself next to me. I'm now glad that I didn't have an ultrasound at my first appointment. All we did then was confirm once and for all that I was pregnant. It feels right that the first time we are seeing proof of our baby is together.

As Dr. Stewart gets her equipment ready, I sneak a peek at Davis. Were his eight-million questions a bit over the top? Yes. Were they also extremely thoughtful and gave me butterflies? Also, yes.

"How you doing?" he asks, taking my hand in both of his.

"I'm nervous. Excited. Anxious. Before, it was just talk, but now..."

"But now this becomes real life."

I nod, loving that he knows how I feel. "Exactly."

He brings my hand to his lips as Dr. Stewart begins the exam.

"Everything is looking good," she says, moving her wand around on top of my stomach. "The baby is right on track size-wise at ten weeks' along."

Was Memphis just ten weeks ago? It feels like it has been a lifetime.

I hear Dr. Stewart talking about size and a few other things, but right now, all I can look at is Davis.

His eyes are transfixed on the monitor. I can tell he is taking in every word Dr. Stewart is saying. His hand is gripping mine tighter each time she says something about where the baby is at in terms of development.

I want to look at the monitor, but I can't take my eyes off of him. Watching his face register the joy and love simply from seeing our child for the first time is a memory I'll never have the chance to have again.

Plus, I tried to look at the monitor. I didn't see anything when she pointed to the place I should have seen something and I don't want to admit that.

"By the looks of everything, clear your calendars for the end of November," Dr. Stewart says, as she begins what I assume is printing out pictures of what we just looked at. "And let's hope you don't go into labor on a Sunday."

My eyes go wide. "Oh my gosh! I never thought of that!" I say, sitting straight up. "What if you're on the road for an away game? What if I go into labor early? What if I go into labor during a game and we can't get ahold of you? What if there's a freak snowstorm? What if—"

Davis chuckles and brings my face to his, doing his best to kiss away my worry. "Don't worry, princess. No matter what, I will be there for you. I promise. Nothing is going to keep me away from the birth of our baby."

"We have plenty of time to come up with a plan," Dr. Stewart says, handing us pictures of the sonogram. "Until then, do everything you've been doing, and we'll see you in a month."

I want to worry. I want to panic. But I can't. Because all I can look at right now is Davis, who is looking at the picture of our baby in pure awe. It's like he's staring at the best gift he could have received on Christmas morning.

I'll panic later. Right now, I'm just going to watch this and let my heart melt a little more for this man.

CHAPTER 25
DAVIS

I'VE ALWAYS BEEN ATTRACTED to Bethany. That was never the problem for us.

And as the days go on and we spend more time together, my attraction and feelings for her are only getting stronger.

I remember the first time I saw her. The sun was setting when she exited the car in front of the bar where we were meeting. As she walked toward me, her long legs on display in that cream dress, I could have sworn the sunlight radiated from her and it almost made it look like she was wearing a crown.

Like a princess.

As I look at her now, standing in the kitchen doing something as mundane as loading the dishwasher, she's just as beautiful as she was that first night. No. That's wrong. She's more. I never knew what people talked about when they said women have a pregnancy glow. But looking at her now? I can see it. Or maybe it's the knowledge that she's carrying my child.

Combine that with the fact we got to see our baby today? There are a lot of emotions flowing through me right now. And they are all for this woman.

I can't believe I was going to deny myself this. I'll never tell Abby, but she was right. For years, I let myself use my family as a shield. As an excuse because I was scared of what kind of partner I would be. Would I be like Mitch? Only half present and then gone when things got too hard? Or would I be the person I had to become when he left? The dependable person who would provide no matter the odds stacked against him?

I was hoping I'd be the latter, but Mitch's blood does run through me. I'm reminded of that every day when I look in the mirror.

But looking at Bethany right now? Knowing that in a matter of months we are going to be bringing a child into this world together? I know that I am the furthest thing from my so-called father. I am going to be the best father and provider I can for Bethany and our baby. And I'm still going to make sure my mom and sisters have everything they need. Just because I'm adding more into my life doesn't mean I have to subtract others.

I know that now. And that knowledge is freeing.

"What are you looking at?" she says, noticing me staring at her as I lean against her kitchen counter.

"You," I say, walking behind her and wrapping my arms around her stomach. Her stomach that is growing our child.

Why does that thought turn me on so much?

"Me loading the dishwasher, does it for you?" she teases as she rinses another dish.

"You doing anything turns me on. I thought you knew that by now."

I begin kissing her neck, which has its desired effect as her body begins to go limp in my hold. "I... I didn't know if you were still attracted to me."

My lips freeze on her neck. How could she think something so outrageous?

I spin her around, lift her up and place her on the kitchen counter, her legs opening and giving me the perfect spot to stand between. "What did you say?"

She doesn't look me directly in the eye. Not liking that at all, I take her chin and lift it so our eyes meet. "There has never been a day since we met that I haven't been attracted to you. Since the day we met, you have driven me so crazy I couldn't say no. You have made me realize that I want so much more out of this life. So why... why on God's green Earth do you think right now that I'm not dying to be inside you?"

I keep hold of her chin, not roughly, but just enough so she can't look away. "Because since we... got back... got together... whatever we are... you haven't tried to have sex with me. And I, well, I puke every morning, and I'm putting on weight and I'm tired all the time, so I figured—"

I don't let her finish. I crash our mouths together and show her just how much she turns me on. She immediately opens her mouth for me, and our tongues find each other, taking everything we want. The counter is the perfect height for me to rub my rock-hard cock against her center, showing her just how much she, in fact, turns me on.

"Feel that?" I ask, taking her hand and bringing it down to my dick. "That is you. That is all you. My beautiful princess. And as to what we are? You're mine. And I'm yours."

Her hand begins exploring, and I almost forgot how good her touch feels. If I was a selfish bastard, I'd let her explore.

But not tonight. Tonight, I need to show her that not only is she the most beautiful woman I've ever seen but that she's desired in a way I didn't know I could desire another.

"Lift up," I command, which she does the second the words leave my mouth. I push up her skirt and take off her panties before spreading her legs even more.

"Oh!"

It's the only sound she makes as I bend down and dive into her sweet pussy. Going down on a woman in the past was always more of a means to an end for me. But with Bethany? I could live here if she would let me. Between the sounds she makes when my tongue hits her clit just right and the feeling of her legs clenching around me when I make her come?

It's fucking heaven.

"Davis!" she says, and I can't believe that she's almost there, but I feel her contracting.

"What, baby?" I ask, replacing my tongue with two fingers. "What do you want from me?"

"You. I only want you."

How can I argue with that? Especially since the doctor has given the green light for sexual activities.

I give her pussy one more lick before I come up and begin taking my pants off. Out of habit, I reach for my wallet when something hits me.

Do we need a condom?

I look back up at Bethany, who is biting her lip while also giving me the sexiest smile I've ever received.

"I'm clean," I say immediately, needing her to know that.

"I trust you, and it isn't like I'll get pregnant or anything," she answers with a smirk, bringing me back in close to her.

While I'd love nothing more than to dive into her right here on the kitchen counter, I can't. This isn't just another roll in the hay between two people sneaking around and denying their feelings for each other.

This is the first time as an us. The first time without anything between us.

The first of many more.

She shrieks as I scoop her off the counter and quickly make my way back to her bedroom. As soon as we find the bed, we frantically strip each other. We are nothing but lips and hands and clothes flying off.

"I've missed you," I say, lying her back and reaching down for one suck on her taut nipple.

"I missed you too," she moans. "Now, please…"

"Please what?" I ask, lining up my cock with her center.

"Make me feel everything you said earlier."

And I do. I drive into her, with nothing between us, and the feel of her hot pussy against my dick is almost too much to handle.

"Fuck, you feel so good," I say, trying to control myself when all I want to do is fuck her hard and fast.

"More," she says, as if she's reading my mind. "Don't hold back. I want to feel all of you."

"All of me." I groan, bringing her legs onto my shoulders. "Give me everything, princess."

And she does. Our hips meet in perfect rhythm as the angle drives her insane. Her hands are reaching for the sheets, the pillows, whatever she can get her hands on. And before I know it, her center is clenching around me in a feeling I've never experienced with a woman.

"Now, princess. Give it to me now."

She does, and I follow right behind her. We come undone with nothing between us, a perfect harmony of pent-up lust, emotion… and, dare I say, something more.

I knew that first night this woman is something special.

Little did I know that she is it for me.

"WHAT DO YOU MEAN, you've never met someone's parents?"

I know my voice got a little loud there, but I'm seriously confused about how he never went through this rite of passage in his life. Then I look over at Davis, who is just laughing at my reaction as we drive to my mom and Mike's house for Monday night dinner.

"I mean, I've never met a girl's parents before. I've never had a dad greet me with a bat or give me mildly veiled threats of treating his daughter right. I've never had to kiss up to a mom."

"How does that happen?" I ask, still confused how this is actually a thing that he hasn't experienced before.

"What?" he asks.

"I'm just baffled how you've never had to meet parents."

"I didn't date in high school," he says matter-of-factly. "When you don't date, you don't have to meet the parents."

"How did you not date?" I turn and face him because I'm genuinely intrigued by how this is a thing. "Did you not go to prom? Or homecoming? Or even out to the movies?"

He shakes his head. "Nope. I was working. My family came

first. When my dad left, I made a vow to my mom and sisters that I would help provide. I was the man of the house and I took that job seriously. It's the reason I was a hard-headed asshole to you for months. That meant every second I wasn't in school or playing football, I worked."

"That's kind of sad," I say, reaching for his hand that's not on the steering wheel. "I mean, I think it's admirable that at a young age you took on that responsibility. I don't know many teenagers who would do that. But I also wish that you could have had a normal childhood."

He shrugs. "It is what it is. So now I ask, how many of your boyfriends did you bring home?"

"Only a couple," I admit. "In high school I had a few boyfriends, and they met Mom and Mike because of circumstance. Proms and what not. Though, I wouldn't consider that the firing squad. Mom was pretty laid-back about things, and Mike had just married my mom, so I don't think he felt right playing the role of my father. Plus, he was my English teacher. Things would have gotten really weird. As of late? None have lasted long enough for me to make it worth my time."

"And I'm worth your time," he says with a cocky tone to his voice.

I lean over and give him a peck on the cheek. "Without a doubt."

We sit in silence for a few minutes and my mind drifts back to a younger Davis. I picture the boy who had to become a man too early in life, working likely at some fast-food restaurant on a Saturday night instead of going to the movies. The boy who barely slept because of everything on his plate.

"Do you regret it?" I ask, curious now that he has hindsight.

He doesn't have to ask what I'm talking about as he turns

into the driveway. "Not even a little bit. I'll never regret putting my family first."

He puts the truck in park and flashes me a smug grin. "Plus, if I had met parents back then, you wouldn't get another one of my firsts."

"Another one of your firsts?" I ask, a little confused. "I didn't realize I had any firsts. I'm going to guess I didn't have the *big* first."

This makes him laugh. "No, you didn't get that first. But the firsts you have, they mean more than any of the other ones."

"Can you tell me one?" I ask with a hint of flirtation in my voice, hoping this gets me my answer.

He leans in and gives me a quick kiss. "You're the first woman I ever spent the night with."

This leaves me speechless. I am? I was?

As I turn this new information over in my head, Davis gets out of the truck to come around to my side to open my door. I tried to open it myself the first night we went out, and I was told to never do it again.

Who knew this man had such a chivalrous side?

"Will you tell me more firsts later?" I ask.

"Of course," he says, taking my hand as we walk up the sidewalk. "But let's get this first out of the way, shall we?"

Now that we're nearing the second trimester and Davis and I have fallen into a consistent groove, we figure it's time to meet the families. We've booked flights to Pennsylvania in June when he has some downtime so I can meet his sisters and Mom. And with rookie camp starting next week, now is as good a time as ever to meet Mom and Mike.

"Are you nervous?" I ask as we approach the door.

"Nah," he says, giving my hand a squeeze. "If Hunter can survive this, then it will be a piece of cake."

The door opens before I have a chance to knock—I now knock whenever I come over—and standing there is a very stern Mike in the doorway.

"Hey, Mike," I say awkwardly, wondering why he's taking up the entirety of the doorframe.

"Hello there," he says, his voice stern and very un-Mike like. The last time he was like this was when he met Hunter.

Oh, Jesus, take the wheel.

"You must be Davis," he continues, stepping slightly to the side for us. "Why don't you come inside. Let's get to know each other a little better."

———

"What do you mean that the SEC is overrated! Helen, are you going to let this man be the father of our first grandchild with that kind of blasphemy coming from his mouth!"

"Now, now, Mike," Mom says, patting Mike's arm like he's a toddler throwing a temper tantrum. "Every person is allowed their opinion. And I don't think I can really have a say about him being the father. That's already sorted itself out."

"Hunter!" Mike yells, turning to look to his left at Hunter, who is trying, but failing, not to crack up. "How does this man work for you!"

Hunter just shrugs. "It's nice to have someone who keeps my ego in check."

"Mike, I'm sorry," Davis says, casually putting his arm on the back of my chair. "But if you take away Alabama, the conference is mediocre at best."

Mike takes his fork and points it across the table at Davis. "We aren't done with this conversation."

"But we are tonight," Mom says, standing up and clearing the plates. "Enough football talk for the night."

"I agree," I say as I start to stand.

"What are you doing?" Davis asks, taking my hand and pulling me back down to my chair.

"Helping clear the table?"

"You will not," Mom says, sweeping the dishes out from in front of me. "You need to stay off your feet."

"You do know I'm still on my feet for hours a day working."

"I do. That means you should be off your feet whenever you can. Davis, can you talk some sense into her?"

"I can try, Mrs. Benson. She doesn't listen to me very well."

"What did I tell you about Mrs. Benson? It's Helen," she says with a smile before she walks with Sadie into the kitchen.

It's safe to say that Mom and Mike are smitten with Davis. As soon as we walked through the door, Mike took him back into the office with Hunter. It was reminiscent of what he did with Hunter when Sadie first brought him home. That lasted for about thirty minutes before they came out laughing and talking football jargon that sounded like a foreign language to me.

Davis then helped my mom in the kitchen. He didn't flinch when she asked him not so casually how many cribs we needed to buy—also known as are you two going to be living together or staying apart.

He explained to her that we're going to start looking for a house, and he made her a promise that no matter what, baby and I will always be provided for.

I'm pretty sure Mom melted a bit at that declaration.

The conversation at dinner was easy and natural. I was worried it would be awkward considering the whole "first time you met this guy was after he got me pregnant thing," but everyone has been wonderful. We talked about our family, he told us a little about his, and we started spitballing ideas for nursery themes.

He wants football. Boy or girl.

I want teddy bears. Either pink or blue ones.

We'll see how this goes down.

"I think she likes you," I say as I reach for his free hand under the table. "Same with Mike."

He gives my hand an extra squeeze. "You could have warned me he and Hunter were going to gang up on me about college football."

"You know I don't know anything about that stuff," I say, leaning back into his shoulder. "For all I know, they were talking about TV shows. It sounds like reality TV."

"I still don't know how none of my football knowledge rubbed off on you over the years," Sadie says, taking back her seat next to Hunter.

"The same way you never listened to my hair or makeup tips," I say, pointing to the messy bun on top of her head that I'm pretty sure is there twenty-four seven. Just once, I'd love to see her with loose beach waves.

"Touché, sister. Touché."

"Enough football talk," Mom says, taking her seat next to Mike. "I want to talk about all things baby."

"Yes!" Sadie says. "First thing's first. Do we have a gender yet? And if you do one of those elaborate reveal parties, I will no longer call you my sister."

I shake my head, suddenly embarrassed that all eyes are on Davis and me right now. "We are going to find out. That's about eight weeks away. As for the reveal party, I am not doing one. I'm not taking the chance that I'm one of those gender reveals gone wrong and end up on the national news. We will stick to telling y'all at dinner one week, then posting on Facebook."

"I like the sound of that," Davis says, bringing my hand to his lips. When I look back at my Mom, I think she's actually going to cry from the act.

"Have you thought about names?" Mike asks. I'm guessing to save my mom from an emotional episode.

"Not really," I say with a shrug. "We still have a few weeks before we have to start worrying about that."

"Names, you say," Sadie says, leaning forward on her elbows as she locks eyes with Davis. "What do you think about names, Davis? Maybe as in, is there a family name that needs to be passed down if it's a boy?"

I laugh at Sadie's horrible attempt to get Davis's first name out of him. Do I want to know? Heck yes I do. But at this point, I'm kind of enjoying the game these two have going on.

"Yes, there is. But I'm not worried about it," Davis says, confidence oozing from his voice.

"Really?" I ask, looking up over my shoulder at him. "Why?"

"Because," he says, placing a slow kiss on my lips. "I think we're having a little girl. And she's going to be just as beautiful as her mother."

If my mother wasn't crying before, she most definitely is now.

It's okay, because so am I.

IT FEELS like forever since the Fury has been on the field.

And even though this isn't our full squad today—this week is just rookies and unsigned players looking for a shot at the big time—it's still good to be back on the field.

"Again!" I yell, signaling for my running back coach to run the agility drill again. Satisfied that he's doing what he needs to, I make my way over to the receivers. Also known as my former position group. The group that now has the best young receiver in the league with Dexter Smith.

"Oh, the offense we can run with you," I say to myself as I watch him make a forty-yard catch.

"You aren't wrong," Hunter says as he steps up next to me. I didn't even hear him approach. "Imagine the plays we can run with him."

"As long as he has someone to throw it to him," I say, trying to gauge Hunter's feelings on Bryce and his offseason antics.

"Let's just hope it's a young kid blowing off steam," he says, patting me on the shoulder. "I have to go pay attention to the defense. Apparently, that's my job now, too."

I laugh. "Better you than me, boss."

He holds up his middle finger as he runs across the field to watch the defense. Happy with what I'm seeing out of the receivers, I head over to watch the offensive linemen.

I'm not like Hunter. I never had big dreams and aspirations to be a head football coach. Whereas he wants to turn the professional football world on its head, I just want a job where I can have some fun while also providing for my family. I want to be a coach who is found reliable and can help a team win. I'm also the coach who gives every rookie an unflattering nickname when camp starts.

It's all about balance.

Coaching offers me financial stability as well as getting to do something I love. Yes, I could have used my MBA to work at a bank, but that didn't sound too fun. Though I would have loved the rush, a stock trader or hedge fund manager was a little too risky. I might not make the kind of money that head coaches do, but between that and my investments, it's more than enough to provide for myself, while making sure Mom's bills are paid, Sara doesn't have to work while in school and helping Abby whenever she needs it.

That's all I ever wanted; to give my family stability and to not have to go to bed each night worrying how they were going to put food on the table or pay the electric bill.

And now I have two more to take care of. But instead of that giving me anxiety like it used to, now I think about it and all I do is smile.

I'm about to have a family of my own.

"Is a shiny new receiver putting that smile on your face or is it someone else?"

The comment comes from Cole Campbell, our left guard on the offensive line and Bryce's best friend. They were in pee wees together before going to the same high school. They both won national championships at Clemson, and because of an injury, Cole fell to the second round last year so we were able to draft him along with Bryce.

He's also the most mature twenty-four-year-old I've ever met in my life. Hence, why his nickname is Dad.

"What are you doing out here, Dad? Miss me too much?"

"You know that's it. Figured I'd come out and see what we have to work with. Not like I'm doing anything else these days."

Cole is one of those players I don't know a lot about personally. I might be his coordinator now, but last year I was the receivers' coach, so I didn't have a lot of interaction with him. From what I know, he keeps his nose to the ground, doesn't party, and is the most responsible player in the locker room of any age, and that's including our veteran tight end who has three kids.

"No girl keeping you busy this offseason?" I ask, half curious and half hoping I can steer him into a chat about Bryce.

"Nah," he says as his gaze turns back toward the group of practicing rookies. "Maybe one day."

Judging from his tone, I would put money on there being more to that story. And that he's also not going to talk about it.

"So, what have you been up to this offseason?"

He just shrugs. "Working out. Went and visited my family for a few months. Just lying low, you know?"

"I hear that," I say, knowing that it's now or never if I want to talk to him about his childhood friend. "Have you talked to Bryce much?"

He lets out a big, frustrated sigh. "No. And don't bother asking me to. I've already tried. He won't listen."

That is the last thing I want to hear. This could be our season. With Hunter's offensive mindset, a defense that has reloaded, and the reigning Rookie of the Year as quarterback, we could be unstoppable this year.

That is, as long as Bryce gets his head out of his ass and shapes up.

Quick.

The talk I had with him did no good. In fact, it might have made him worse. *The Nashville Banner*, the local newspaper and where Sadie used to work, rarely prints gossip. But Bryce has been so out of control lately that even they are writing about it. The other night a video went viral of him dancing on a bar with two women before making out with each of them within seconds of each other.

I don't know what has gotten into him. But if he doesn't clean up his act, he's going to be out of the league before he really even made his mark.

"I tried to talk to him," I say, wanting Cole to know that it's not all on him. "He pretty much blew me off."

"Yeah, he's good at that," Cole says, still looking out at the players. "He's done this from time to time. Rebelled. He did it our freshman year of college, but it never made the news. And it wasn't nearly this bad. Before, I knew what to do. But now? Now I don't even think that will work."

This gets my attention. "What is it? You tell me and we'll make it happen. He's the future of the franchise. You both are. Whatever needs to be done, you tell me and I'll do it."

Cole finally turns to look at me, a sad look in his eye. "That look in your eye. The one from earlier. Is she special?"

Confused by his question, but wanting more information, I go along with it. "Yeah. Yeah, she is. We're actually having a baby together."

"Then you know. What would happen if she left you? That you thought, albeit selfishly, she'd always be in your life, but then for whatever circumstances, one day she up and leaves. What would you do?"

My blood temperature spikes from just the thought of it. "I'd go nuts. Probably off the deep end."

Cole nods and looks back to the position group. "That's Bryce right now. He's off the deep end. He never thought she'd be gone. I've tried to talk to him. His sister has. We don't know what to do."

Fuck. This is all because of a girl? I remember last year when he started off rough, Hunter said it was a personal matter, but he worked through it so it was completely forgotten.

Is this the same thing? And if Cole is right, can it be fixed? If this is a personal matter, we can only help Bryce so much before he has to do something about it himself.

I can fix his throwing motion. I can fix a play that's not working.

But this? I don't know if I can help him fix this.

"What can I do?" I ask Cole.

"I wish I knew, Coach. I wish I knew." Cole sighs and gives my back a slap before walking away. "Oh, and congratulations on the baby."

"WHAT DO you mean you won't tell me his name!" I cry out, though I'm only half mad that my efforts have again been derailed. "I thought I could bring you to my side! What happened to our girls' day this afternoon! I thought we bonded."

Abby and Sara both fall back into Abby's couch in a fit of laughter. All Davis can do is plaster on a smug smile as he puts his arm around me.

"We did. Never did I ever think I'd be able to go makeup shopping with Davis's girlfriend. Hell, I never thought Davis would have a girlfriend. And I really wish I could tell you," Abby says, straightening herself back up. "But that man has sworn me to secrecy. Plus, he has all the dirt on us. If it was just me, I'd dish away, but I'd rather he not one day tell my daughters what I was like in high school."

"You're damn right I would," Davis says, a smug smile on his face. "I told you, princess. They have sworn a vow of silence."

"If it makes you feel better, Bethany, I also hate our last name," Sara says as she stands up from the couch. "I would have changed it too, except I'm holding on to the hope I'll get married and not have to go through the paperwork. I don't tell anyone unless I know they are going to be around for a very long time."

I snap my head to Davis and turn on my best overly dramatic southern accent. "You had your last name changed? I thought we were just trying to figure out your first name! This is brand new information! Who are you even? I'm having a baby with a complete stranger!"

"That's it. You're dead," he says, jumping up from the couch and running after Sara.

"I didn't know about that part being a secret! I'm sorry!"

Sara's voice trails off and all Abby and I can do is laugh.

"There wasn't enough of that in our house growing up," Abby says out loud, though I don't know if she really means to voice it.

"What was he like?" I've been dying to ask this question and now seems like the perfect chance.

Abby sits back into her couch and doesn't answer right away. Instead, she's looking in the direction that Davis and Sara ran off, like she's trying to see through the walls.

"It's like I grew up with two different brothers."

"What do you mean?"

She lets out a sigh and turns back to face me. "I like to call our childhood pre-Mitch and post-Mitch. He did tell you about our so-called father, right?"

I nod. "Yeah, but not a lot. I get the feeling he doesn't like talking about him."

Abby lets out a humorless laugh. "That's the statement of the year. The Davis before Mitch left was so full of life. Not that he's not now, but before he was the definition of a carefree kid. There wasn't a room he couldn't charm or a crowd he couldn't make laugh. He didn't get into big trouble, but he was mischie-vous. Then, the day we realized that Da—Mitch—wasn't coming back, it's like a light switched off for him. He made it his mission to take care of us. I don't even know where he got that idea in his head from. Mom surely didn't ask it of him. But once he made up his mind that he was going to help financially provide for the family, we couldn't talk him out of it. Lord knows, Mom and I tried. We hated seeing that light in his eyes go out. I know he still kept up the act around people at school and his teachers. They had no idea what was going on at home. But to those who knew him, who really knew him, we never saw that same spark again."

My heart hurts as Abby tells me this, and I subconsciously put my hands over my stomach. I can only hope that our child will have that same playful side.

For some reason, at that moment, I let myself imagine a little boy. But it's not Davis. Abby showed me pictures earlier. This little boy I'm imagining does have Davis's brown hair, but it's lighter. The lightest brown hair can be. And his eyes aren't the same blueish-gray color as Davis's. No, they are lighter, almost as if they are a combination of the two of ours.

For the first time since I found out I was pregnant, I let myself envision a little boy. A boy with Davis's smirk who is a tad bit ornery in the best way. A little boy who might be tough on the football field, but deep down is a mama's boy. One who gets to have the spark in his eye forever because I'll make sure I do everything in my power to make sure it never fades away.

"That is, until I met you."

Abby's words bring me back from my daydream. "I'm sorry. What did you say?"

Abby stands up and comes to sit next to me, taking my hand in hers. "I never, ever, thought that Davis would find his spark of happiness again. I don't know if you've realized this about my brother, but he's quite hard-headed."

"I've noticed."

We both laugh before Abby continues. "I might bug him every week about settling down, but I really thought I was talking to an empty room. Then one day he talked about you. You were the first one he's ever told me about. Then I met you and… now I see it. The spark is back in his eyes. The way he looks at you? It might not be the same trouble making look he used to have, but for the first time in years, there is life in his soul. And I have you to thank for that."

I laugh because that's the only thing that's keeping the tears away. "I'm pretty sure a faulty condom also had a little something to do with it."

"While that might be true, don't for one minute discourage how crazy he is about you." She looks up and Davis and Sara are on their way back to her living room. She quickly leans in, close enough to whisper now. "I knew you were someone special before I knew you were going to make me an aunt."

I look at her confused, and all she does is nod as Davis and Sara retake their seats.

He talked to Abby about me before I told him about the baby?

If I needed another piece of reassurance about how he feels about me, then this is it. I've always believed him, but that twat waffle inner voice of mine always perked up with thoughts of "this is working out too well" and "don't you think this happened a bit too fast?"

But knowing that he talked to Abby about me before I told him I was pregnant? That's everything.

"Uncle Davis!"

My head snaps to the doorway to see a little girl no more than four years old running as fast as her little legs can carry her toward Davis and me. Before she crashes into us, Davis quickly kneels to the ground and scoops the little one up.

"How's my Livvie doing?" he says, scattering kisses on her face. "What did you do today?"

"Went to park!" she says between giggles.

"We were quite fond of the swings today," Abby's husband, Joe, says as he comes in the house with a sleeping Sophia in his arms. "One fell asleep on the way home. One picked up her fourth wind."

"Uncle Davis! I want to show you my toys!" Olivia yells, dragging Davis up the stairs. "Come on!"

I laugh as I watch Davis being manhandled by a four-year-old. Though it is nice to see him with his nieces, today was our adult day. Joe volunteered to take both girls to the park to give us girls time to get to know each other. Davis had some things he needed to take care of at his mom's facility, so we decided to go shopping. This mama was in need of some maternity clothes.

And of course, no girls' day shopping trip is complete without a trip to Sephora.

I have a feeling that by the look Abby is giving him right now, his efforts today earned him some husband points.

"Thank you for taking them," she says as she starts to stand up. "Want me to go lay her down?"

"Nah," he says, waving her off. "I got it. I'll see you guys in a bit."

As soon as Joe goes up the stairs, I see movement coming down it.

And it's a sight that I will never forget for the rest of my life.

Davis, my two-hundred-pound, muscled, former football player, is walking down the stairs in a blond wig.

With a tiara.

It is freaking adorable. And weirdly sexy.

"We're having a tea party!" Olivia says. "Come on, Uncle Davis! Bethy! Come play too!"

We've now been in Pennsylvania for two days. The first day we laid low and recovered from a day of travel. Yesterday, we made our way over to Abby's house, where I officially met everyone. From the second I met this little girl, my heart melted. She's everything I could want in a daughter. Spunky and sassy, while also sweet and kind.

And she loves her uncle Davis.

She's not the only one.

Since we've been here and seeing him with his family, I've seen a side of Davis I could only hope existed. I know there are a lot of layers to this man, but seeing him with his nieces? With his sisters? It confirms what I hope for deep in my soul.

This is a man who knows the worth of family.

This is the man I want to have a family with.

This is the man I want to spend the rest of my life with.

"What are you looking at, princess?" he whispers as Olivia "makes" more tea.

I almost crack a joke about how right now, technically, he's the princess. I also almost say those three words that are on the very tip of my tongue.

I don't say either of those things. Instead, I say what's in my heart.

"I'm looking at our future."

He smiles, taking my hand in his. "Do you like what you see?"

I nod and say three different words instead. "It's simply perfect."

EVERY TIME I go to enter my mom's memory care facility, it takes me a second to gather my resolve.

I wasn't there when the memory lapses started. I was away at college and had to get my updates from Abby and Sara. At first, we thought it was just the byproduct of getting older.

Then one day Sara got home from school and she wasn't there. She wasn't working either of her jobs that day. Her car was in the garage, and the front door was unlocked. Sara panicked, called Abby, and the search began. They ended up finding her a few blocks away at a park where she was sitting on a bench, none the wiser about what she had done or how she had gotten there.

We knew then it was time to get her help.

I've only made it here a few times since then. But every time I stand on this sidewalk, staring at the doors that take me inside, I'm reminded that Mom—the woman who kept us together when everything could have fallen apart—is in there. And this is her life now.

No more singing Motown in the kitchen. No more of her knitting while we watch TV. No more pushing us on the tire swing in our backyard.

That woman is still there, but she's not. She's never going to get better. And this walkway reminds me of that every time I'm here.

Even more so today. I have no idea how she is going to be when Bethany and I walk into her room? Will she recognize me? If I tell her Bethany's name, will it register for more than a few seconds? Will we be robbed of the moment when we tell her we're having a baby?

Will she ever be able to meet our baby and know who it is? Will my child ever get to know the woman who did everything in her power to keep our family together when it could have crumbled?

I hate this disease. Today, more than ever.

"You okay?" Bethany asks, giving my hand a squeeze. "We don't have to do this if you don't want."

I take a breath and bring Bethany around to my front, wrapping my arms around her waist. Her arms instinctively go around my neck.

"It's always hard walking in," I say, allowing her touch to give me resolve. "Yesterday she was napping when I was here, so I didn't want to disturb her. But now? Now I know I'm going to see her and I'm always... I just never know how she'll be."

"It's okay," Bethany says, her soothing voice having its desired effect. "No matter what kind of day she is having, we will make the best of it. And we'll do it together."

"You're right," I say, placing a kiss on her forehead. "Let's go tell my mom she's going to be a grandma again."

I walk through the front door and go to push the button for entry. One of the best features of this facility is its security and round-the-clock, in-person monitoring they have of the residents. However, when I push the button, nothing happens. Normally, it signals a worker to buzz me in. Right now? Nothing.

"That's weird," I say, pushing the button again. "It worked just fine yesterday."

"Maybe it's broke?" Bethany says as she tries to pull the door open. Just when I'm about to tell her it won't work, it opens right up.

"That's not supposed to happen," I say, my anger growing slightly. "The security here is supposed to be state of the art."

"Oh my goodness, I am so sorry!" A woman in her mid-forties says as she comes rushing toward us. "Mr. Davis, I'm so sorry about that. I don't know what happened with our alarm, but it went offline for five minutes. Security is double-checking all of the residents now, which is why there was no one to let you in. Trust me when I say that this has never happened before."

"Thank you for the explanation," Bethany says, taking my hand in both of hers before I can snap at this woman. "Technology has its quirks sometimes. We appreciate the explanation."

I let out a breath, glad that Bethany stopped me from making a scene. "Yes. Thank you, Ms. Hathaway. Can we see my mother now?"

"Of course. Right this way."

I don't need directions to Mom's room, but I have a feeling that Jennifer Hathaway, the director of the facility I met with yesterday to talk about my mom's care, needs this more than I do.

"Here you go," she says, ushering us into a room that looks more like a studio apartment than a nursing home room. "She's having a good day today."

"Thank you," I say, as I gently knock on the door. "Mom? It's me. Can I come in?"

Bethany and I slowly walk into my mother's room, not

wanting to startle her. Though, I doubt she can hear me with the sound of *The Price is Right* playing at full blast.

"Mom!" I say a little louder, hoping to get her attention. I'll have to ask Jennifer about her hearing.

"What do you want, Richard!" she says, muting the television as we walk in. "I heard you the first time."

Well, at least she remembers my name.

My birth name, that is.

"Richard!" Bethany whisper-yells. "Is that a part of the Alzheimer's, or did your mother just out your name?"

"I should have known she would do it," I say in defeat.

"Oh, you have so much explaining to do, mister."

"Are you two just going to stand there and have a conversation, or are you going to tell me who this is, Richard?"

My mom is sitting on her reclining chair, looking slightly annoyed that I interrupted her television time and confused as to why I'm not alone. But the best part of how she looks? Her eyes look clear. Not confused. She knows who I am from the second I walk in.

Jennifer is right; today is a good day.

"Hey, Mom," I say, walking over to her and giving her a kiss on the cheek. "How are you feeling?"

"Today is good," she says, turning off the television. "Now, enough stalling. Who is this beautiful woman?"

I smile. "Mom. This is Bethany Hall. Bethany, this is my mom, Marie."

"It's so nice to meet you," Bethany says, holding her hand out.

"Nonsense," Mom says, holding out her arms. "Come over here and give me a hug."

Bethany smiles and walks into my mother's embrace. The sight hits me in the heart in a way I wasn't expecting.

"I've been waiting fifty-five years to do that," Mom says as

Bethany comes and takes a seat next to me on her small couch. "About time."

I laugh, loving how much she sounds like herself right now. "I was making sure she was perfect."

Mom turns her gaze to Bethany. "Do you fall for his smooth words? You know half the time it's a bunch of crap, right?"

Bethany laughs. "I can't resist them, ma'am. It's probably why I'm here today."

This makes Mom laugh. "I like you. But don't ever call me ma'am again. I might be getting old. I have trouble remembering some things. The least you can do is just call me Marie."

Bethany smiles. "I can do that."

The three of us fall into conversation. We tell her about how we met through Hunter and Sadie—though we leave out the part where we spent four months of that time as friends with benefits. She tells us about a recent field trip they took to a botanical garden that she enjoyed, though the way she's telling it, I don't know if it was last week or last year. She struggles a few times with remembering certain things like Olivia and Sophia's names, the name of a recipe she used to love making, and a few times stumbles over Bethany's name. But for the most part, it has been smooth sailing.

Which will make telling her the big news so much easier.

"Mom, there is something we want to tell you," I say, bringing Bethany a little closer to me.

"If it's that this lovely woman here is pregnant with my grandchild, then you should have told me that a lot sooner."

My jaw drops in shock. I look over to Bethany, whose eyes look like they are about to jump out of her head.

"How did you know?" I ask, and if the answer is Abby told her, I'm going to beat my sister's ass.

"Oh, Richard," Mom says, and I hear Bethany snicker a little bit at the use of my real name. "I've been pregnant four times. Some were on purpose, some were gifts from God. I might not remember a lot of things most days. But I'll never forget the look of someone who is expecting. The subtle ways she's been holding her stomach? The glow on her face? My dear, pregnancy looks wonderful on you and I am so glad you are going to give me another grandchild."

Bethany stands and rushes over to my mom, giving her a big hug. But I replay those words over in my head.

Pregnant four times? That's not right. There are only three of us. I'm not going to correct her though. I don't want it to trigger anything if that was just a lapse in words.

Instead, I take the moment to look at two of the women most important to me in this world. I can usually keep my emotions together, but seeing this before me? It's a struggle to keep the tears at bay.

With my schedule, I don't get here too often. Hell, probably the next time I see her will be after the baby is born.

Will she remember then what we told her today? Will she know me? Or Bethany?

I wish I knew. But at least today, we all get this. We get to enjoy this moment together.

I'll take that as a win.

"ARE we just not going to talk about the truth bomb your mom dropped today... Richard?"

I waited until we were back in our hotel room before I asked Davis... I mean, Richard, to talk to me about the little tidbit of information his mother disclosed.

Now that we are here, he has nowhere to run.

After months of dancing around the topic, I'm finally going to know the true story behind his name.

Oh, I wish Sadie could be here for this one.

"You think you have jokes," he says, coming up behind me and putting his arms around my waist as I take my earrings out at the bathroom vanity. "And here I thought you were a nice girl. A southern lady. Who knew you would manipulate my sweet mother into telling you my secrets?"

"I did no such thing." I gasp, turning around so I'm now leaning against the bathroom counter and touching his hard chest. His chest that feels darn good against me. "She offered that information freely. I can't help that I'm such an easy and appealing person to talk to."

"Easy and appealing, huh?" he says, his mouth attacking my neck in a swarm of sucks and kisses that make my body go weak. "Actually, this dress makes things very easy. And I find you very appealing."

"You can't get out of this conversation through sex," I say, though not with as much resolve as I would have liked. I mean, his tongue is tracing circles on my neck that is sending a straight shot to my core.

"Fine," he grumbles, picking me up and sitting me on the counter. "What do you want to know?"

The giddiness in my voice can't be hidden. "You're seriously going to let me ask?"

"You can ask three questions about it. And you can't tell Sadie because I want free food from her. Then I'm getting you naked. Choose wisely. And hurry."

He still tries to distract me by bringing his finger up the side of my leg and traveling underneath my dress. I have found that sundresses are a savior for a pregnant woman in the summer. They are flowy, comfortable, and don't make me feel like I'm roasting all the time.

It's also easy access for Davis—I mean, Richard, or Dick... oh, I like the sound of Dick. Pregnancy brain is off the charts real. Regardless, the easy access is an added benefit for both of us.

"Quit trying to distract me," I say, doing my best to ignore his traveling hand. "Why don't you go by Richard?"

He lets out a sigh and his fingers stop searching. I'd be more upset if I wasn't about to get the answers I've been wondering since the day we met.

"My grandfather's name was Richard. My mother named me after him. And she hated it when I tried to go by Ricky or Rick. I even tried Richie. That made it for a few months before my teacher called me that when she sent a note home and I got grounded for a month. Mom said she gave me that name to honor her father, and that I was to respect it. So, much to my dismay, I was Richard. She is also the only person on this Earth who calls me that."

"Okay," I say, still a little confused by the secrecy of this all. "So you have an old-fashioned name. Is that a reason to not go by it?"

"You try being an eight-year-old kid whose jackass classmate figured out that Richard is a form of the name Dick."

I laugh, because hello, was just thinking about Dick, but there is more. I can tell. "What are you not telling me? Is your name unfortunate? Yes. Is it easy access for bullies? Also, yes. But this seems all a bit extreme. What's the scoop, sir?"

Davis looks up at the ceiling and lets out a breath before meeting my eyes again. "I just want you to know. You are the only one besides my mother and sisters who are about to know this."

I take my finger and make a cross over my heart. "Your secret is safe with me."

"The first name would have been bad, but I could have gotten through it," he says, taking another breath before continuing. "But then there was also our last name. That... that was the dagger, the literal sword that I could not fall on."

I beg him with my eyes to go on. "What is it? You can't just leave me hanging like that."

He smiles. "You've already asked three questions."

"I'll make it worth your while later if I get a few extra," I say seductively, letting my hand fall down and grazing his dick.

He lets out a moan. "You play dirty."

"I learned from the best. Now, spill it."

"Fine," he says begrudgingly. "My legal last name now is Davis. It was my middle name. When we fill out the birth certificate, our baby, if we agree to it, will have the last name of Davis. It was legally changed to that the day I turned eighteen."

"Should I ask from what or why first?"

"Because," he says, pulling me a little closer, "for one, it is the worst last name to have in the history of last names. I was teased mercilessly for it. And it was Mitch's name. His actions might have turned me into the man I am today, but he doesn't deserve to have his name carried on. So the day I could, I stopped it. I would have changed my first name, too, but I couldn't do that to my mother, so I opted to just go by my initial and given middle name, which is now my last name. Hence, Davis."

I stare at him, not believing he is keeping me in suspense. "Are you not going to tell me? I'm dying over here."

He laughs. "You promise you will not tell anyone? Not even Sadie."

I cross my heart again. "Scout's honor. Now tell me."

I don't know what I'm expecting. But what comes out of his mouth next? I could have had a hundred years to mentally prep for this, and I still wouldn't have been ready.

"Semen."

I shake my head a little.

Did he just say?

"Excuse me?"

"Yup. My name growing up was Richard, aka Dick Semen."

I try not to. I summon all the power I have, and even some from the baby, to not laugh.

But it's no use. I laugh. I laugh so hard I almost pee my pants.

I'm having a baby with Dick Semen.

"Oh, you think that's funny?" he asks, scooping me off the counter. "I'll show you funny."

Before I know it, we are landing in the center of the king-size bed and his mouth is on mine. If he wanted to get me to quit laughing, this is definitely the way to do it.

"You want funny, huh?" he says, sliding down the strap of my sundress. "Is it funny when I do this?"

His mouth moves down my neck, over the tops of my breasts, before he pushes my bra down, freeing my breasts that are larger than they have ever been in my life.

"Not funny." I moan as he takes one nipple in his mouth and twists the other with his fingers. In my first trimester, they were so swollen I couldn't bear him touching them. But now? I'm craving his mouth on them. I need him there. He switches it up and puts his mouth on the other, and I've all but forgotten the admission of his name and even what my own name is.

He releases my nipple and leaves me panting on the bed, half-dressed and turned on as well. "If that's not funny, then how about this?"

He sits me up, bringing me on his lap as he unsnaps my bra and lifts my dress over my head. I think once I'm undressed he's going to continue whatever magical thing he was doing to me with his mouth, but instead, he just lays me down, stripping me of my panties, and runs his hand across my stomach before he gets off the bed.

"You think this is funny?" he asks, taking his shirt off over his head with one motion.

"No," I say breathlessly.

"How about this?" Next to go are his shorts, showing his hard cock that is begging to be released from his black boxer briefs.

I shake my head. It's hard to find words right now as I watch this magnificent man strip for me.

"Maybe this?" he asks, stripping off his briefs, freeing his perfect cock.

"No," I barely say as my hand begins traveling to my center that's begging for any kind of release.

"Well, then maybe this?"

He slowly crawls into bed, taking my hand that was just rubbing my clit and sucking on my two fingers.

Holy hell, that's hot.

"Davis," I moan, shocked I can find words at this point I'm so turned on.

"Shh," he says, covering his mouth with mine in a kiss that is pure fire and lust. "No more talking."

I couldn't talk anymore if I tried. All I do is feel as he enters me, his cock filling me in a way only he can. His thrusts are fast and hard and perfect. I don't know how every time he knows what I need, but he does. The man can read my body better than I can, which is evident by the orgasm he gives me in a matter of minutes.

"Davis!" I yell, hoping that the walls in this hotel are a little soundproof.

He doesn't let me recover from the orgasm. Instead, he scoops me up under my back and brings me to where I'm sitting on his lap. Our eyes are locked on each other as I ride him, taking from him everything I want and everything he will give me.

"You're mine," he says, holding me still as he drives into me. "Forever."

"Forever," I repeat as I fall apart again, only this time he's right with me. I grab on to his shoulders, burying my face in his neck as my orgasm rolls through me. Unable to hold us up anymore, Davis collapses on the bed with me lying on top of him.

We don't say anything for a few minutes. I revel in feeling his heartbeat beneath me and get lost in the feel of his fingers tracing my skin.

This man. I've learned so much about him on this trip. And not just the reveal of his name. I see him as a son. As a brother.

As an uncle. As the provider he has become. I see the love he has to give and the love he has for his family.

I realize that I'm one thousand percent, head over heels, crazy in love with this man.

"I love you," I say, not able to hold the words in any longer. "I love you so much."

His fingers stop, and for a second, I'm nervous that I should have kept my mouth shut. Is this like the other times? When I would think there is more to a relationship than there is? Does he not feel the same about me?

But before my brain can go down too many dark alleys, he lifts my chin so I'm looking in his eyes. And all I see is nothing short of love.

"I love you so much," he says, leaning forward and kissing me deeply. "You're it for me, Bethany Hall."

I don't know how we got here. Lord knows, we didn't take the conventional route, but at this moment, I don't want to be anywhere else.

WHEN I STARTED GETTING interested in finances and stocks, real estate never really captivated my interest. The thrill of watching stocks go up and down? That's exciting. Betting on the housing market? Not so much.

Now, I can tell you everything there is to know about the Nashville real estate market. I'm also an accomplished bluffer.

It's driving Ken the skeezy real estate agent insane.

"It's going to go fast. It will likely sell for seven-fifty K," Ken says in his best used car salesman voice. "If you want it, you better make a quick offer."

"I don't know," I say, pretending to check out a nonexistent fault in the open-concept first floor. "We looked at a similar one two streets over that's just sold for six seventy-five. And that had more square footage."

"Well," the agent stutters, trying to think of a reason, "this one has newer appliances. State of the art."

I don't get to make a comeback to him because at that moment, Bethany comes rushing into my arms. "Did you see the kitchen? And the deck? Imagine how many parties we can throw!"

I laugh and pull her aside to the office that sits just to the right of the entryway. I don't want Ken, the realtor who is hosting the open house today, to know that by far, this is the best house we've seen. And by the look in Bethany's eye, this is her favorite as well.

Once we decided on where to look, it was full steam ahead. This neighborhood will add a commute for both of us to work, but it's going to be worth it. This house is move-in ready, never lived in, and ten minutes from Mike and Helen.

We've looked at our fair share so far. One was too small. The other was way overpriced. Another we liked, but it needed too much work, and with being halfway along with the pregnancy and training camp opening soon, we don't have time to fix up a house.

But this house? This house has the layout she wants, the number of rooms I want, and comes at a price tag we are more than comfortable with.

And it has a pool. With a fence. I would pay all the money in the world to have access to Bethany wearing a bikini every day in the summer, pregnant or not.

"What do you think?" she asks, looking around the room that I envision to be an office. "It's perfect, right?"

I pull her into my arms before giving her a quick kiss. She's so damn adorable when she's this excited. "I do. It has everything we need."

I don't know why at this moment it hits me that this comment would have scared the absolute piss out of me just a few months ago. Buying a house? Putting down roots? Those were things for some other guy. Some guy who didn't have another family who relied on him.

Now? Especially after visiting Mom, Abby, and Sara? I realize what an idiot I was. I can have it all. I can help them and still have love and happiness of my own.

All it took was the right woman to show me that.

"Want to see where I think the nursery should go?" she says, grabbing my hand and leading me out of the office.

"I have a feeling you're going to show me no matter what," I say, though I notice as we climb the stairs that Ken is talking to another couple in the living room. "If we want to put an offer in, I'd like to do it before we leave. I don't want to lose this place."

I send a text message to my realtor, letting him know that I'll be in touch with him soon, as Bethany yanks my arm and pulls me into a bedroom.

One that looks awfully big to be a nursery.

"This is where you want the nursery to go?" I say in confusion as I look around the room that is obviously the master suite.

"No," she says before she literally jumps into my arms and starts kissing me. "This is going to be our bedroom."

"Princess," I say when I can catch my breath. "What are you doing?"

She doesn't answer me. Instead, she takes the opportunity to start rubbing her pussy against my growing cock as she continues to kiss the life out of me.

I love second-trimester Bethany.

I mean, I love all Bethanys. I meant what I told her in Pennsylvania and every day since. But second-trimester Bethany? The one who loves sex almost as much as Flaming Hot Cheetos, is horny all the time and is happy about everything? I'd like to keep her.

"Bethany," I say, already hating myself for what I'm about to say next. "This house is going to be ours. Trust me on that. We will have plenty of time to break it in. There are other people here. We should get going."

She gives me a pouty lip before unwrapping her legs from around me. But just as I think we're going to leave the room, she takes my hand and yanks me toward a closet, shutting the door behind us.

"What are you…"

I can't even finish the sentence because I realize Bethany is on her knees in front of me, undoing the zipper to my jeans.

"This is going to be our house," she says, stroking my cock. "And I love that you are doing this for me. For us. And I want to show my gratitude."

I can't answer before she takes me fully in her mouth. Usually, she is gentle when she and I have done this. Hesitant, even. But now? This woman is determined to give me the best blow job of my life.

And she's succeeding. Her hand and mouth are working in tandem, and that is already making my balls tight. And when she goes to lick the underside of my cock, I almost lose it right there and then.

"Fuck," I groan, hoping my voice isn't too loud. Then again, maybe if they hear us, then they will leave, and the house will be ours.

"Don't hold back on me," she says, still working me with her hand. "I want you to come in my mouth."

Jesus tap dancing Christ.

I have never come in her mouth. Then again, most of the time, when she goes down on me, it's before we have sex, and I know I'm going to finish inside her. Now just the thought of her swallowing me does me in.

"Bethany… shit!"

I don't know how loud I yell that as I release into her mouth. And I honestly don't care. I just got the best blow job of my life from the mother of my unborn child in a house we haven't bought yet while there are people in the other room.

There is nothing hotter than that.

She slowly releases me from her mouth, and I hurry and help her off her knees before I take care of my... situation.

"Where did that come from?"

She giggles, and even in the dark, I can tell she's doing her best to fix her hair. "I wanted to break in this house correctly."

I kiss her nose as I finish tucking my semi-hard cock back into my pants. "You know I'm never going to be able to look at this closet without thinking about this."

"Good," she says, opening the door. "Maybe that will be our sneak away spot once the baby is born."

We both laugh as we leave the closet but stop in our tracks as soon as we see the scene in front of us.

Ken, the realtor, and the couple I noticed downstairs, both staring at us with horrified looks on their faces.

"What are you doing?" Ken says, though if he really looked at us, he would absolutely know what we are doing. I look at Bethany, whose hair gives away that something was going on in the closet. That and she hasn't stopped giggling since we exited the closet. I'm guessing my face has the smile that every man who has ever gotten a phenomenal blow job knows.

Judging by the look on Ken's face, he's never received a blow job from a woman in a closet. Or maybe ever.

"Excuse me!" Ken yells, now annoyed with us. "I asked you what you were doing."

I laugh and pull Bethany to me. "I'd like to put in an offer on this house. How does cash sound?"

CHAPTER 32
BETHANY

I THINK I've handled pregnancy quite well now that I'm through my first twenty weeks.

I battled and conquered the morning sickness. I've adjusted my diet and made sure that I'm taking all my vitamins. I even gave up Diet Coke.

And I really love Diet Coke. I love it more than my current pregnancy craving, peanut butter and pickle sandwiches.

Don't knock it till you've tried it.

That being said...

Shit! Shit! Shit!

Fuck! Fuck! Fuck!

Fuck! Shit! Dammit all to hell!

There, I feel better.

Except I don't.

It's why I'm standing on Sadie's doorstep banging on her door to let me in. I need to figure out what to do, and she drew the short straw to help me fix this.

"What in the—?" Sadie asks as she opens the door. "Bethany? What are you—"

I don't give her a chance to finish the sentence as I barge

into the condo and unceremoniously flop onto the couch and scream into the pillows.

"I'm going to go get you some water. Though I wish I could get you something stronger."

Same, sis. Same.

I make myself sit up and take a breath. I'm freaking out over nothing. The baby is healthy. The baby is strong. Everything on the ultrasound was perfect.

Except now I know a secret I'm not supposed to know, and I don't know how to handle that.

Hence, the freak-out.

"Okay, what the hell is going on?" Sadie asks, handing me a glass of water before taking a seat next to me on her sectional. "Is everything okay with the baby?"

I nod. "Yes. I just came from my twenty-week check. Everything is great."

"Then, what's the problem? And where is Davis?"

Oh, Davis. If Davis was with me at this appointment, none of this would be an issue.

Yes! This is all his fault. He doesn't get sex for a week!

Oh, who am I kidding. I feel so guilty right now, I'll probably give him a blow job before and after dinner. Hell, maybe even while he's eating dinner.

"We had a scheduling mix-up between the appointment and the coaches' meetings he had today," I say, starting to calm down a bit. "So, I went to the appointment alone."

"Wasn't today the day you were going to find out the sex?"

I nod, taking a big gulp of water. "Yes. But I told him... I promised him I wouldn't find out. That we would do it together. So, I was all prepared to tell Dr. Stewart to put the results in a little envelope and we would open it up together tonight."

"I'm guessing that didn't happen."

I shake my head. "Dr. Stewart got called in for an emergency c-section, so the nurse practitioner saw me."

Sadie's eyes grow large. "Oh, no…"

"Oh, yes."

"You know?"

"I know."

I don't know why I didn't tell the nurse from the moment she stepped into the room that the father wasn't here, and I didn't want to know the gender without him. I could have said that. I should have said that. But we got to talking—turns out she gets her hair done at the salon by one of my best stylist friends—and next thing I know, she's squirting the gel onto my stomach.

Looking back, I also could have told her right then, too. But at that point, we began talking about hair styles that need to go away. If you ever want to distract me, bring up this topic. I could go on for hours.

Next thing I know, she's saying the words I'll never forget.

"Bethany, she looks great!"

And that's how I found out Davis and I are having a little girl.

"No!" Sadie gasps as I deliver the not-so-funny punch line.

"Yup," I say in defeat. "We're having a girl. You were right."

"Screw me being right. I can't believe she slipped like that! And Davis… oh hell, how are you going to tell him!"

I collapse back into the sectional in defeat. "That, my dear sister, is the million-dollar question."

I hate it. I hate this. He didn't get to be there for the first appointment when I found out I was pregnant. I have wondered from time to time what his reaction would have been. I thought that I could make that up to him by being there when we found out the gender.

I pictured it a dozen times. Him sitting next to me, holding my hand as we watch our baby on the screen. Then, the doctor would do her thing and ask us if we wanted to know. We say yes, but not now. We have her put it in an envelope so we could find out later at home.

Then, later, we would open it together and celebrate whether or not we were having a baby girl or boy. We'd profess our love for each other and this child and have a perfect night celebrating.

But no. None of that can happen now.

Because Nurse Nancy ruined it.

"What if you pretend you don't know," Sadie says. "Make another appointment, and then when the doctor reveals the gender, you act super surprised. Boom, it's like today never happened!"

"I thought of that," I say defeatedly. "Except I'm a horrible liar around him. I can't even lie about eating the last cookie. He'd know immediately."

"Hmm," Sadie mutters. "And we agreed to not have a gender reveal party. Though we are in a different situation, I don't think we've resorted to that yet."

"No we have not," I say. "I'm not letting the next people to know the gender of my baby be a bakery or a balloon company."

We both sit in silence for a few minutes. I know I'm being dramatic about this. I know I could just wait for him to come home tonight, sit him on the couch and tell him what happened. I'm sure he would understand. He'd be a little upset, but at the end of the day, he is just going to be happy that we have a healthy baby girl who's planning on making her way into this world at the end of November.

But then my heart hurts that he doesn't get a moment. I want to give him that moment.

"I got it!"

Sadie's exclamation makes me jump a little. "Good Lord, woman, you scared the pee out of me. Which isn't hard to do these days."

"I'm sorry, but I have an idea. Though it is a little dramatic and over the top."

I raise an eyebrow to her. "I thought I was the over-the-top, dramatic sister."

"You are. I guess you're rubbing off on me."

I laugh, grateful that I can laugh about something right now.

"What's this plan?"

Sadie gets a devilish smile on her face. "You want to give Davis a moment? I can make it happen. But you need to give me a few days."

My eyes go wide. "A few days!"

She grabs my hand and gives me a squeeze. "Yes. Put on your best lying face and be willing to distract that man with sex for forty-eight hours. But I promise you, it will be worth it."

"RUN IT AGAIN!"

I don't know how many times I've yelled that today since practice started. I know it's about ten times too many for a quarterback who should already know the playbook, yet he's the one fucking up every time.

This is our second day of camp. We don't have pads on yet, but I'm liking what I'm seeing for the most part.

The offensive line looks great. Cole is stepping up as a leader, and if you don't have a good line, you don't have a good offense. The running backs are doing everything I have asked of them. The receivers are running good routes.

They just can't catch. And that's not their fault. Can't catch a ball that is five yards off the mark.

"What the fuck is his problem?" I mutter as Hunter and I watch another drill break down because Bryce goes the wrong way.

"I can't believe he looks this bad," Hunter says. "The press is going to eat him alive."

I look over to the media gallery that gets to watch the morning session of practice and can hear the cameras click with every movement—correction, every wrong movement—Bryce makes.

Fan-fucking-tastic.

"Cole said it had something to do with a girl. Know anything about that?"

Hunter shakes his head. "Last year, when he and I talked, he wasn't specific, though I had a feeling. But this? This is nothing like last year. Last year he looked lost. This year he looks like he doesn't give a fuck. He has another few days like today and we need to be looking at other options for quarterback. I benched him last year, and I'll do it again. I can't wait around for him to get his head out of his ass."

I let out a defeated breath as Hunter signals for the players to huddle up and head to the locker room for their lunch break.

"Bryce!" I yell, wanting to catch him before he heads inside. He lazily jogs to me, which pisses me off more than any missed throw he just made.

"Care to tell me what all that was?" I ask as discreetly as possible as there are still some players and media outside.

"Not my fault they weren't where I put the ball," he says in a cocky tone. "New guys need to figure me out."

It takes every ounce of strength I have not to ring this kid's fucking neck. "You didn't run one drill right. Now that I'm up close to you, I can tell you're hungover. What the fuck is wrong with you? And if you tell me nothing, I swear to God..."

"It's not your problem, and quit trying to figure me out," he says in a defensive tone as he turns away from me.

I grab his shirt before he can walk away. "Not a fucking chance. You're benched for the rest of the day. You come to my camp again hungover and lazy, you can find yourself a new team."

He just stares at me before he starts laughing. "You think

you can do that? My contract is worth more than yours and half the team's combined. You can't do anything to me."

"Try me," I say, getting in his face. "Now get the fuck out of here. I don't want to see your face for the rest of the day."

Bryce rolls his eyes but stomps toward the locker room. I follow him to make sure he doesn't cause a scene in the locker room as he packs up his stuff. Luckily, he doesn't. He quickly changes, grabs his bags, and storms out of the locker room. As I watch it unfold, I catch Cole's eye as he watches his best friend leave without a word. He looks to where Bryce had been standing, then back to me before giving me a slow nod.

He gets it. He doesn't like it, but he gets it.

Once I know Bryce is gone, I make my way back to my office, thankful for a few hours of quiet time. If I could get everything figured out with Bryce, my life would be just about perfect. The coaching staff with Hunter at the helm is clicking better than any staff I've worked with. Every player, save for Bryce, came to camp in shape, focused, and hungry. We have a favorable schedule this year, so it's playoffs or bust.

Then there is my personal life. Bethany and I closed on the house quickly. I have a feeling real estate Ken wanted to be rid of us as fast as possible. We have everything moved, unpacked, and we are settling into our new life together.

And soon we will find out if we are having a boy or a girl. I hate that I couldn't be at her appointment the other day, but I know the wait will be worth it.

It also doesn't hurt that second-trimester Bethany is still here, which means that she is always ready. Whenever. Wherever.

I never thought I'd say that my dick is tired, but it is. It's a good problem to have.

I don't even realize that I've nodded off at my desk until I hear a banging on my office door. I shoot up to see Hunter standing there, laughing his ass off.

"Bethany wearing you out?" he teases, tossing me a pre-wrapped sandwich that we have catered for lunch each day of camp.

"In the best way possible," I say, digging into the turkey and cheese before we have to go back onto the field.

"I must say, this looks good on you," Hunter says, taking a seat across from me.

"What's that?"

"Happiness."

I let that sink in. While he's one hundred percent right, I can't let him know that.

"Who says I wasn't happy last year? You've known me going on two years and you think you know everything that is the book of Davis?"

Hunter laughs. "No, you asshole. But I can tell when someone is putting on a show. I did it for most of my life, so people didn't know about the real relationship between me and my dad. That always happy-go-lucky guy front you put on? The one who pretended he didn't have a care in the world? I knew at least half of it was bullshit. But now? Seeing you with Bethany? The way you talk about her and the baby? That, my friend, is true happiness. And I'm glad you've found it."

Well, damn, maybe he really does know me.

Close friends aren't something I had growing up. Sure, I had buddies I ate lunch with or played ball with, but no one who really knew me. Honestly, the closest friend I had was Abby. In college, I still kept people at arm's length. It was all I knew how to do at that point.

Now? Now I have family on multiple levels. I have friends who I can call on when I need it.

He's right. I am happy.

"All right, enough of this mushy shit," I say, crumbling the sandwich wrapper and tossing it in the trash. "Don't we have football to coach?"

Hunter laughs and gives my back a slap as we walk out of the offices and toward the practice field.

Everything seems normal until we step outside, though. Normally, there is rap and heavy rock music blaring from the practice field speakers. Instead, I hear a ballad, and I'm pretty sure it's one of the Motown songs my mom used to listen to. The one about having sunshine on a cloudy day.

I take another few steps onto the field, confused as ever. When I get a full view, I see the team doing their normal warm-up routine. Only it's what they are wearing that is throwing me off. They each have on their normal practice jerseys and shorts. However, each of them has a pink mesh vest over top.

What in the actual fuck?

The strength and conditioning coach who runs warm-ups blows his whistle and every player drops to the ground. I have to blink my eyes to make sure that I'm seeing what I think I'm seeing.

Standing in the middle of my professional football team is Bethany, wearing a pink dress and holding something in her hands.

I run over to her, paying no attention to anyone around me. "What are you doing here?"

She laughs nervously. "I wanted to give you your moment."

"My moment?" I say confused. "What do you mean?"

"The other day, at my appointment..." Bethany trails off, fighting back tears, though I still don't know why she's crying. "The nurse accidentally told me what we were having. And you weren't there, and I feel terrible about it. I should have told her. I should have stopped her."

She takes a breath, and I take the opportunity to wipe away a tear from her cheek. "It's okay. But why didn't you tell me that night?"

Another tear gets loose. "Because I felt horrible. And I know we said no big gender reveals, but you deserve to have a moment you'll never forget. I want to give you another first."

Now it's my turn to get choked up. I look around again. All of the players wearing pink have stopped stretching and are now looking at us. I listen a little close to the song that is still playing. I catch Hunter's eye, who is standing next to Sadie, who looks like she is crying.

"Are you saying?"

My question trails off and she nods. "I am."

"We're having a girl?"

She nods again. "Congratulations, Daddy. We're having a girl."

Applause roars from the players and coaches as I pick Bethany up and twirl her around, kissing the life out of her.

A girl. I'm having a little girl.

The next several minutes are a mixture of back slaps, congratulations, and sneaking a few moments with Bethany when I can. When the scene calms down, I pull her to the sideline where Hunter and Sadie are standing, both with conspiratorial looks in their eyes.

"You," I say, pointing to both of them. "This has the two of you written all over it."

Sadie just shrugs. "My sister needed my help, Reginald. And I figured this would be the best way for you to find out and not be mad at the nurse who spilled the beans."

I laugh. "You're right. And my name is not Reginald. Isn't that right, Bethany?"

Sadie's eyes go wide as she shoots a look to Bethany. "You know! And you haven't told me! I helped you coordinate this whole thing, and you've been keeping this from me! How dare you!"

The girls walk off with Sadie still going on about sisterhood bonds trumping baby daddies. All Hunter and I can do is laugh.

"You're right," I say.

"About what?"

"Happiness. I am. I've never been happier in my entire life."

Davis: When I get home, you better be waiting for me naked in bed.

I READ THE TEXT AGAIN, a little bounce to my step as I climb the stairs to our bedroom.

Our bedroom.

I still can't believe everything that has happened in such a short amount of time. At this point last year, I didn't even know who this man was. Heck, Sadie and Hunter hadn't even come out publicly as a couple. I was still going out on bad date after bad date, and Davis... well, I really don't want to think about what he was doing.

Now? We have a baby due in about four months. We have a house that I can see myself and Davis growing old and raising a family under its roof. I've found a man who loves me the way I've always wanted to be loved and whom I love equally in return.

In no way did I do this in the order I thought it needed to be done. First comes love, then comes marriage and all of that. But who's to say what is the right order? At the end of the day, isn't the result all that matters? I have the man of my dreams, a baby girl on the way, a career I love, and a house we plan on making a home. If I had to go through every bad date, every guy who ghosted me and do this all over again in the wrong order to get here? I'd do it again in a heartbeat.

I now understand the line from *Steel Magnolias* about wanting thirty minutes of wonderful rather than a lifetime of nothing special. I never truly understood that until now. But this. This is what Shelby meant. This is the wonderful. And I'll take as many minutes as I can get.

> Davis: I will be home in ten minutes. This is your warning.

After today's grand announcement of the gender of our baby, Davis unfortunately couldn't come home with me right away to celebrate. Something about limited practice time and the league rules. All of that confuses me.

However, he did promise that he would make it up to me the second he got home. And by the tone of these text messages, I'm not going to be disappointed.

I hurry and strip the sundress over my head, quickly disposing of my bra and panties as well. As I make my way to our bed, I catch my reflection in the full-length mirror by our closet.

Just in the past week or so, my baby bump has gone from "is she pregnant or gaining weight?" to "Yup, she's preggo." I've always been slender—being five foot seven helps narrow me out—so this ball that's sitting in my belly right now is pretty obvious.

What's it going to look like in a few weeks? A month? Am I going to have one of those bellies that just looks like a beach ball took residence in my body?

"You are fucking stunning."

I look up and see Davis standing in the doorway, looking at me with pure desire in his eyes.

"I didn't hear you come in," I say, making my way toward the bed.

"No," he says as he begins to walk to me. "Stay right there."

I can't take my eyes off of him as he slowly walks toward me. Though his eyes are on nothing but my stomach.

He obviously knows that my bump has started to show. But that's over clothes or under covers when the lights are off. This? In the daylight with not a scrap of clothes on my body? This is the most naked I've ever felt in front of a man before.

"Do you know how sexy you are right now?" he says, standing behind me and wrapping his arms so his hands are sitting on my bump.

I meet his eyes in the mirror and almost melt from the intensity of his gaze. "I don't."

I don't get an answer right away. I don't complain though. He's currently kissing the top of my shoulder, traveling up to my neck, and slowly moving his fingers up and down the sides of my body. I can feel myself getting wetter by the second.

"You have always been sexy to me," he says, his fingers still exploring my naked body, one hand tracing my bump as he takes hold of one of my breasts. "I remember that first night I saw you, the physical attraction I felt for you was instant. But here? Now? Seeing you carrying our child? You are, without a doubt, the sexiest woman I have ever laid eyes on. And you are all mine."

He spins me around and our mouths meet in perfect unison. As my fingers slide through his hair and his hands pull me into him, I can only hope that this part of us never wavers. That even after a child, and whatever else the future has in store for us, that we always have this.

The passion. The desire.

The love.

"Now, princess, I believe I told you to be naked in bed waiting for me. And while this isn't a bad view to come home to, there are things I plan to do that will be much better for you if they are done lying down."

I giggle as Davis scoops me up and carries me the few steps to our bed.

"Why do you call me that? And no more of this 'it's my secret' crap."

He lets out a small laugh as his fingers travel down my body, headed straight to my center.

"The first night we met. When you stepped out of the car, the way the sunlight radiated from you, it looked like you were wearing a crown. That, and you were the most beautiful woman I had ever laid eyes on."

My eyes go wide at his admission. I was *not* expecting that.

"I thought you were making fun of me," I say a bit shyly. "I thought it was because I always had my hair done, or because I wear so many skirts. That's why I didn't like it."

"Never," he says, his eyes locked onto mine. "From the moment I met you, I knew you were someone different. Someone special. It might have taken me a while to realize it, but you're not just my princess. You're my queen. My love. The woman who is about to give me a baby girl. You're my forever, Bethany."

His lips are on mine before I have a chance to respond, which is fine by me because he has left me thoroughly and utterly speechless. And a tad bit emotional.

Our tongues are tangled in a perfect symphony, and his fingers have found their way to my opening, slowly entering me and beginning to explore. I slowly reach down and slide off his pants, taking his cock into my hand, slowly stroking it, loving the feel of his hardness against my skin.

"I want you inside me," I say, not being able to stand any more of his fingers teasing me.

"Your wish is my command."

He strips off the rest of his clothes and before he can position me in the way he wants to, I push his shoulders down and swing my leg over his body, seating myself on top of him. By the look in his eye, this was a good decision on my part.

I lean forward to align myself, my heavy breasts dangling in front of his face. He takes full advantage of the position, taking one in his hand and bringing it to his mouth. The sensation of his lips around my nipple feels so good, I can't help but slowly rub my pussy on his cock.

"Quit teasing," he groans, taking my ass in both hands and lifting me up. "Ride me."

He takes his cock and lines us up, allowing me to sit back and feel every inch of him enter me. My hands go to his chest as I slowly find my rhythm, loving not only the way he fills me but the look in his eyes.

"So goddamn beautiful," he says, taking my hips and slowly beginning to move me faster. "I could watch you all day."

His words only spur me on. Before I know it, my pace is quickening. His thrusts are meeting mine, and by the look on his face, he is as close as I am to finding release.

"Yes," I say, loving how even though I am on top, right now, he's in complete control. "So close."

He doesn't say another word. Instead, he flips me over, somehow never leaving me, and begins rapidly pumping into me. His finger comes to my clit, and with just one flick, I'm done for.

"Davis!"

Thank goodness we don't have any close neighbors,

because I'm sure they would have heard me clear as day. If they didn't, they surely would have heard him seconds later.

"Fuck. Bethany. Fuck!"

Neither of us moves for a long time after we come down from another set of earth-shattering orgasms. I actually might have fallen asleep when I feel Davis's fingers start to trace my sides.

"You know," he says quietly, his fingers still exploring, "I pictured something like this once."

"Hm?" I ask, my voice heavy with sleep.

"Right before you called it off. I pictured you in my bed. I wondered what it would be like to wake up with you. For us to have lazy days on the couch, and nights where we couldn't keep our hands off of each other."

I turn toward him. "When was this?"

He kisses me gently before answering. "The night you told me we were done."

"Oh, really?"

"Yeah," he says, now a bit confused. "Why is that so funny?"

I lean in for a deeper kiss, one which he obliges. "Because that night, I had the same thoughts. That was the night I knew my feelings had grown. And I had to leave you before you could hurt me."

"Are you serious?"

I nod. "Funny how things work, huh?"

I'm greeted with another kiss. This one more intense. "I'd leave you all over again if it's how I end up here."

CHAPTER 35

DAVIS

I REALLY THOUGHT I was doing fine.

I have not panicked once since Bethany said those few little words that changed my life forever. She might say I lost my mind when I asked her to marry me. That's still up for debate.

I didn't even freak-out the first time I heard the baby's heartbeat. That was a whole different feeling. I remember feeling shocked. Almost paralyzed when I heard that thumping. I knew Bethany was pregnant, but at the moment, it felt real. Yet, I didn't panic. I cried like a baby. But I didn't panic.

How do I know I didn't panic then? Because if that was panic, then what I'm doing right now is full-on hysteria. The racing of my heart? The shortness of breath? The feeling I have that the room is spinning and there's nothing I can do to stop it. This is panic.

The worst part is it came out of nowhere. One minute I'm fine, the next, I'm talking to Wes, our veteran tight end and father of three.

"Getting everything ready?" Wes asks as we leave the practice field.

"For sure. We're ready. Baby could come tomorrow and everything would be great."

Wes laughs. "I wish I was as confident as you are before my first. Hell, I was so nervous putting together the crib it took me a week. I was so scared I was going to screw something into the wrong hole and that it would break the second we put the baby in it."

Oh shit. The crib. "Well, we still have to get that."

"Did you two decide on a stroller? Personally, I like the travel ones. Easier for transporting."

"Oh... We... We haven't settled on one yet."

"Oh," he says, a bit surprised. "Well, if you need any help, let me know. I also know a guy who started this line of baby carriers for men..."

I have no idea what the fuck else Wes said. All I knew was at that moment, I might have set up my insurance to cover the baby and started her college fund, but I forgot to buy a fucking stroller and a crib for her to sleep in.

"McAvoy!" I yell, charging toward Hunter's office. What kind of fucking father am I? How do I forget to buy a damn stroller and crib?

"What?" he asks, looking up from his pile of paperwork. "What the hell are you yelling about?"

"Are you doing anything important?"

"Just going over the scouting report. I know it's just preseason, but I like to be prepared. Why are you breathing heavy? Are you okay?"

"I'm fine. I'm not fine. Fuck. Just get your keys and let's go. We have shit to take care of."

———

"When you said, 'we have shit to take care of' this is not what I had in mind."

Hunter's remark comes as I stare at no less than thirty options of cribs at a store that is called Everything Baby. Felt like a good place to come to buy all the things that I forgot to get.

Some provider I am. If the baby comes tomorrow, she'll be sleeping on the floor.

That's a lie. I would be. Because I'm pretty sure Bethany would have kicked me out of bed and Baby Girl Davis would be on my side of the bed.

How have we not done any of this yet? We talked about it a few times. But first, we wanted to wait to find out the gender of the baby. Then training camp hit, and next thing we knew, any free time we had was spent unpacking boxes and getting the house settled. Now preseason is here, and pretty soon, games are going to start, and holy hell, I am not ready.

Well, that all ends today. My baby *will* have a place to sleep by the time the sun sets.

"Don't you think Bethany is going to want to pick some of this stuff out with you?" Hunter asks as I eye the seemingly endless amount of cribs in front of me. "I might not be a dad yet, but I at least know that Sadie would kill me if I did these things on my own."

"I'm sure she will like what I pick," I say, eyeing a white one with a better headboard than we have on our bed. "Plus, I know how she wants the nursery. I can get the changing table and the dressers and the nursing chair all today. How hard can this be?"

"How does she want the nursery?"

"Girly. Pink. Bows. I got this."

Hunter grabs me by the shoulder so I'm now looking at

him. "Are you listening to yourself? Are you really telling me that Bethany, the woman who has three pairs of shoes for every occasion, is going to be okay with you picking out your baby's entire nursery without her input?"

I hear what he's saying. He's right. But I can't leave here without something.

"I'm not ready," I admit, plopping down on a rocking chair that is the most uncomfortable thing I've ever sat on. I'm definitely *not* buying this.

"Talk to me," Hunter says, taking a seat next to me. "What happened today? I thought everything was okay?"

I let out a heavy sigh. "It was. Or so I thought. I thought I had everything ready. Then I talked to Wes."

"The man who just looks at his wife and gets her pregnant?"

I laugh. "Yeah. He was asking me pretty basic questions of things we were getting ready for, and we didn't have any of them done. It made me panic. It made me... I don't like to be unprepared."

Hunter slaps me on the back. "Dude. Cut yourself some slack. You still have more than two months before the baby gets here. You just moved into a house. You don't have to get it all done today."

"Except I do," I say, urgency coming in my voice. "You never know what's coming tomorrow."

Hunter raises an eyebrow at me. "What are you not telling me? Is everything okay with you two?"

I let out a breath. "Yeah. It's just... when I was growing up, one day my dad was there. The next day he was gone. Haven't heard from him since. I was thirteen."

"Fuck, man," Hunter says. "How come you never told me this?"

I shrug. "Not really one of my favorite subjects, you know?"

"Yeah," he says as he leans his elbows on his legs. "But what does that have to do with this? I know you. You aren't just going to one day leave. You would never leave Bethany hanging like that."

"I know," I say, standing up, pulling at my hair in frustration. "But I also know what it's like to be unprepared. The day before my dad left, we didn't have to worry about if we had enough money to cover groceries and utilities that month. We didn't have to worry about rationing food. Then, the next, we did. I had no idea what to do. I was unprepared. I vowed to myself that day I'd never be unprepared again. That I would make sure we were ready for anything, so my family didn't have to suffer. And here I am, a baby on the way and nothing ready for her. I just... I need to do this, Hunter. I need to feel like I did something to help prepare for this. For her. For Bethany."

Those words have been living in my brain for months now, I just wouldn't admit it. Now that I've said them out loud? I feel the weight lifted off my shoulders.

"All right then," Hunter says, standing up. "Let's get my niece a crib."

"OH, yeah. Right there. That's the stuff. Yes. Yes!"

"Mom!" I yell, scaring the very nice woman who is currently buffing my feet. "Can you please not make sex noises when you're getting a pedicure?"

"But it feels good," she defends, turning her attention back to the magazine she's reading. "I can't help it if I vocalize when I'm feeling good."

"Don't remind me," I say under my breath as Sadie tries not to crack up in the seat next to mine.

Pedicure day sounded like a great idea two hours ago. Now that I'm having flashbacks to the day I heard Mom and Mike having sex? Not so much.

Mom, Sadie, and I used to do this all the time. Not at first, though. Sadie and I are the same age and were even in the same class in school, but I wouldn't have considered us close. We had nothing in common and no mutual friends. We didn't hate each other, we really just didn't know each other.

I remember the first time the four of us got together when Mike and Mom were dating. We just sat there staring at each other with nothing to talk about. Mom and I were the definitions of girly girls, and Sadie was a tomboy who was raised by Mike the sports fan.

Then one day Mom took Sadie and me to get our nails done. For the two of us, this was a semi-regular outing. For Sadie? It was a first. And that was when we found out that there was a little bit of "girl" in that tomboy.

Since then, we try to go every few months. And since my feet are starting to swell in ways I didn't know feet could swell, and it's getting harder each day to reach my toes, Mom thought lunch and pedicures were what the doctor ordered.

I'll never turn down lunch and pedis.

"So, enough about Helen's sex noises. Let's talk names," Sadie says.

"I told you, I'm not telling you Davis's name. You have to find it out on your own."

"Whatever," she says, waving me off. "I'm talking about baby names. What are you thinking?"

"Oh! I really love Gretchen," my mom says. "You know you were almost a Gretchen."

Sadie and I look at each other and give each other a gagging look.

"What was that for?" Mom asks.

"Gretchen was the queen bitch of our high school," Sadie explains. "Bethany and I might not have been in the same circles back then, but that didn't mean we both didn't hate Gretchen."

"Fine," Mom says, a little defeat in her voice. "What is your suggestion then, Sadie?"

"You mean, what is about to be the name of my future niece because Bethany is going to love it so much and it's absolutely perfect?"

"Oh, really?" I ask, wondering when she had planned to tell me this amazing name. "Well, don't hold back, sis."

"Ready?" she asks, doing a little drumroll on her legs. "Magnolia."

I slouch a bit in disappointment. "That's your great name?"

"What?" Sadie yells a bit too loudly for a packed salon. "You love *Steel Magnolias*. It's a perfect name! You could call her Maggie. Or Nola. What is the matter with it? I thought I did so good!"

"I take it you haven't watched *Hart of Dixie* yet?" I ask. She shakes her head in confusion. "Watch two episodes. You'll know why. That character ruined that name for me."

"Fine," Sadie says defeated. "So, what have you and Davis talked about?"

"Honestly, we've vetoed more than we've put in the good column," I say, staring at my toes that are currently having a bright pink being painted on them. "We aren't fans of anything that starts with the same letter of our names. We don't want people to think we did that on purpose. I suggested Emma, but he wasn't a fan. He suggested Memphis, but then I asked him if he was going to be the one to eventually tell our daughter that her name is where she was conceived. He quickly put that idea into the no column."

Everyone gets a laugh out of that. "Hey, that could be your thing! Maybe all your children could have 'where they were conceived' names. If you have a boy and you're here, his name could be Nash. Or take a road trip to watch a Tennessee football game and he could be Knox. The possibilities are endless!"

"No, thank you," I say, slipping my flip-flops back on. "We'll find the perfect name. It will just take time."

We gather our things and tell Mom goodbye before Sadie takes me back to my house. Even though I told her I was more than capable of driving, she insisted on picking me up today. Though I think it was just an excuse for her to come to the house and try to snoop to see if she could find anything that signaled Davis's name.

She's never going to guess it.

I've been thinking so much recently about how much things have changed between Davis and me in such a short amount of time, but the same could be said for Sadie and me. After Mom and Mike got married, we got closer, but I still wouldn't have called us besties. Then, last year, Sadie needed an ear when she caught feelings for Hunter. I was there with an open ear and a bottle of wine. During that process, she became my best friend.

What if Hunter hadn't been hired as Fury's offensive coordinator? If he didn't get the job, he would have never met Sadie. They would have never fallen in love. Maybe she and I wouldn't have gotten as close as we are now? They wouldn't have set Davis and me up on a date.

I wouldn't be pregnant.

Crazy how one event can trigger so many things.

I'm pulled from my nostalgia as Sadie turns onto my street and something catches my eye from my driveway.

"What is Hunter's truck doing here?" Sadie asks as she pulls into the driveway. "I thought he and Davis were going to be at the facility all day?"

"I did too." I open up the garage door to see Davis's truck there as well. Now I'm really confused.

"Maybe they decided to work here?" I say, opening the door that goes from the garage and leads into our mudroom. "Change of scenery?"

Sadie and I aren't even two steps inside the house when we hear a loud crash come from upstairs, followed by the loudest yelling of the word *fuck* I've ever heard in my life.

"What the hell?" she says as we both take off toward the noise. Well, she takes off, I quickly do a half-walk half-waddle.

When we get upstairs, the scene before us is one that I never thought I'd see. In the room that is going to become the nursery are Davis and Hunter. They are surrounded by what looks like a million pieces of wood and screws, and they have no idea we are here.

And Davis is wearing a tool belt. I didn't even know he owned one of those.

"I told you that piece *A* needed to connect to piece *D* with the *E* screw. Not the *F*."

"How the fuck am I supposed to be able to tell!" Hunter says. "They all look the fucking same!"

"I told you to read the directions! Do you want your niece's crib to fall apart!"

"I don't need any goddamn directions!"

"Just hand me the fucking *E* screw!"

"Oh, I'll hand you something!"

What in the name of Jolene is going on in here?

Sadie and I bust out laughing at the scene in front of us, which catches their attention.

"Bethany! You're home early!" Davis says frantically, trying to recover from something. I just don't know what.

Hunter chimes in, trying to right himself as well. "Sadie! You're here too!"

"Oh, this ought to be good," Sadie says, chuckling next to me. "Hunter. Why don't we leave and you can tell me all about how you got roped into this?"

Hunter all but runs out of the room as Sadie and I continue to laugh at the scene before us.

I can't walk more than two steps into the nursery without stepping on a piece of wood or a screw. When I finally make it in, I see the box leaning against the wall. Pictured on it is the most gorgeous crib I have ever seen.

"Did you buy a crib?" I ask, my hand going to my stomach like I do a lot these days.

"I wanted it to be a surprise," he says hesitantly as he walks toward me. "Do you like it?"

I look at the mess on the floor, then to the box again. There could have been two hundred cribs to pick from, and I doubt I would have picked any other one. "I love it."

"Oh, thank God," he says, relieved at my reaction. "Hunter had me worried you'd be mad that you didn't get to pick it out. I wanted to put it together for you before you got home, then we didn't realize how many pieces were involved—"

I cut his ramble off with a kiss. "You're just lucky you have good taste," I say, looping my arms around his neck. "Now, I'm going to need you to help me with something else since you are all about trying to make me happy today."

He wraps his hands around my back. "Anything, princess."

"Apparently, I have a thing for guys in tool belts. And I think we need something fixed in the bedroom."

In a second, Davis throws down the directions he's holding and scoops me into his arms.

"Just call me Mr. Fix It!"

I don't know when he's going to finish building the crib, but it's not going to be tonight.

WHEN I ACCEPTED Hunter's offer last year to become his offensive coordinator, I did it because I knew I was attaching myself to something special. Hunter, even though I won't tell him this to save his ego, is one of the brightest football minds in the business. He's not the youngest head coach in history by accident.

Becoming his offensive coordinator means I get to help run an innovative offense with a man I respect who is also becoming my best friend. I couldn't ask for more in a job.

What I didn't foresee happening is being the offensive coordinator of a team who is led by the Rookie of the Year in one season to that same player not being able to throw ten yards the next.

"Are you sure this is what you want to do?" I ask Hunter, standing next to him in his office as we wait for Bryce to come in. We are not even two hours removed from our latest loss—by a team we beat by double digits last year—and Bryce looked like he had never thrown a football before.

"When I benched him last year, it helped get his head out of his ass. I hate that I have to do it again, but we can't function as a team with him right now. He's a liability."

Last season when we started off bad—as in couldn't score a touchdown and lost our first four games—we didn't know what was going on. Nothing was working. I remember spending hours with Hunter trying to figure out why the offense couldn't click.

This year it's the same start, only this time there is one specific culprit. Not only is his play suffering, but his antics have become regular national news. Bryce has gone from football's golden boy to football's bad boy in the span of months. Sports radio's new favorite topic is "where was Bryce last night" and usually, the answer is drunk with a flock of women around him.

"I've got your back," I say to Hunter as I see Bryce slowly walking into Hunter's office. He doesn't knock. Instead, he just slouches in, drops into one of the chairs like a high school kid who got called into the principal's office, and doesn't care that he's about to get detention.

"Bryce," Hunter begins, but before he can say anything else, Bryce interrupts.

"I know. We sucked today. Your new shiny wide receiver can't catch any of my passes. He needs work."

"Dexter has nothing to do with this," I say, feeling defensive of my former position group. "It's not his fault that he ran the correct route and his quarterback underthrew him by ten yards."

"Like I said," Bryce continues, cockiness oozing from his voice. "The receivers need to be where I put it. Not the other way around."

"Who the hell are you?" Hunter asks as Bryce rolls his eyes. It takes all the power I have not to smack that look off his face. "I'm being serious, Bryce. You aren't the kid we drafted. You aren't the player who led us to the playoffs last year. You aren't the leader of this franchise like you're supposed to be. This guy... I don't know this guy. And I don't want to."

"No one says you have to," Bryce says, beginning to stand up. "Just leave me alone and let me play football."

"We aren't done," I say, pushing him back down into his chair. "You want to play football? Then start fucking playing football. What you showed us today was pathetic. If you want to start playing football, quit the partying, get your priorities straight, and get your head back in the game."

"Here we go again with the partying," he says, the annoyance in his voice clear as day. "What I do outside of this facility is none of your damn business."

"It is when it affects your play," Hunter says, his voice growing sterner. "And it is. Bryce, you're a liability right now. Today's loss? That is all on you. Until you can prove to us that you are the leader and player we drafted, you're benched."

His eyes go wide. "I'm what? You can't bench me. I haven't violated anything in my contract. I'm your star."

Hunter laughs. "Damn right, I can. And I am. I never thought I'd have to do this again after last year, but here we are. Maybe this time it will work. As for your contract? Consider this me helping you to make sure you didn't break it."

Bryce shoots up from his chair and slams his hands against Hunter's desk. "Fuck this! This is all his fault!" he yells, pointing to me. "This fucker has been on my ass since the summer. He tell you to do this?"

"While I take stock of all recommendations from my coaching staff, this decision I came to on my own," Hunter says with a calmness I don't know if I could pull off right now. "If you can't clean up your act on your own, we will demand you go to a rehabilitation center to get treatment."

"Treatment!" Bryce yells so loud that teammates are now

starting to gather outside Hunter's office. "I don't need fucking rehab. I'm fine. Why can't you just get off my ass?"

"We are on your ass because despite what you think, we care about you and we don't want you to run your life into the ground," I say, trying to keep my tone even. "This is for your own good."

Bryce looks at me, a humorless laugh coming from him. "You know, it's funny that you've been telling me to clean up my act all summer. Like you have the right to fucking talk."

My blood is now officially boiling. "What is that supposed to mean?"

"I remember last year you were partying with us. The fun uncle coach. Isn't that what they called you? Now I hear you knocked up McAvoy's sister-in-law? Real responsible, Coach. Great role model. Maybe take your own advice and get your shit right before you come after me."

Oh, fuck no, he didn't.

In that moment, I don't even think. I just charge. I'm two steps from clocking my own player before I feel Hunter's arms wrapping around me, picking me up and holding me back. Bryce's eyes are inviting me to try something, but before he can get any further, Cole comes into the office, stepping between us.

"You need to go," he tells Bryce. "Get the fuck out of here and get your head straight."

"Shut the fuck up," Bryce yells, shoving his best friend in the chest. "How many times have I told you to mind your own fucking business, too? You aren't my father."

"And how many times have I told you I'm not fucking going anywhere," Cole says. "I promised you when we were kids that I'd protect you. And that's what I'm doing. Do what coach says. Get out of here. Go home. Get help. Do something.

But I'm not protecting your ass anymore until you're the Bryce I know. This guy? This isn't him."

Hunter lets go of me as we watch the scene unfold in front of us. Cole's eyes are challenging Bryce to try something, or to defy him. I've always thought of Cole as a gentle giant. But right now? This man would rip off the limb of his best friend if he made a wrong move.

"Go," Cole says again, putting his hand on Bryce's shoulder.

Bryce doesn't say anything before he turns to leave. Cole doesn't either, but turns to us, nods his head, and exits the office.

"Did we do the right thing?" Hunter asks. "I feel like we just made it worse."

"Only time will tell," I say. "Only time will tell."

CHAPTER 38
BETHANY

"IT'S ADORABLE! THANK YOU!"

I don't know how many times I have said those words today. By the looks of the unopened presents on the table, I'm going to be saying them at least twenty more.

But I don't care. Today is the baby shower, and my heart is overflowing with love.

And it's not about the presents. Though they are wonderful, needed, and thoughtful. But it's about the people who are here with me.

Mom and Sadie did an amazing job planning this. They invited my friends, coworkers, and my favorite hair clients, including Ruthie, who swears she's not mad at me that my date with Gavin didn't go as planned. They were even able to coordinate with Abby and Sara to make sure they were here. It hurts my heart Marie wasn't able to travel, but it hasn't been a good few weeks for her, according to Abby, so the doctors didn't want to take any risks.

The shower isn't even the best part of the weekend. Tomorrow is a Fury home game and the whole family is going to watch from one of the boxes. It's not only my first professional football game, but it's the first time Abby and Sara have been able to see Davis in action as a coach.

I'm ready. I have my Fury gear that is now decked out in rhinestones. He has been quizzing me all week to make sure I at least have an idea of what is going on so I don't have to keep bugging Sadie, who will be attending as the fiancée of the head coach, and not as a reporter.

Turns out, I know more than we both thought I did. I know the quarterback throws it. I know if the other team scores it's bad. I know somebody did something wrong when the yellow flag is thrown. And I know if I don't know the answer when he quizzes me on football knowledge, I just distract him with sex.

Football is officially my favorite sport.

"Now that is just precious!" Mom says as I hold up a onesie that says "Daddy's Little Cheerleader" in Fury colors.

"You better hope he never loses his job!" Ruthie belts out. "That kid will need a whole new wardrobe!"

I try to hide the worried look on my face as I glance at the gifts we've received. Ruthie isn't far off. Besides the bigger items that people bought for us—the girls at the salon chipped in for our stroller that is nicer than my car, and Mom and Sadie bought us the rest of the furniture for the nursery—every piece of clothing is either baby girl pink or Fury orange.

At least our daughter is very on brand with her parents.

"Don't worry about what she said," Sadie whispers, handing me another gift. "He's under contract for four years. Unless things go horribly bad, he and Hunter are safe."

I might be just learning about football, but even I know this season isn't off to the best start. They just won their first game last week, and Bryce is MIA. The company line in the media is he's rehabbing an injury. The truth is, no one has heard from him since he was benched and stormed out of the locker room. The whole thing ate at Davis for days after it happened. He feels horrible that he couldn't do more to help him. I tried to console him as best I could, but I don't know if it helped. The team has done its best to move forward, but it hasn't been easy.

If Sadie is right, they aren't going to lose their jobs this year. But what happens if next year it's more of the same? Or worse? What happens if the whole coaching staff is fired? Could they do that?

"Oh my gosh, that is the most adorable thing I have ever seen!"

At this point, I'm unwrapping the presents on autopilot as the thousands of scenarios play through my head.

What if he's fired? We have a house here. I have family here. We said this was where we were going to raise our family.

Would we split our time between Nashville and wherever he ends up? Would we live here while he lives wherever he found a job? I can't imagine being anywhere without him for that long of a time, but if his job takes him to a different city, he'd have to be there. Can I just pack up and leave?

Would things be different if we were married?

We've talked about a lot of things in the past few months. Yet somehow, the topic of marriage hasn't come up since that first night when he asked me out of shock and panic.

I know he loves me. And I love him more than I thought possible. If he were to ask me today, without a doubt, I would say yes. But he hasn't.

When I told him no, it was because I wanted him to be sure. It's not that I'd *never* marry him. I just didn't want him to propose because he felt he had to.

I shouldn't be worried though. It will happen. Is he waiting for the baby? Yeah. I bet that's it. We have enough going on. We're committed to each other. We bought a darn house together.

It's fine. Everything is fine. Right as rain.

A collective gasp breaks me from my thoughts. Since I'm not opening a gift, I look around to find Davis walking in, looking as handsome as ever. He's wearing black slacks, a light pink button-down with his sleeves rolled up, and that smile I can't get enough of.

"Hello, ladies," he says, oozing charm, as he walks over to me, placing a kiss on my lips while gently rubbing a hand over my now very large bump. "How are my girls doing today?"

"We're great," I say, clearing my head from the thoughts earlier. "What are you doing here?"

"Well, I can't let you have all the fun," he says, which gets a good laugh from the ladies in the room. "Plus, I heard one of these presents is for me."

"Of course, you would think something is for you," Abby says.

"Am I wrong?"

"Sometimes I hate you, big brother," she jokes, giving him a kiss on the cheek and handing him a package. "This is for both of you. From Mom."

I'm not telling a lie when I say it takes all of my willpower not to cry as soon as Abby says that. As for Davis? He doesn't even pretend to hide himself wiping away a few stray tears.

"Go ahead," I say gently, giving his arm a squeeze.

He clears his throat and begins gently unwrapping the paper. His hands are shaking a bit, so I lean over to help him take the top off the box. Inside the box is the most beautiful, softest, pale pink, baby blanket I have ever seen.

"She still knits on her good days," Abby says as we look at it. "She wanted to give you guys something she'd made all by herself while she still could."

There is now not a dry eye in the house.

Davis, blanket in hand, stands and goes straight to where

his sisters are sitting. The three of them embrace in a hug that is the most touching thing I have ever seen.

As I go to put the box down, something inside catches my eye. It's a note, and it's addressed to me. My fingers can't open it fast enough.

Bethany,

Every baby girl should have a pink blanket, and my grand-daughter should be no different.

I'm about to tell you something none of my children know. I was pregnant a fourth time. After Sara. No one knew besides Mitch, but I miscarried early. As you know, Davis was named after my father. Abby and Sara were named after women on my ex-husband's side of the family. I always wanted to name a child after my grandmother, and don't ask me how I knew, but I knew that baby was a girl. The kids never knew Grandma, but she was the strongest woman I had ever met. Survived the Depression and raised a family with my grandfather fighting in the war. When Mitch left, I asked myself, "What would Grandma Charlotte do?" And the answer was survive. And that's what we did.

I tell you this because I want you to know that I saw the strength in you the second I met you. I saw the strength that my grandma had. That I tried to have. That my kids had when they were too young to ought to need it. You are the absolute perfect woman to love my son. Thank you for loving him. And I'm glad I got to meet you before it was too late.

Love,

Marie

"YOU KNOW we don't have to put everything away tonight?" I say as I bring in the last two boxes of baby items from the truck.

"I just want to get a jump on it," Bethany says from her spot on the floor as she folds another onesie that is so small, I have no clue how it will fit a baby. "I plan on doing most of it next week when you guys are on the road."

The nursery currently looks like the baby store exploded in here. There are clothes everywhere. Tons of boxes of diapers to put away. Everything a baby could want is here.

Our child is already so blessed.

We are so blessed.

The sight of a pink blanket laying at the bottom of the crib catches my eye. I don't know how I didn't completely lose it when I opened that today. Knowing my mom made that? That even though her good days are dwindling, she was still able to create something so beautiful for my daughter? It's too much to think about.

At that moment, the small box that has been sitting in my pocket all day taps my leg, reminding me it's there. Before my sister dropped that surprise gift on me, I was planning on proposing to Bethany at the shower. But after opening that beautiful gift, I couldn't.

No worries. It just wasn't the right time. I'll know it when it comes.

"Today was amazing," she says, holding out a stack of onesies for me to put away. I do before taking a seat next to her on the floor. She immediately leans back into me, my hand instinctively going to her stomach, where I feel our little one kick.

"That feeling will never get old," I say, placing a kiss on her temple.

"I'd love it if she kicked more during the day. Currently, her favorite time is at three a.m. She's already exhausting me."

I laugh. "She's a night owl like her dad."

"Well, then does Dad want to try and eliminate a few more names for his mini me?"

This has become our nightly ritual. Neither of us has come up with names we like, so instead, we have continued to throw out names we don't like. Last night we eliminated Heather, Jessica, and Kathryn for no reason except they didn't feel right to us.

"I heard the name Layla today. I gave it a test run. Doesn't fit."

"I agree. No to Layla."

"What about you? What's your veto of the night."

She doesn't say anything for a minute, and I feel the air in the room shift.

"Actually. I might have a name to keep this time."

This surprises me as I turn her toward me. "Really?"

"Yeah," she begins nervously. "What do you think about the name Charlotte?"

Charlotte.

"I love it," I say, playing it around in my head again. I don't know why, but it just... fits.

"I do too," she says, a smile growing on her beautiful face. "And if you don't mind, I'd like her middle name to honor my mom. I was thinking her middle name could be Elizabeth. It's my mom's middle name."

Charlotte Elizabeth Davis.

"It's perfect," I say.

"You think?" she asks.

"It is the most perfect name for the most perfect baby girl in the world."

Like a magnet, our lips come together, sealing this moment in the only way we know how. I never knew I could have this much love in my heart. How did I survive for so long thinking that my heart had a limit on how much love it could hold? That I couldn't have more people get close to me because it would take away from others?

There is no limit when it comes to love. There is no cap on how much you can love. You don't have to ration it out to people who are worthy.

My love for Bethany grows every day. From what started as simply physical attraction has grown into a love I can't imagine my life without. I already love Charlotte and I haven't even met her yet. I love the children I want to have with this woman in the future.

When our kiss breaks, neither of us moves. Instead, we just look at each other, our foreheads touching, and nothing but love in our eyes.

This. This is the moment.

Not when she told me she was pregnant. Not today, in front of a bunch of people. Not something elaborate like Hunter did for Sadie.

Just the two of us. Right here. Right now. This is where I ask her to marry me.

"Do you remember what you told me after you said that you wouldn't marry me?"

She laughs slightly. "I said that the next time you ask me to marry you, it needs to be because you can't imagine spending the rest of your life without me, not because you were panicking."

I position her so I'm now fully facing her, taking both of her hands in mine. "You also once said that you wanted a proposal that was just for you and your partner. It didn't have to be fancy, just something special that only the two of you would know."

I see the tears begin to well in her eyes. "I did say that. I can't believe you remembered."

I lift myself up, now facing her on one knee. "Bethany, as I sit here tonight and think back on our story, it's nuts to think that we are here today. I know this wasn't the order it was supposed to happen, but I don't regret one minute of our journey. I don't regret you ending things all those months ago. It made me realize you were more to me than I was ready to admit to myself. I don't regret having this baby before we even knew if we'd last, because I already know she's going to be the greatest gift either of us has ever received. I don't regret you telling me no the first time I asked you to marry me, because then we wouldn't have had this moment."

I pause, allowing myself a minute to breathe, and take the ring from my pocket. Bethany's tears are now full-on sobs, but I need to keep going.

"I love you, Bethany Hall. I didn't know I could love someone like this. You showed me I could be the man you needed, even when I didn't think I could be. You helped me see that one day I can be the father neither of us had. And not just to Charlotte. I want to have a whole bunch of babies with you."

This makes her laugh. "We'll talk about that later."

I wipe away a tear with my free hand. "What do you say, princess? Spend the rest of your life with me?"

She frantically nods her head as tears come streaming down her cheek. "Yes. Yes. A million times yes."

With shaky hands, I put the ring on her finger, thankful that Sadie was smart enough to tell me to go up a ring size just in case. As soon as the ring is on, our lips collide, kissing with a passion I've never felt before.

This woman. She bewitched me from the first moment I laid eyes on her. I remember feeling a jolt of energy the first time we touched. I thought it was strange, but I never thought anything of it.

Now, I know what it was. It was the universe telling me that I was done for.

EVERY FOOTBALL TEAM hits a point of the season when it goes into cruise control. Yes, you want to win. Yes, you want to keep preparing for the next opponent because every win counts in some way.

But it also comes to the point where if they don't know it by now, it's never going to happen.

This is where we are at the beginning of November. Somehow, despite Bryce not playing since the beginning of the season, we have just as many wins as we do losses. By some miracle, we aren't the laughingstock of the league, considering our franchise quarterback hasn't been heard of since that fateful day when we told him he needed to get his act together.

We thought he might come back in time for the bye week. That's always the week for teams to hit the reset button. That was three weeks ago, and the week came and went without a word from Bryce. Well, we got a message from his agent that he was alive but that it was best for everyone that he sits out the rest of this season. We placed him on injured reserve, gave a bullshit line to the media about an old injury that flared up, and kept going about our season.

One where we are probably not going to make the playoffs.

The fact that we are still mathematically in contention is actually a miracle, though it's a long shot. Once Bryce left the locker room, the mood drastically shifted. The offense didn't seem as tense. The veteran quarterback we picked up to hold us over is doing a well-enough job. The defense is keeping us in games, and we've managed to win a few. It could have gone a hell of a lot worse.

I might sound like a horrible coach, but the thought of playoffs right now is the last thing on my mind. Bethany is in the final weeks of the pregnancy, and things are becoming very real. We've hit the thirty-seven-week mark, and Dr. Stewart said everything looks great. I'm freaking out daily because I think she should be at home resting. She's fighting me every step of the way. Not only is she still working, when she isn't at the salon, she is in what I've read to be the "nesting" stage.

She also insisted on coming down here to meet me for a lunch date. I've learned to pick my battles. I knew I wasn't winning that one.

"Hey there," Hunter says as he lightly knocks on my open door. "Got a minute?"

"For the boss? Anytime."

He laughs as he takes a seat in the chair across from me. "It's still weird when you call me boss."

"Would you like me to call you something else? I gotta admit, that's a little weird, but if that's what you're into, we don't need to let Sadie know."

He grabs a loose football from the corner of my desk and chucks it at me. I catch it with ease.

"You forget sometimes that I was quite the receiver back in the day."

"Why didn't you try to go to a bigger college?" he asks, his voice back to being serious. "I've watched your tape. You were good, man."

I shrug, tossing the football back to him. "I didn't want to be too far from Mom and Abby. Mom was starting to show symptoms then. Though at the time we didn't know what it was. Abby was around, but Sara was just a kid. Pitt was the closest college who offered me a full ride, so I took it."

"I get it, man. I just wonder..."

I shake my head. "I don't. If I've learned anything over this past year, it's that everything happens for a reason. If I hadn't gone to Pitt, I might not have had the chance at the graduate assistant position. That introduced me to the coaches in Denver and put me on track to come here. I wouldn't mess with a day. Who knows how else it would have turned out?"

"You might not be sitting at my old desk," he says, tossing the ball back to me. "And you might not be on the way to becoming my brother-in-law."

"Like I said, I wouldn't change a thing," I say, a smile growing on my face as I watch Bethany slowly walk down the hall toward my office. Hunter catches my gaze and just shakes his head.

"God, you're whipped," he says, standing up.

"I learned from the best."

He kisses Bethany on the cheek before turning back to me. "See me before you leave. I have scouting reports for this week."

"Am I interrupting?" she asks as I guide her to a chair. "I know I'm a little early, but I didn't know how long it would take me to walk from the parking lot."

"I don't know why you walked at all. I hate that you're even out. You should be at home resting."

She just waves my comment off. "I'm pregnant, not dying. I'm fine. Plus, I'm craving a wrap from that place across the street. And you wouldn't deny your pregnant fiancée food now would you?"

It's her ace card and she's been playing it a lot these days. But she's right. If the woman asked me right now to find Dolly Parton to preside over our wedding and baptize our child, I'd make it happen.

"Of course not, princess. How are you feeling today?" I ask as I straighten up the folders on my desk and grab my cell phone. "Any discomfort?"

She gives me a look that would make a weaker man crumble to the ground. "I'm thirty-seven-weeks' pregnant with a future soccer player who has taken up residence on my bladder and Braxton Hicks contractions are hitting me. What do you think?"

I've learned this is a trick question.

"I think you look beautiful," I say, walking back to her and placing a kiss on her cheek. "Are you sure they are just Braxton Hicks?"

"Yes, and good answer," she says, taking my offered hand to stand up. "Speaking of your daughter, she is signaling to me that it's time to go to the bathroom. I'm going to do that before we go."

Before I can respond, my phone vibrates from my pocket.

"It's Abby," I say, though I'm confused as to why my sister is calling me on a Monday afternoon. We had our weekly talk last night.

"Well, answer it," Bethany says. "I'll go do my thing, then we'll go."

"You remember where it is?"

She nods and walks out of the office as I answer the call.

"Abby? What's up?"

"Davis..."

Abby's voice is panicked and mixed with what sounds like traffic noises.

"Abby? What's wrong. Talk to me."

"It's Mom. She's missing."

Four words. That's all it takes for my blood to go cold.

"What do you mean, she's missing? She lives in a secure facility! What the fuck do you mean she's missing!"

"I don't know," she says, evident she's trying to hold back tears. "I just got the call. I don't know anything yet. I'd never ask this of you but—"

"I'm on my way. I'll be there as soon as I can."

I hang up the phone before she has a chance to respond.

Mom.

Missing.

I know she hasn't been having many good days, but this... this hasn't happened since right before we found her the treatment facility. The last time she got out, she was so disoriented we didn't know what to do.

Where could she be? Where would she go?

I have to go. I have to find her. My family needs me.

I sprint down the hall to Hunter's office. "Hunter! The plane. Is it available?"

He looks up at me, confused about my sudden request. "It is. Why do you need it?"

"It's my mom. She... she's lost. She wandered away from the treatment facility. My sister just called me—"

"Go," he says as he picks up his office phone. "Don't worry about anything here. Take the plane. We're home this week, and we don't need it. Take all the time you need. I'll make the arrangements."

I turn to leave his office when I see Bethany walking toward me.

Shit.

I can't leave her. She's three weeks away from having our baby. What kind of father would I be if I leave her right now?

"Davis?" she asks, clearly seeing the worry written on my face. "What's the matter?"

"It's," I swallow, now finding it hard to say these words, "it's Mom. She... she's lost."

"Lost?"

"Apparently she wandered off. I don't know. Abby didn't know much. All we know is she's missing."

"Well, then, what are you doing here?" she says, marching back toward my office. "You need to go!"

I look at her, confused and torn on what to do. "I can't leave you."

"The hell you can't," she says, finding my keys on my desk and tossing them to me. "Your mom and sisters need you. Get your butt to Pennsylvania."

I stand there stunned, not even sure what to say.

Bethany lets out an exasperated breath as she walks to me with my coat in hand. "Richard Davis, you listen to me and you listen to me good. I am fine. I have Mom and Mike and Sadie and Hunter. We still have three weeks before Charlotte graces us with her presence. You need to get on a plane this instant and find your mama, do you hear me?"

At this moment, I realize two things. One, that when Charlotte is ever in trouble, Bethany will instantly turn into a stereotypical southern mother.

Two, I love this woman more than I even realized.

"Thank you," I say, leaning in and kissing the ever-loving hell out of her. "I'll be back as soon as I can."

She takes both of my hands, placing one over her heart and one over her stomach. "Find her. Then come back to us. We'll be here waiting. I love you."

"I love you more," I say before I give her one more kiss, then run as fast as I can to my truck.

"HAVE YOU HEARD ANY UPDATE YET?"

Mom's question pulls me from my daydream. One where I'm holding Charlotte in the blanket Marie made for her, smiling up at Davis after she's born.

"No," I say, grabbing a potato to start peeling. Anything to keep me busy as I sit and wait. "Nothing new."

Davis texted me when the plane landed in Pennsylvania to say that he made it, but I haven't heard from him since. I didn't expect I would hear from him. He has much more important things to do than text me every ten minutes.

When there is an update, he will let me know. And until then, I sit and wait.

"They are going to find her," Mom says, bringing me a glass of water as she comes to sit next to me. "We have to keep the faith."

I'm trying to, but the longer she is missing, the more I worry. After Davis left to take the team plane to Pennsylvania, I decided to come to Mom and Mike's for the day. It's Monday, so I was going over tonight for weekly dinner anyway. Something didn't feel right about going home to an empty house. But now, sitting here, it doesn't feel right doing nothing, either. Though every time one of these fake contractions hits me, it's a reminder of why I'm here and not there.

For being fake, they are quite uncomfortable.

"I hate that I can't be there helping," I say, putting down the potato. "I could be another set of eyes."

"I know, sweetie," Mom says, wrapping her arms around me in a side hug. "All we can do is send them good thoughts and hope that everything works out."

I try to think back to the day we went to visit her. The facility is large, so she could be somewhere on the grounds that they haven't checked. Though I doubt that. It's also in the middle of a residential neighborhood with a lot of side roads. She could have gone down any number of them.

I hate this. I hate this for Davis. I hate this for Abby and Sara. I hate this for Marie.

God, she must be scared. Or is she? Does she know what's going on? Does she have any idea how many people are trying to find her right now?

"I can't believe my baby is having a baby," Mom says so softly I almost don't hear her.

"That was random," I say, though I'm glad for the change of conversation.

She just shrugs. "I mean, I've obviously thought about it. But seeing you here, all belly, it just hit me today."

"What do you want to be called?" I ask, adjusting in my seat after another cramp hits me. This one wasn't too bad.

"I guess I haven't thought about that yet," she says, taking a sip of her Diet Coke. God, how I miss Diet Coke. I think the minute this baby is out of me, I'm going to request an IV drip of Diet Coke into my veins. "I don't want to be Grammy. That just sounds..."

"Old?" I say, finishing her sentence with a laugh.

"Yes. I don't like that. Grandma would be fine. Maybe Gigi? Do I look like a Gigi?"

I shake my head. "I'm pretty sure Sadie told me that Hunter's mom already requested Gigi on the day that they told her they were engaged."

Mom laughs. "Both of my girls are growing up. I remember the day we first moved into this house. It feels like so long ago now. But I still remember how nervous I was."

This takes me by surprise. "You were? But you and Mike were so in love. What was there to be nervous about?"

"Oh, sweetie," she says, taking a seat next to me, her hand resting on top of mine. "I was nervous about everything. It had been you and me for so long. Honestly, I had forgotten what it was like to live with a man. And even when your da... even when he was there, he really wasn't. I was nervous that you and Sadie wouldn't like each other. I was nervous that I'd screw something up just when I finally thought I found happiness. I was nervous that once we got here, Mike would change his mind. I still wonder sometimes how I got so lucky, but I thank the heavens every day I'm here now."

"Do you ever wish he would have stayed?" I ask. That question has been on my mind for as long as I can remember, but I've never asked.

"Oh God, no," Mom says, shaking her head. "Your sperm donor, because let's be honest, that's all he is, gave me the greatest gift of my life. I can't imagine my life without you. You have given me so much joy and I'm so proud to be your mama. But if he would have stayed? He would have only brought us down. He wasn't ready to be a dad. He left because he knew that. I don't hold any ill will toward him. I did for many years, but I don't anymore. He tried and he just couldn't do it. Him leaving made us who we are today. And I quite like how we turned out."

"I love you, Mama," I say, wrapping my arms around her the best I can with a beach ball in my stomach. "The only way I know that I'm going to be able to do this is because of you."

"I love you too, baby girl," she says, giving me a kiss on the cheek. "But you have something different than I did. You have Davis. That man, I know you were worried at first, but he is going to be the most amazing father."

"How do you know?"

She laughs, standing up from her seat. "Because I see the way he looks at you. That man would rather die than let you down. Your daddy never looked at me that way. But Davis? That man would move Heaven and Earth and walk through hell for you. That is the man you want by your side forever. That is the man to start a family with."

Mom gets up to check on dinner. I reach for my phone, instinctively checking to see if there is any word from Davis, even though I know there won't be. It's six thirty in Nashville, which means seven thirty in Pennsylvania. It's November. It has to be completely dark by now. And cold. God, she must be so cold.

If they don't find her tonight...

No. I won't let myself go down that road. He will find her. She will be okay.

She has to be.

Another pain hits me, this one a little bit longer than the others. When it subsides, I decide to get up and stretch my legs. But before I can even take a step, the oddest feeling happens between my legs.

No.

It can't be.

It's too early.

I haven't had a symptom all day except... well, shit. Were those contractions? Like real ones?

I take a deep breath and look down at the floor.

Oh shit.

"Um, Mom?

"Yeah, sweetie?"

"How do I know if my water broke?"

She turns to look at me, her eyes growing wide. "It will feel like you peed yourself. Why?"

I look down at the puddle on the floor and back up to her. "Well, then someone better go home and get my bag. I think I'm fixin' to have a baby."

I FEEL like I have walked down this street a dozen times.

I haven't, it just feels like I have since every fucking street in this goddamn neighborhood looks the same.

Where in the hell could she be?

As soon as I got the call, I raced to the airport. Two hours later, I was in Pennsylvania.

Turns out the security system shorted out again. Mom was outside when it happened, as it's an unusually warm November day for Pennsylvania. Somehow, when they were doing a check on all the patients to make sure that they were safe and secure, Mom wandered off.

It could have happened to anyone, they said.

Well, it didn't. It happened to my mother. And now she's been gone for going on eight hours. When the sun went down, so did the temperature. She has to be freezing. If I don't find her soon...

I turn down yet another side street, looking every direction I can to see if anything catches my eye. Abby and her husband are out looking, as well as the local police and a group of staff from the center.

How far could she have gone? The staff and police seem to

think she has to be somewhere in this neighborhood, but I'm starting to doubt them.

I check the time on my watch again. It's almost eight o'clock. The sun is now completely set, but I can't make myself stop looking. She's out there somewhere.

I should call Bethany. It's not like I'm doing anything except looking back and forth right now. But just as I go to pull my cell phone out of my pocket, something catches my eye. A shadow moving in a backyard.

I check the front of the house and there is a for sale sign posted, which makes me pick up my pace. As soon as I get to the backyard, I see her clear as day. Mom, sitting in a tire swing, slowly swinging back and forth.

I hurry up and grab my phone, ignoring the twenty texts and missed calls, and message my sister that I found her and send her my location. I slip my phone back into my pocket and gently start making my way toward her.

"Mom?" I say, hoping to not startle her. "Are you okay?"

"Dinner isn't ready yet," she answers without looking at me, a sadness to her voice.

The way she says that makes me pause. Dinner isn't ready?

Then it hits me. She's not here right now. She might be physically here, but in her head, she's not. If the answer she just gave tells me anything, she thinks I'm a kid.

"Mom, it's dark out. Why don't you come with me?" I say, taking a few more steps toward her.

When she turns to look at me, the sadness in her eyes nearly breaks my heart. "I'm not coming inside, Mitch. You can heat up leftovers."

Mitch? Does she think I'm...?

"Mom, it's me, Dav... It's Richard, Mom. How about we go inside?"

She smacks down the hand I just offered to her. "Shut up,

Mitch. I know you aren't Richard. He's at school. And I'm not coming in with you."

Fuck. I should have known better. I remember when she was first diagnosed, one of the therapists told us that if she was ever having an episode to not scare her. To go along with it. It's the best thing to do so as to not to agitate her.

That means, right now, I have to pretend to be the man I hate more than anyone else on this planet.

"Okay, Marie," I say, her name feeling foreign on my tongue. "What do you want me to do?"

"I want you to leave me be. You left us. You walked away. Don't you dare think about coming back."

I don't know what to say to this. Is Mom reliving a real event? Did Mitch try and come back? She had always told us that once he left, she never saw him again.

"I just want to make sure you're okay," I say, hoping she thinks Mitch is still talking.

"Okay? I'm not okay. I lose my Charlotte and the next day you leave. Of course, I'm not okay!"

What did she just say?

"Who is Charlotte?" I ask, wondering if this is just a coincidence. It has to be, right?

"You know who Charlotte is. She was our baby, Mitch. But I lost her. I lost our Charlotte. And then the next day you go and leave. And now you're back. You need to leave. Let me be in peace. I don't want the kids to see me like this or know you were here."

I stand there in front of my mother, who thinks I'm my father, stunned silent.

Is all of this real? Did this really happen? It sure as hell feels like it did, even though I have no idea what is going through her mind.

If all of this happened, then Mom was pregnant, but lost a

baby right before Mitch left. And she was going to name her Charlotte? Does Bethany know this somehow?

And why did he come back? What did he have to gain from coming back? Was he trying to get her to forgive him? Did he forget something? I guess we'll never know since no one has spoken to him in more than fifteen years.

"Mitch, you need to leave," Mom says, wiping the tears from her eyes. "The kids will be home from school soon. You made your choice. You left us. You chose her. Now leave us be."

What did she just say?

Mitch had an affair? That's why he left?

I don't know why I'm shocked by this, but I am.

"Leave, please," she says as I hear the sound of cars pulling up to the house.

I know this next move is risky, but I can't just walk away from her right now. She might think I'm my piece of shit father, but I can't let this be how I leave her as I see Abby and the team from the hospital coming toward us.

"I'm so sorry. I'm sorry I couldn't do more." I lean in and kiss her forehead, meaning those words as both identities. As Mitch, I hope wherever the bastard is that he's sorry for hurting her and leaving us. As for me? I'm sorry that she felt she had to live with this pain, with these secrets, for all this time.

Her mind might be betraying her right now, but she is still the strongest woman I know.

———

"She's resting comfortably," Jennifer says, greeting Abby and me in the small waiting area at the facility. "Again, I would like to profusely apologize for this. I... I just feel awful."

I want to rip her a new asshole. I want to scream that she better get that fucking door fixed. That I will pay for it personally, so this never happens again.

But I don't, because I know it will do no good. That, and Abby threatened me that I would never have another child if I cause a scene. It could have happened to anyone. All that matters is that Mom is back in her room and safe.

"Thank you, Jennifer," Abby says. "We'll be by to check on her in the morning."

"That will be no problem. Come whenever." She shakes our hands and walks away.

"Holy fuck, that was scary," I say, collapsing back into the chair, my body and mind exhausted from the day.

"You're telling me," she says, taking the seat next to me. "What happened with you and Mom?"

I sit up and rest my elbows on my knees, not knowing where to start. "Do you know if Mitch ever tried to come back?"

"Not that I was ever told. Did he?"

"Apparently. At least, that's what Mom was remembering tonight. If it was real. She... she thought I was him."

"Can you blame her? When she's in a state like that? You're the spitting image of him."

"Don't remind me."

"What else did she say?"

I take a deep breath, preparing myself because this is news that I still haven't come to grips with. "Mom thought Mitch was back. In her mind, by my guess from what she was saying, it wasn't long after he left. She told him to go back to the woman he left us for."

"I always knew that bastard was cheating on Mom," Abby says, the anger clear in her voice.

"Yeah, well, are you ready for the rest?"

This surprises her. "There's more?"

"When I got there... She was crying on a tire swing. Just like the one we used to have as kids. She... she was crying over a lost child."

"A lost child?"

I nod. "She said she was pregnant but lost the baby. She was calling her Charlotte. She said she lost the baby and the next day Mitch left."

"Oh my God. I had no clue."

"I don't think anyone did."

"Poor Mom."

"Want to hear the most fucked-up part?"

Abby's eyes grow wide. "That *isn't* the most fucked up?"

"The night after Bethany's baby shower, we were doing our nightly elimination of baby names and she said that she had a name that she liked and wanted to see what I thought about it. Abby, she said Charlotte."

If Abby's eyes were wide before, they are all but popping out of her head at this point. "You have got to be shitting me."

"We both love it. That's our baby's name. We're... I'm... we're naming our child after the sibling we never knew."

Abby gets up from her chair to sit on the arm of mine, wrapping her arms around my shoulders. "Mom is going to love it. Hopefully, she still has a few good days so we can tell her."

I pat Abby's arm when I feel a vibration go off in my pocket.

"Oh shit," I say, scrambling for my phone. "I never called Bethany to tell her we found her. She has to be worried sick."

"Good move, Richard," she says, moving back to her seat. "Why are you staring at your phone like you've seen a ghost?"

I didn't realize the color in my face drained that fast. When I check my phone for the first time tonight, there are dozens of missed texts and calls from Sadie, Hunter, and Helen.

I ignore all of them and immediately call Sadie, who answers on the first ring.

"What's going on, Sadie?"

She takes a deep breath. "First, tell me if you found your mom."

"Yes," I say, already standing and walking out of the facility, Abby not too far behind. "Now, what's the matter? Bethany? The baby? Is everyone all right?"

"They are fine," Sadie says, though her voice has an urgency to it. "But you need to get here sooner rather than later."

"Spit it out, Sadie," I say, now sprinting to my rental car.

"She's in labor, Davis. And if I were a betting woman, this baby is going to be here before the sun is up."

CHAPTER 43
BETHANY

ONE OF MY guilty pleasures during pregnancy has been to watch videos of women doing ridiculous things to speed up or induce labor. Some of the dances they did were pretty entertaining. It was also pretty interesting to see what food combinations they were willing to try, all in the name of an old wives' tale that said it would jump start labor.

Who would have known that I needed to be watching videos of how to keep a kid inside me, because that would have been a lot more educational at this point.

This kid is ready to come out. But she needs to hold her damn horses until her daddy gets here.

"Ahhhh!" I yell, another contraction tearing through me. It's three in the morning, I've been having consistent contractions for nine hours now and this kid is one accidental push away from crowning.

Davis and I talked about the possibility of him missing the birth. The weeks surrounding my due date were away games. There was a very good chance he would be on the road when I went into labor. But knowing that he's on his way back, I need to do everything I can within reason to wait for him to get here.

I don't want him to miss this first.

"You're doing great," Sadie says, placing a cold washcloth over my forehead. "What do you need?"

"What's his status?" I ask, trying to even my breathing as I feel another contraction coming on.

"I haven't felt my phone vibrate, so likely nothing."

I shoot her a death glare. "I'm sorry. I didn't know we were going to assume things tonight. *What. Is. His. Status!*"

"Okay, hold on," she says, pulling her phone out of her pocket with hesitancy because I'm even scaring myself right now. "The last text was a half hour ago, and he just landed. Hunter is waiting with a car for him so they could go as fast as they could. He's on his way."

I had Sadie look up for me earlier how long it would take to get from the airport to the hospital. According to the map app on her phone, fifteen minutes.

If Hunter knows what's good for him, he better make it here in ten.

"I don't want him to miss this," I say, trying to hold back tears. He missed when I found out I was pregnant. He missed the accidental gender reveal. I don't want him to miss this as well.

I don't want him having to regret making an impossible choice. He made the right one. He did what he had to do for his mom and sisters. But if I can do anything to make sure he doesn't have to miss this, then I'm going to do it.

Maybe if I just cross my legs she won't come out? Seems reasonable.

"I know, sis," Sadie says, taking hold of my hand again. "You know he's doing everything he can to get here. You just need to keep breathing."

We always had a backup plan if Davis was out of town

when I went into labor. Though at the time, I thought I'd be using it because of a football game. First, Sadie wasn't to contact him until we were one hundred percent sure I was in active labor. Tonight, we just amended that to make sure she did not tell him until she had confirmation Marie was safe. I didn't want to have him make that decision, and making sure she was safe was the top priority.

Sadie is also my backup birth coach if Davis isn't able to be here. Mom wanted to be in the room with me, but frankly, she's just too nice. I need the drill sergeant. I need Sadie.

But now that I'm here? I want Davis. I want his strong hands holding me. I want his soothing voice telling me everything is okay. I want him to be here with me the first time we lay eyes on our daughter.

"How are we doing?" Dr. Stewart asks, taking a seat at the bottom of my bed.

"I…" I don't get to finish that sentence because another contraction comes roaring through me. This one is the worst yet.

Holy hell, these things are no joke.

"Bethany, I know this isn't what you want to hear, but it's time to start pushing. We can't wait any longer."

I flash a panicked look down at Dr. Stewart. "What do you mean, it's time? He's not here yet. Just give him a few more minutes. He's on his way."

"Bethany, if we wait any longer the baby will be in danger," Dr. Stewart says, doing her best to be patient with me. "We tried, but we need to do what's best for the baby now. It's time."

I nod, tears now pouring down my cheeks as my birthing team gets into position.

How did this happen? I wasn't supposed to go into labor

for another three weeks. Those contractions earlier today? Those were supposed to be Braxton Hicks.

Why can't one thing in this whole freaking pregnancy go according to plan? I had come to terms with not doing things in the right order when it comes to Davis and this baby. Why can't one little tiny thing like having the baby on time with my fiancé here be an option?

Though, honestly, it's fitting. This whole freaking thing has been off track since day one. Might as well keep on going. No sense trying to right our journey now.

"Are you ready, Bethany?" Dr. Stewart asks as I see a man sprinting past my labor and delivery room.

"Davis!" I scream, knowing that's who just ran past my room.

"What?" Sadie asks confused.

"Davis, he just ran by. Go get him! Now!"

Sadie looks at Dr. Stewart, who signals for a nurse to go chase down Davis. I've lost track of minutes and seconds, so I have no clue how long it takes for the nurse to find him. But when I see him through the window of my room, he isn't moving as fast as a man who's about to miss the birth of his daughter should be moving, in my opinion.

"Richard Davis Semen, you get your fucking ass in here right now!"

Everything stops in the room. Every doctor and nurse just stare at me. And Sadie? I'm pretty sure I just sent her into shock.

"What did you say?" Sadie asks, her voice laced with excitement. "Is that his name? Like his real name? Oh my God, this is the best day of my life."

I shoot her another glare. "Get my fucking fiancé in here NOW!"

Before she can move, Davis comes crashing into the room

and sprints to the side where Sadie is no longer, taking my hand and kissing it.

"I'm so sorry, princess. I'm so fucking sorry."

"Apologize later! We have a baby coming!" I say, biting through a contraction. "It's... FUCK!!!"

ON NOVEMBER 9, three weeks early, Charlotte Elizabeth Davis was born at 3:58 a.m., coming in at seven pounds, eight ounces. She has a full head of brown hair like me and has blue eyes that are clear like her mom's.

She is the most beautiful thing I have ever seen, next to her mother, of course.

And I almost missed it.

If not for the grace of a good tailwind, Hunter driving one hundred miles an hour across Interstate 40 and a little luck, I would have missed the moment my daughter came into the world.

I almost let this beautiful little girl down before she even knew who I was.

I'm really nailing this fatherhood thing out of the gate.

"You look exhausted," Bethany says from her bed where she is nursing Charlotte.

"I'm fine," I say, shaking away the yawn that is fighting to come out of me. "You're the one who should get some sleep."

"I'll sleep when I'm done here," she says, smiling down at our baby girl.

I sit next to Bethany on the bed and just watch her nurse for a few minutes. I don't know which of these two I'm more in awe of right now.

That's a lie. It's Bethany. This woman... this woman who just gave me a child... she is so fucking strong. She was prepared to have this baby on her own if I would have said no to her all those months ago. She was ready to have it without me if the curveballs of life kept me away. She fought with everything she had to make sure she gave me the best chance of being able to see the birth of our daughter.

And what did I do? Ignored text messages and calls all night while I was hundreds of miles away.

"What's the matter?" she asks, looking at me out of the corner of her eye. "I know that look. Where's your head at?"

That's the question of the year. I have no idea where my head is. The last forty-eight hours are such a blur. Did all of it really happen in that short of a time span?

"How did you come up with the name Charlotte?"

Though that's not the first question on my mind, it has been one that has been nagging me since the episode with my mother. It can't be a coincidence, can it?

Bethany takes a breath and situates Charlotte to burp her. "In the box with the baby blanket, there was a note for me. In it... she told me about a miscarriage she had. And that she was going to name the baby Charlotte, after her grandmother, but didn't have the chance to. She didn't ask us to name her that, but... it just felt like we should."

I lean in, needing to feel her lips against mine right now. I don't know what I did in this life to deserve this woman, but I know I don't.

"When I found Mom... she was sitting on a tire swing. It was like one we used to have in our backyard. She was talking about a baby named Charlotte. It freaked me out. On top of that, she thought I was my dad. It was like I was living in two worlds at once."

"Oh, Davis," she says, giving me another kiss, the one of reassurance. "I can't imagine what you had to have been going through."

I shake my head. "I didn't know what to do. I hated being away from you, and I wanted to get back to you as soon as I could. And I didn't even know then you had gone into labor. I wanted to help my mom, but having to do it while she thought I was my asshole father was not my first choice. Then everything happened so quick to get her back and safe. Then I forgot to check my phone. If something would have happened to you or the baby..."

I trail off, the emotions and feelings of the past few days finally catching up to me. Bethany puts Charlotte down in her bassinet and brings me into her arms.

"You did everything you could," she says as she runs her fingers through my hair. "You had no idea I was in labor. I had no idea I was in labor. The system breakdown at the center was an accident. It was a perfect storm. But at the end of the day your mom is safe, Charlotte is healthy, we are fine, and we have a perfect little girl we get to take home with us in a few days. That's what counts."

I nod, hearing her words but not really fully letting them digest. Even two hours later, as I'm holding Charlotte while Bethany sleeps, I let her words wrestle in my head.

I still can't find peace with them.

All I can think about are the what ifs.

What if I wouldn't have made it back in time? I know we had a plan in case, but I never would have forgiven myself if I missed the birth of my daughter because I forgot to check my phone.

What if something were to have happened to her during

delivery and I wouldn't have been here? What if there would have been a complication with Charlotte? Or, God forbid, something happened to Bethany?

If any of those would have happened, I don't know if I could have lived with myself.

Then there are the what ifs with my mom's situation. What if I wouldn't have been able to find her and I would have learned my daughter was born while I was wandering the streets of suburban Pennsylvania? What if she didn't respond to me and I couldn't have brought her back? What happens the next time? Because she might not get lost again, but there will be more episodes that I'm going to need to be there for my family.

But then there is my family here. The one I created with the woman who has shown me I could love.

This is why I said I never wanted this. I'm only one man. In the first hours of my daughter's life, I've already been pulled in more directions than I know how to bend. Now I'm worried that I will continue getting pulled and will finally break.

I rub Charlotte's back as I take a glance down to my chest to look at my sleeping daughter. Feeling her little body against my chest is the most surreal feeling in the entire world. Right now, she's counting on me for warmth. For love. And I'll do everything in my power to give her anything she needs.

But does that mean letting down others? When something like this happens again, which family am I going to let down the most? The one who raised me or the one who is now my future? I'd rather cut off my own arm than disappoint either of them.

The worst part is the little voice in the back of my head. I've pushed him away for months, making myself think I could be enough for everyone in my life. But right now, as I hold my sleeping daughter, he comes back to the forefront of my brain, louder than ever, and says the words I've been denying for months, though right now I'm realizing are absolutely true.

I don't know if I can do this.

CHAPTER 45
BETHANY

WE HAVE BEEN HOME for four days.

I think Davis and I have argued for the better part of three of them.

Take last night, for example. We made a deal a long time ago that he would take at least one late-night feeding. If my memory serves me correctly, he volunteered to do it on his own. I believe his exact words then were, "I'm a night owl, it's the least I can do." So each night before I go to bed, I make sure I have at least one bottle pumped and ready to go for Davis' shift.

When Charlotte woke up for her three a.m. feeding, I rolled over and nudged him. I'm still trying to figure out if what happened next actually happened or is a product of my post-partum imagination.

"She's up. There's a bottle downstairs."

Davis grunts and rolls back over. "I'm tired. Can you do this one?"

"I did the last one. You promised me one a night. Please, I'm exhausted."

"Join the club."

That was his response. A "join the club" and a snore a few minutes later.

Frustrated as all get out, I got up, went to my daughter's room, and whipped out the boob. After I was done, I decided it was best for all involved if I didn't go back to bed, so I slept in the rocking chair in Charlotte's room. It might not have been the most comfortable, but it saved me from accidentally smothering my fiancé with a pillow.

I don't know where his sudden mood shift has come from, but I'm not a fan. I thought everything was fine in the hospital. Since that first day, he's been distant. Quick to the trigger. If it's not a fight, it's a dismissal.

I don't know who this man is, and I pray to the heavens that this isn't some sort of new Davis. Because if this is Davis as a dad, we are going to have big problems.

I'm not expecting him to give everything up to help me, but a little bit here and there can go a long way. Since we've been home, he hasn't changed one diaper. He has fed her twice. Yesterday, I asked him to get me a Diet Coke because I can have Diet Coke again, and his response was, "what do I look like?" and he walked away.

During all of this, he was in the kitchen. Two steps from the refrigerator.

I'm hoping today is better. It's Sunday, but Hunter told Davis that he was not to show his face in the stadium today, even though they have a home game. I'm hoping for a nice easy day with minimal arguments, a chance for both of us to catch up on some sleep, and maybe, if I'm lucky, a shower.

Because I don't remember the last time I took one of those.

Needless to say, it takes me by surprise when I see Davis coming down the stairs, bookbag in hand, and decked out in his normal Fury coaching attire.

"What are you doing?" I ask, checking the time to see that it's just after eight a.m.

"Going to the game," he says, like it's the dumbest question I've ever asked. "Did you make coffee?"

"No," I say, following him into the kitchen. "I didn't think you'd be taking it to go."

"Fine, I'll do it myself," he says, annoyed as he heads into the kitchen and pops in a K-cup.

"Why are you dressed like you're going to the game?" I ask, trying to keep my voice down so as not to wake up Charlotte, but I'm having a hard time. "I thought you weren't coaching today. Hunter told you to stay home."

"Hunter isn't the boss of me."

"Actually, he is."

The sound he lets out is somewhere between annoyance and dismissal. And it's pissing me off. "Don't get literal on me, Bethany. It's my job to coach. We have games on Sundays. I'm going to coach my team."

"I thought you would want to take this time to be here with me and Charlotte? We've had a long week. Take the day and relax. We both could use some down time."

He's standing facing away from me, almost like he's willing the coffee machine to brew faster. I step up behind him and put my hand on his shoulder, hoping to ease some of the tension for him.

Then he does something that throws me more off guard than any way he's been acting the past few days.

He shrugs off my touch.

Never, not once since the day we met, has he ever done that.

I take a step back, wondering what is going on. "Who are you right now?"

He turns to face me, and the look on his face is confused. Like I just asked him what color the sky is.

"What do you mean who am I? I'm the one who has to pay for this house and buy our kid diapers. I'm the man of this house, and I'm trying to go to my job so I can provide for my family like I'm supposed to."

Whoa. That came out of left field.

"Why are you being like this? And when has money ever been a concern for us that you can't take one day off? You're acting like I forced you to buy this house. You wanted it as much as I did, and now you're throwing it in my face?"

His eyes grow cold as he puts on the lid of his coffee cup. "Hard to say no to someone in the position I was in."

Did he really just make a reference to the closet blow job? By the look he is giving me right now, he sure as shit did.

The *audacity*.

I have never wanted to punch a person as much as I do right now. But I don't. Because I'm a fucking southern lady.

"That was completely uncalled for."

He lets out a heavy sigh but doesn't apologize. "I'm only one man, Bethany. And today I have to go to work. Maybe tomorrow I can be a dad. I'm leaving."

I stare at him as he puts on his shoes and grabs his coat.

That's it? That's how we are going to leave it? Somehow, in the months of dating and preparing for Charlotte, we never fought. This is completely foreign territory for me.

I just know that I hate him leaving today with us angry at each other.

"When will you be home?" I ask, desperation clear in my voice.

"When it's done."

That's all I get as he walks out of the door.

"What you're telling me is that Richard is acting like a real dick?"

I shoot a look over at Sadie. "Please don't talk like that while you are holding your niece."

She rolls her eyes. "You know she is going to hear a lot worse from my mouth over the years, might as well get her accustomed to it from the start."

I fall back into the couch, flipping on the television to turn on the Fury game. "I know. I'd just rather her not hear it this young. Plus, this isn't a laughing matter. Something is seriously wrong with Davis and I have no idea what it is."

I don't know how long I stood in the kitchen stunned this morning after Davis walked out. I do know the only thing that got me moving was the sound of Charlotte crying. Feeling confused and not really wanting to be alone today, I called Sadie and asked her to come over. Since she doesn't cover the Fury anymore, her Sundays are more open.

"Okay, let's think back," she says, switching arms as she holds Charlotte. "He started acting funky when you came home from the hospital?"

I nod. "Yeah, but even when I was there, he was starting to act a little aloof. But I didn't think anything of it. We were so tired, and everything was a whirlwind. I just chalked it up to that."

"Makes sense. I probably would have done the same thing."

"I thought we were good, Sadie," I say, unable to hold back the tears anymore. "Everything was going great. I hate to say that it changed the second the baby was born, but unfortunately, that's the case."

We sit in silence, well, except for the sound of my tears that I can't control, neither of us really sure what to say. What can we say? It's not like either of us has a pathway into Davis's head. For a while, I thought I did. I guess I didn't.

"Oh, turn it up," Sadie says, signaling me to grab the remote. "I always love to hear what the announcers say when they talk about Hunter. I think this guy is going to lean into his age."

Sadie is right. The announcer goes on and on about Hunter being the youngest coach in pro football history and that just last year he was the offensive coordinator.

"But today, McAvoy's offensive coordinator isn't with us as he is home with his fiancé, welcoming their new daughter into the world." The television flashes to a picture of a newborn Charlotte. *"We want to wish Coach Davis and his fiancée, Bethany, congratulations. Now, calling plays today for the Fury is running backs coach..."*

I snap my head to Sadie, who does the same to me.

"What did he tell you he was doing today?" she asks.

"He said they had a game, and he didn't care that Hunter told him to stay home."

Sadie looks back to the television and back to me again. "If he's not at the game, and he's not here, then where is he?"

I stand up and begin to nervously pace around the living room.

If there was an accident, we'd know by now. He left the house more than five hours ago. The television is making it sound like he's here. He told me he was there.

I collapse back onto the couch and I can feel my face drain of color. Sadie hurries and puts Charlotte in her carrier and rushes over to me.

I'm pretty sure she starts talking to me. I have no idea what she is saying. All I know is that my worst fear is happening.

He wasn't ready.
He wasn't ready and he left.
He left me. He left our daughter.
Just like my own father.

"YOU ARE some kind of fucking asshole."

Hunter's voice should startle me as he takes a seat at the bar next to me, but it doesn't.

Part of me knew he'd show up sooner or later.

The other part of me is just drunk, so I don't give a flying fuck about anything.

"This is where you spent your day? Back to the bar where you used to pick up nameless women to get your dick wet?"

I look around the sports bar by my old apartment. "Yup. Right here. Though, no women today. Just booze. My man Patrick here kept my glass full!"

I raise my glass to the bartender, who is now ignoring me. That's kind of rude.

Also, Patrick looks like a woman now.

I meant to go to the stadium this morning. I had every intention to. Being in the house with Bethany and Charlotte was becoming too much. Over the past week I drummed up every what if and hypothetical scenario. I was starting to feel suffocated. I needed out. So I was ready to defy Hunter and coach in today's game.

Then, on my way to the stadium, all I could hear was the

sound of disappointment in Bethany's voice. I replayed the fight that I started for no other reason than I'm an asshole over and over in my head.

The part where I told her I bought our house because I was getting a blow job. How I dismissed her touch when she was trying to soothe me despite me being a grade A asshole.

I don't deserve her sympathy.

I don't deserve her.

I don't deserve to be a father.

So, instead of driving to the stadium, I somehow ended here. Where I've been for the past... fuck, I don't know. I've been here all day.

"What are you doing, Davis?" Hunter asks, his voice full of disappointment. Seems like I'm good at getting that reaction from people lately.

"I'm getting drunk," I say, finishing off my glass, hoping he will drop this conversation and leave me be.

"I mean, what are you doing here? Why are you not at home with your fiancée and newborn daughter? When I said take the day off, this isn't what I meant."

I shoot a look at Hunter, who has the gall to look at me like he's upset. At least I think he does. There's two of him right now.

Both look pretty pissed off.

"It's too much," I admit. Damn, drunk me for being honest.

"What is too much? How much you've had to drink? Because that I will agree with you on."

I set down my glass and turn to face Hunter. "Everything."

"You're going to have to be a little more specific than that."

I try and gather my thoughts before responding. Which is hard because I'm pretty sure I killed a good amount of brain cells today. "I almost missed it, Hunter. I almost missed her being born."

"But you didn't," he says. "You did everything you could to make it there for her. And you did. You got to hold that little girl of yours in the first moments of her life. You were there for both of them."

"But I wasn't," I admit, hating having to say this, knowing I'll live with it for the rest of my life. "Bethany had to go through labor alone. Yeah, I know she had Sadie, but I should have been there. I promised her I was going to be there and I wasn't."

"Davis, no one could have predicted what happened to your mom happening at the *exact* same time that Bethany would go into labor three weeks early."

"But it did happen," I say, my anger starting to creep back up. "I had to choose between my two families. There was no right or wrong answer. Do I say no to helping find my mom who doesn't know what day it is half the time, or do I stay with the mother of my child? This is why I never wanted a family of my own. Having to make these choices. This is why I stayed single. This is why I denied Bethany for so long. I don't want to have to make these choices. My mom and sisters count on me. Bethany and Charlotte now count on me. I can't be in two places at once. And before my child was even born, I had to make that choice."

"We all have to make choices sometimes," Hunter says, looking at me confused. "You know that Bethany wasn't going to be upset if you missed the birth, right? She understood. Did she want you there? More than anything. But do you know what her instructions were to Sadie when she was in labor?"

I shake my head because I obviously don't.

"She said specifically, 'until he says that Marie is found and safe, you do not tell him I'm in labor.' She knew where you needed to be. There was a backup plan for her. There wasn't a backup plan to finding your mom. Bethany was prepared to sacrifice her want to have you next to her during the birth of your child so you didn't have to make an impossible decision."

She did that? I know Sadie asked me if Mom was safe before she told me she was in labor, but I didn't realize it was because it was on Bethany's demand.

"That doesn't change anything," I say, though I'm finding it harder to believe my own words. "This isn't going to be the last time I have to pick between my two families. I'm always going to disappoint someone. It was the first, but it won't be the last time. I can't do this, Hunter. I can't fucking do this."

"Can't do what?" Hunter asks, his voice now pissed off. "Can't be a father? Can't be a son? Can't be a brother? Can't be a partner to your fiancée? What are you going to give up? Who are you going to disappoint, your words, not mine, when you tell someone that because you are one thing you can't be another?"

I don't answer, but only because he's right. I hate when he's right.

"I'd love to hear this conversation," Hunter continues, clearing his throat. "'Hey, Bethany. Engagement is off because on the chance something happens with my mom or sisters again when something big in our life is happening, I don't want to disappoint you guys. So I'm just going to end things here. Disappoint you from the fucking get go. Tell Charlotte I'll see her at her graduation.'"

"I wouldn't ever—"

Hunter cuts me off. "Or maybe it will go like this. 'Hey, Abby. I know I'm your brother and power of attorney for our mom, but I'm going to have to dump all of that onto you and Sara because you might need me sometime down the line when I have to be there for my future wife and child. Sorry. See you at some point.'"

"That's not what I mean—"

"Oh. Maybe this one will be the best. 'Hey, Mom. Hope you're having a good day today. I'm just going to let you know that I can't help your daughters anymore because I'm a dad now.'"

"Shut the fuck up!" I yell. I can see eyes across the bar flashing toward me. "That isn't what I meant."

"Then what did you fucking mean?" Hunter asks, his voice more even. "Because I just laid out your three choices if it's really too much for you. You have to pick."

He's right. I hate to say it, but he's right.

Until the day I die, I will do everything in my power to be there for Mom, Abby, and Sara. But Bethany and Charlotte? I would rather take a bullet to the chest than not be there for them in every way I can.

"How do I do this?" I ask, my voice now barely above a whisper. "How do I be enough for all of them?"

Hunter laughs. "You don't be."

"What?" That isn't the answer I was expecting.

"What you want to be for everyone? It's an impossible feat. But you know what you do have that not every man can have?"

I think I know where he's going with this, but I let him finish because I'm a glutton for punishment.

"You have women around you who are stronger than most men I know. Bethany? She might seem all sweet and southern, but that woman had every hospital worker at her will that night to give her just another minute to try and get your pathetic ass there. Your sisters? I might have only met them once, but I'm pretty sure they can shoulder a little more than you let them."

"I don't want them to have to worry about things I can handle," I say, all of a sudden feeling like the thirteen-year-old boy who had to become a man in a day. "I can handle it."

"But you obviously can't," Hunter says. "No man can. It's

admirable you want to do everything. But you're right. You are only one man. But the women in your life around you? They are damn good ones, and you are going to piss all of them off if you keep this shit up."

I laugh. "I hate it when you're right."

He smiles and begins to stand up. "Last question."

I let out a breath. "What's that?"

"How are we going to sober you up so Bethany takes you back? I really don't want you sleeping on my couch tonight... or in the future."

I REMEMBER the day I realized I wasn't like other kids—that most kids had a mom and dad.

I was in first grade. We were making Christmas cards, and our teacher told us to make ones for all of the relatives in our family.

My mom was an only child, and her parents passed away before I was born, so I only had the one card to make. I remember Gretchen, the girl who grew up to be the queen bitch of my high school, teasing me because I only had one card to make.

"You don't have a daddy? What is wrong with you?"

When I got home from school that day, I was crushed. I remember crying to Mom, wondering why other kids had a mommy and daddy and I didn't. She explained to me that some families have a mommy and daddy, some just have mommies, some just have daddies, and some have two mommies or two daddies. But the important thing was that no matter how many parents you have, as long as they love you with all their might, that's all that counts.

As I sit here and hold Charlotte, looking down at the beautiful little girl I am blessed with that is the perfect mix of Davis and me, I wonder if I'm going to have that conversation with her? Am I going to have to one day tell her that it's okay that you don't have a daddy, because I have loved her enough for the both of us?

I hope I don't have to, but the longer Davis stays away, the more I can't shake the feeling that this isn't going to end well.

I tried to call his cell as soon as I realized he wasn't at the game. It went straight to voice mail. The second the game was over, Sadie called Hunter, and I know he left to go look for him as soon as he could.

Sadie messaged me a while ago saying that he found him. And while I'm glad he's safe, it doesn't help knowing that now hours have passed and he's still not home.

"If it's going to be you and me little girl, then it's going to be you and me," I whisper to Charlotte, who is currently fighting to keep her eyes open. "You and me against the world."

I pull her to me a little tighter, not wanting to put her down in her crib. It's funny, the parenting books say that your children need to feel your skin and feel close to you in the days right after their birth. Little did I know I'd need her just as much as she's needing me.

We must both drift off because I'm startled awake by the sound of a door opening. When I open my eyes, I see Davis standing against the door of the nursery, looking a bit worse for wear. He doesn't say anything, instead just nods his head, silently asking me to follow him.

I don't want to, but if he's leaving, I can't let him go without saying my piece. And I can't let him just leave. If he's going to do this, he's going to look me in the eye and tell me he's leaving.

I stand up, put Charlotte down in her crib, and make my

way to our bedroom where I find him already sitting on the bed.

"Are you coming back just to leave again?" I ask, needing to not beat around the bush with this one.

He looks up at me, his eyes bloodshot and confused. "I don't want to. But if you want me too, I will."

I laugh, though it probably sounds like an evil one. "I don't want you to leave. What I do want is the man you have been the last few days to kick rocks and never come back."

Davis smiles, and I hate that he has that effect on me. Will that ever go away? How can one smile melt me so instantly? It worked on me that first night we met. I have a feeling it will work on me until we are old and gray. "He was a pretty big asshole."

"The biggest," I say, walking to sit on the bed, though there is significant space between us. "What happened? What's going on? I'm... I'm so confused right now."

He takes a deep breath and reaches out his hand for mine. I don't move closer but place my hand in his.

"My entire life, all I've wanted to do is not let the people in my life down," he begins. "It started with Mom and Sara and Abby. It was my teammates when I played football. It's my players. But now, more than ever, it's you and Charlotte. I'd rather cut off my arm than disappoint you."

"Then why have you been acting like you have?" I ask, still confused. "Because the last few days? Even though you've been here, that man, that man is not who I fell in love with. That man doesn't have a place in this house."

"I know. And I will never be able to say I'm sorry enough. It's just..." he pauses, slightly turning toward me. "Knowing that I almost missed the birth because of having to choose others, it started getting to me. I've been playing what-if scenarios in my head for days now. What if it happens again?

What if I can't get to Mom because you need me? Or what if I disappoint you because Abby needs me and I need to go to Pennsylvania? It was just too much and I..."

"You started acting like an asshole?"

"Yeah," he says, a little laughter in his voice. "I started acting like the biggest asshole of all."

I take in a deep breath, letting that all settle in. It makes sense. While him leaving Charlotte and me is my worst nightmare, not being able to be enough for the ones he loves is Davis's.

"You know I wouldn't have been mad at you if you missed it," I say, hoping he knows that. "I wanted you to be there, yes. But finding Marie was the most important thing you could have done that night."

"I know," he says, inching himself a little more toward me. "All I could think about was that our daughter wasn't even born yet and I almost let her down."

Now it's my turn to face him. "Richard Davis, you listen to me and you listen to me good."

He takes my other hand in his. "I love it when you go all southern mama on me."

This gets a smile out of me. "Hush and listen while I say what I need to say. Your daughter would not have known if you were there or not. And if she ever did? I would have told her that her daddy was being brave and making sure that her grandma was safe and sound. And that if anything were to ever happen to you, he'd make sure he does the same thing for you. Because you... you're the only man I want to keep us safe. You're the only man I want to raise this child with. But if you're going to retreat into yourself and be an asshole when you start feeling overwhelmed? That I won't accept. We're teammates. We're partners. If we're going to do this, we have to do it together."

He doesn't answer. With words at least. Instead, his hands travel to my face, bringing our lips together.

And just like that first night, I feel the zing from my head to my toes.

"I love you," he says, pressing our foreheads together. "I love you so much. Can you forgive me?"

Little does he know I forgave him the second I sat down on this bed. "Possibly."

He quirks his eyebrow at me. "What do I need to do to make it up to you?"

"Two things," I say, my voice growing more playful.

"Name them."

"One. Never, ever, and I mean ever, act the way you did this morning."

"Done," he says, taking my hand and bringing it to his lips. "I will never be able to say I'm sorry enough for that. What else can I do?"

I smile. "You owe me a few middle-of-the-night feedings. Oh, and some more foot massages."

He laughs. "Consider it done, princess. Consider it done."

LAST YEAR during the championship game, I was sneaking out during halftime with Bethany for a quickie in Hunter's garage.

Oh, how much has changed in a year.

"What are you doing?" Bethany asks as I pull her into the bathroom, already kissing every part of her neck I can. "Davis, we can't do this."

Well, not that much. So what if I'm still trying to sneak moments with my girl? I think it's a good thing.

Especially since Aunt Sadie and Uncle Hunter are here to watch the game with us. And watch Charlotte while I sneak away with her mama for a few minutes.

"I'm kissing my fiancée because it's been an hour since I've done so last and that's unacceptable," I say, finding her mouth and willing her to open for me with my tongue.

I don't know if I'll ever get tired of kissing this woman. Or making love to her. Or watching her with Charlotte. It baffles me that I was stupid enough to think at one point I could live without her. Without them both.

"We can't do this," Bethany says, though her roaming hands say otherwise. "Hunter and Sadie are in the next room!"

"I don't care," I say, sneaking my hands up the front of her shirt to get a feel of her full breasts. "Let's make it our tradition. Every year during halftime we sneak away for a quickie."

She laughs, her hand searching for my growing erection. "What happens when you are in the game? I don't think we can do it then."

"We'll cross that bridge when we get there," I say, hoisting her on the counter, our lips crashing together in a frenzy.

Despite being in playoff contention until the final week of the season, the Fury did not make the postseason. However, the year could have gone a hell of a lot worse considering our franchise quarterback sat out for pretty much the entire season and is still off the grid.

To be honest, I'm kind of glad we didn't make the playoffs. Charlotte is almost three months old, and she changes every day. Being able to be here for her and see all her little milestones is something I'll never take for granted. Bethany is back to work part time at the salon, and I'd be a liar if I didn't say I love the days that all I do is the job of daddy.

I even considered giving up coaching and being a stay-at-home dad. Maybe trade some stocks in between changing diapers? Then Bethany reminded me that additional cooking responsibilities go along with that job, so I figure I'll stick with the football thing.

Plus, Hunter is bound and determined that he and I are going to be the youngest head coach and offensive coordinator duo to ever win a championship. And the man is nothing if not determined.

I've had to make a few trips to Pennsylvania for Mom and Abby—we decided to move her to a facility closer to Abby to make it easier on her. Mom is getting great care and the miles are easier on Abby.

Bethany and Charlotte came with me once, and seeing my

mom hold her grandchild was easily one of the best moments of my life. It wasn't a great day for her, so I'm not completely sure Mom registered what was going on. But when we told her the baby's name was Charlotte, her face lit up in a way I hadn't seen for years. Then she snuggled her granddaughter tight as she was wrapped in the pink baby blanket.

It's a memory I'll cherish always.

And then there is Bethany. I don't know how I can love her any more than I already do. I knew she would be an amazing mother, but seeing her with Charlotte makes me want to put another baby in her immediately. I have been told that's not happening until we are married.

So I booked a venue for July. I would have done a court-house ceremony, but I know how much a wedding means to Bethany. We've done everything else out of order; the least I can do is give her the wedding of her dreams.

"If we're going to do this, let's do this now," she says, hurrying and sliding down my joggers and boxer briefs.

"I love it when you talk dirty," I say, quickly removing her leggings and panties. It only takes me a second before I'm lined up and entering her with ease.

She might say she doesn't want another baby just yet, but she hasn't made me wear a condom since we got the okay from Dr. Stewart to "resume intercourse." Yes, that's what she called it when I asked the question. And as far as I know, she's not taking birth control.

I smile to myself as I think that Charlotte could be getting a brother or sister sooner than we think.

The thought of Bethany being pregnant again spurs me on, making my thrusts faster than normal. I'm not even thinking about how she's only balancing on a small piece of counter.

"Davis," she whispers in my ear, wrapping her legs around me tighter. "You feel so good."

"Fuck, I love you," I say. "I love you so fucking much."

Our pace is now furious and I feel her tighten around me. "Come for me, princess. Now."

I move my hand to the top of her clit, and with two strokes, Bethany comes completely undone.

"Davis!"

It takes all I have not to yell her name as I empty myself inside her.

Holy fuck, that was intense.

Neither of us moves for minutes, both finding ways to catch our breath.

"That was..." I say, but am unable to finish the thought.

"My new favorite tradition," she says, leaning in for one more kiss.

But before it can go too far, we are stopped by the sound of banging on the door.

"Richard! Bethany!" Sadie yells, still banging her fist against the wood. "We know what you're doing!"

"We don't care!" I yell, sneaking one more kiss as we finish putting our clothes back on. "And just because you know my name now doesn't mean you have to use it."

"I can and I will," Sadie says. She has been calling me Richard every chance she gets since she found out my real name. Though the bet was technically a draw since Sadie didn't guess, neither of us won. Being the nice guy I am, I still gave her the interview—after she bought me lunch, of course. "And when you two are done in there, your daughter has decided to invent a new definition for 'blowing through a diaper.' I did not sign up for that today."

We look at each other, each of us smiling from ear to ear.

"I'll take the diaper if you take the feeding tonight?"

I lean in and kiss her one more time. "You've got a deal, princess."

EPILOGUE

BETHANY

FOUR YEARS LATER

SOME TRADITIONS ARE MEANT to be broken.

For the first time on championship Sunday since I met Davis, we haven't snuck away at halftime for a mid-game quickie.

And I couldn't be more excited about it.

The Nashville Fury has won the league championship for the first time in franchise history. It has been years of hard work, frustration, and determination, but Hunter and Davis did what they set out to do all those years ago.

They are the youngest coach and coordinator duo ever to win a title.

And I couldn't be prouder of them.

"They did it, sis. They really did it."

The words come from a very emotional and very pregnant Sadie as we watch Hunter receive the championship trophy. I bring her into a side hug as Hunter hoists the trophy above his head, his team cheering behind him as they all hold up their phones to capture the moment.

"Look at him up there," Hunter's mom, Francine, says. "I'm just... I'm just so proud of him."

Sadie gives my hand a squeeze as she goes to stand next to Hunter's parents as I take in the scene in front of me. Standing off to the side of the makeshift stage in the middle of a huge stadium are Mom and Mike, along with Hunter's parents, who are basking in the moment of their son winning the championship. Bo, Hunter's dad, keeps pointing to the jumbotron to show Camden, my nephew, his daddy on the screen.

Unfortunately, Abby and Sara couldn't make it. It's the middle of the school year and Abby didn't feel right about having the girls miss, and Sara just started a new job with a tech company in Seattle. Then there is Marie. Hopefully, she's watching and understands what her son just did. Though these days, it's unlikely. She's still with us physically, but mentally each day it gets a little worse.

Then there is Charlotte and me. I'm watching her dad in awe of the accomplishment he just made. She's more interested in the balloons and confetti that are still raining from the rafters. As much as Davis tries to get her to take an interest in football, she wants nothing to do with it. She is my daughter through and through.

And he loves every minute of it. What no one knows is that last night Charlotte wanted to have a spa night at the hotel, and my husband's toes are painted pink because he can't say no to his daughter.

Maybe things will be different with our next one. The one that Davis doesn't know about yet.

We didn't mean to wait this long between kids. In fact, we tried for a few years with no luck. But in classic Davis and Bethany fashion, nothing happens the way we plan. We had all but given up and resided ourselves to Charlotte being it for us.

I took the test this morning. And I can't wait to tell him.

I look up on stage, where Hunter is still giving his television interview with the championship trophy in hand. I would guess most everyone here and those watching on television are watching Hunter speak. But me? I'm taking in the moment behind him.

The moment where Bryce and Davis are hugging, basking in the glory of what the two of them accomplished tonight. At that moment, I look to my right and see Bryce's wife crying, holding her very pregnant stomach. We share a look, and somehow without speaking, we have a full conversation with our eyes.

My look is meant to say thank you. I don't know if we'd be standing here if she hadn't come back into his life.

Her look is soft and welcoming. Though she hates taking credit for what she did for Bryce, everyone knows she's the one who pulled him from the gutter.

It's almost unreal to think that just a few years ago we wondered if Bryce was ever going to play again. Now? Now he's taking the championship trophy from Hunter, holding it above his head as the MVP of the game.

Yes, I know what that stands for. And yes, I know that because Davis quizzed me last night.

As the television announcer turns his attention to Bryce, Hunter and Davis start exiting the stage. As soon as they step off, they turn to each other and embrace in one of their manly back-patting hugs.

Sadie and I like to tease them about how much they man hug, but today they get a pass. It wasn't easy for the two of them to get here. But they never gave up on each other or the team. And now they can call themselves champions.

They part ways, and Davis makes a beeline for Charlotte and me, scooping her up with ease and planting a kiss on me that I feel in every inch of my body.

"Daddy!" Charlotte shrieks. "You won!"

Thank God, she at least knew they won. Her favorite part of the day was the halftime show and the fact I allowed her to drink the complimentary Diet Coke that I wasn't drinking.

She really is my daughter.

"I did!" he says, placing her on his hip. "Did you have fun?"

"Can I take some of these balloons home?" she asks, her voice so sincere.

He laughs, putting her down. "Of course. Go get some right there by Gram and PopPop."

Charlotte goes running to Mom and Mike as Davis brings his hands around my waist.

"We did it," he says, his voice more emotional.

"You did it," I say, wrapping my hands around his neck. "I love you."

He leans in and kisses me. Nothing too X-rated, but enough to make me know that tonight is going to be a fun night.

Thank God, Gram and PopPop are keeping the kids tonight for both Sadie and me.

"I can't believe this happened," he says, still holding on to me. "I didn't think this would ever happen. And now that it has? I don't know how you can top this feeling?"

I smile and bite my lip. "I bet I can make it better."

He wags his eyebrows. "You ready for that quickie? I bet we can sneak into the locker room."

I laugh, shaking my head. "No, but I still think you'll be just as excited."

"Well, I'm now officially intrigued."

I raise up on my tiptoes and lean in. "I'm pregnant."

He immediately pulls back to look at me. "You are? We are?"

I laugh, nodding my head. "I took a test today. We're having another baby."

He picks me up and twirls me around, shouting for everyone to hear that we're pregnant again.

All I can do is laugh and enjoy this moment.

Who would have thought that two people who were so different and wanted such different things could be so happy? I know things didn't go the way I had planned, but if that's what needed to happen for me to be here right now, I'd do them all over again.

And I'd do it with him every single time.

That's right! Another baby is on the way for Davis and Bethany. And you'll never guess Baby Boy Davis's name. Find out in the Extended Epilogue!

ACKNOWLEDGMENTS

Confession time: Like Bethany's pregnancy, this book wasn't supposed to happen. When I first dreamed up the world of the Nashville Fury, it was Hunter and Sadie, then Bryce, then Cole (spoiler for the heroes of the next two books). Davis was never in the plan. He and Bethany were just supposed to be side characters to help Hunter and Sadie along the way. Heck, he didn't even have a first name.

Then something happened. Something in my brain made me write a chapter about their blind date. Then something made me write that they were having a not-so-secret... we'll call it relationship.

I might not have known it when I dreamed up this world, but Davis and Bethany were always meant to have a book. Thank you to Kelly and the rest of my readers who made me see that. This book made me laugh, cry and scream in frustration while writing it, but at the end of the day, I love it so much. I hope you did as well.

As always, I need to thank my parents. I've lost count of how many times I've come to you guys with a change in life plans, and never once have you tried to steer me toward a safe course. You've allowed me to follow my dreams and my path, and for that I am forever grateful. And like always, the free rent is appreciated.

To Kelly. I don't know if Davis is here without you. You

knew he needed a story before I did. Thanks for the friendship, critiques and support. Book friends are the best friends.

Julia, Georgia, Mae and Claire: How did I write a book before I met you ladies? All I know is I don't ever want to write one without y'all again. I'll bring the pie.

Evie, Adriana, Tori, Molly and Anjelica: Each and every one of you got a "HALP!" message from me in this book. Thank you all for responding. I love each and every one of your faces.

Corinne: Thank you again for giving me my start. I'm not here without you.

Elaine, thank you for once again dotting the Is and crossing the Ts I forgot to. Marla, thank you for your detailed eye. One day I'll stop overusing common phrases. Michele, thank you for your keen eye and being an amazing cheerleader. Amanda and Angie, thank you for saying yes. Jill, you are amazing and I love every time we work together. Kari, you once again brought my cover idea to life in ways that I didn't think imaginable. You are a true talent and I'm hiring you forever.

Bloggers: Thank you for taking a chance on me. I know there are so many authors out there and I'm blessed that you chose to read my book. Y'all make the book world go round.

To my ARC, Book and TikTok Squads: I don't know what I did in this life to deserve all of you. Thank you for your support, your endless cheerleading, and following me wherever you do. I love you all.

ABOUT THE AUTHOR

Known for her witty sense of humor, Chelle Sloan is a former sports editor who after years in the newspaper business, decided to become a romance author. You know, because that's the normal path to writing happily ever afters.

An Ohio native, she's fiercely loyal to Cleveland sports, is the owner of way too many tumblers and will be a New Kids on the Block fan for life. She does her best writing at Panera, or anywhere that's not her office.

When she's not writing, you can find her in the kitchen attempting to become a baker, fixing up her condo (badly and by watching YouTube videos), or falling in love with a book.

As for her own happily ever after? Maybe one day...

Stay up to date with all things Chelle & join the VIP Squad!

ALSO BY CHELLE SLOAN

THE NASHVILLE FURY, PRO FOOTBALL SERIES

Off the Record: A secret office romance

Off Track: A surprise pregnancy romance

Off Season: A second chance romance

Off Limits: A sibling's best friend romance

NASHVILLE FURY WORLD

Off the Market at Christmas: A childhood friends-to-lovers romance

LOVE ONLINE SERIES

Thirst Trap: A social media romance

Match Maker: A fake dating romance

Run Run Rudolph: A celebrity, holiday romance

ROLLING HILLS

The One I Want: A single dad/nanny romance

The One I Need: An accidental marriage romance

The One I Love: A friends to lovers romance

The One I Hate: An enemies to lovers romance

GUIDE TO LOVE SERIES

Runaway Bride's Guide to Love: A brother's best friend romance

Single Mom's Guide to Love: A marriage of convenience romance

Roommate's Guide to Love: A fling to forever, single dad, romance

Good Girl's Guide to Love: A fake dating, football romance